Heather Graham's Christmas Treasures

Heather Graham

13Thirty Books

13Thirty Books
Print and Digital Editions
Copyright 2014

Discover new and exciting works by Heather Graham and
13Thirty Books at www.13thirtybooks.com

Print and Digital Edition, License Notes

DEDICATION

To all who believe in the spirit of the season . . .
No matter what their faith may be!
Not the tinsel and gifts, but the caring and the brotherhood!

Peace to all – and a happy and healthy New Year.

And, of course, thank you for reading!

ACKNOWLEDGMENTS

My family, my friends, both near and far, often seen and dearly missed,
Merry Christmas.

ONE LITTLE MIRACLE

"Sweet Jesus, Mary, and Joseph!" Anna Maria cried, terror deep within her gray eyes as she stared out over the white-capped waves before them. "'Tis a pirate ship; see how brazen her skull flies from the mast!" She crossed herself once, then again, and still one more time. "Dear Lord, save us!"

Tessa Dousseau, standing with Anna Maria at the bow of their armed French sloop, *Mademoiselle,* narrowed her eyes and stared across the waves, feeling hot tremors of fear and excitement and dread come sweeping in a fever down her spine. Indeed, the ship appeared to be a pirate ship, bearing down on them swift and hard, regardless of the gray-clouded, ominous skies, regardless of the wild, reckless waves that crashed and rose, white-tipped as if touched with snow.

The *Mademoiselle* was a fine sloop, and when she had been built, it had been intended that she carry thirty guns and a crew of more than a hundred hale and hearty men to operate those guns. But somehow, she had left port minus fifteen of her guns and dozens of men. There hadn't been time to outfit her properly, not with winter so swiftly on its way. And Tessa's father, the Comte de la Verre, had been very determined that he would have Tessa set upon the French isle of Dejere well ahead of Christmastide—for she was his idea of a gift for a friend.

It was nearly the first of November now, and they were within twenty-four hours of their port.

Facing a pirate ship...

"Oh, dear God, please—" Anna Maria began again, and Tessa started as she saw her lady's maid sink to her knees at the bow of the ship. Then Tessa's fingers curled more tightly around the wooden rim of the bow as she remembered how she had prayed those very same words, again and again, all the long way out here at sea.

Dear Lord, please. Dear Lord, please...

She had begged and prayed for a miracle to release her from her father's bargain. Day after day, hour after hour.

She had considered jumping into the sea—not to take her own life, but to swim to some distant shore.

But now it seemed that her prayer was about to be answered, and in the most dreadful, horrifying way. There was a pirate ship upon the sea. She was outfitted with the English flag—and a skull-

and-crossbones—both whipping hard against the wind from the ship's flag mast.

"Ladies!" Tessa could hear Don Juan Diego, the *Mademoiselle's* Spanish captain, bellowing out to them. She swung around, seeing him in his elegant coat and white-lace cravat and perfectly powdered wig, and wondered how her father had ever imagined that such a dandy was fit for this commission at sea. Don Diego's face seemed nearly as white as his powdered wig. "You must hasten below, my lady!" he charged Tessa. "We've a murderous English scoundrel ahead of our bow! This is that wretched creature, the dreaded Red Fox, the only fool English captain to warn his enemies with his colors bright and bold. You must go and hide from the fighting!"

"You will best him, Don Diego!" Anna Maria cried, leaping to her feet.

"We've a battle ahead, a fierce one!" Don Diego promised. Then he shrugged. "A battle, or perhaps surrender. This pirate does not butcher men as so many others do. He seeks the gold of ransoms. Perhaps—"

"You cannot let him take us, Don Diego!" Anna Maria cried in horror.

"A battle would be fiercely bloody."

"But the Lady Tessa is to wed Raoul Flambert, Comte de Sierre, and the Royal Governor of Dejere! You cannot trust her to the likes of an Englishman!"

Tessa decided not to remind Anna Maria that Tessa's mother had been English, that Tessa had spent most of her life in England, until very recently. Besides which, it didn't matter to her. Pirating was a wretched profession, and no man had a right simply to pluck the treasures from another man's ship—no matter what his nationality. And pirates were horrid, hairy men with rotten teeth, bowed legs, and rancid, insect-infested beards. She would rather die than surrender to such malignant men.

"My father would be heartily disappointed in your cowardice, Don Diego!" Tessa said firmly, her eyes, deep blue like the sea, flashing an earnest warning. It didn't help, of course, that she had warned her father of the privateering activities going on when he had determined this course of action. But her father had received a fantastic sum—in gold—for her marriage portion, and he had waved a hand at the idea of pirates. "They go after the treasure ships, my dear. The *Mademoiselle* will carry no cargo more precious than you, Tessa, and so the pirates will all stay at bay."

Not this pirate. Perhaps he didn't know that the only precious cargo aboard the ship was a bride bought and paid for in gold. There was French furniture aboard, linens, silks, all the things that went with a woman who would soon be wed. There was the little jewelry she possessed. Perhaps even these meager pickings would do for this wretched English pirate Red Fox.

A cannon suddenly boomed, and just off the bow of the ship, a tremendous spray of water erupted from the sea. Tessa was startled by the little tremor of terror that suddenly tore at her heart. She didn't want to die. She hadn't wanted to ever reach Dejere, and her fate there, but neither did she want to die. She gritted her teeth very hard together, grasping the rail at the bow to maintain her balance as the ship rocked upon the sea, as the mates and seamen screamed and cried out and went running in confusion.

"Hold her steady, hold her steady!" Don Diego called to his first mate at the raised helm above them.

"It was a warning shot!" Tessa heard herself cry. "Don't run from him so swiftly! Fire back!"

"Get below!" Don Diego, very red-faced now, commanded her. "You must go below—"

"But I am not frightened, Don Diego," she lied to him, eyes narrowed. "I will not so swiftly submit to the barbaric tactics of a pirate!"

"Mademoiselle! We are not properly armed!" Don Diego cried to her.

There was another burst of fire from the not-too-distant cannon. The shot just missed the ship. Water spewed up again, falling back upon them like rain droplets.

"Send up the white flag!" Don Diego shouted.

"You whiny coward!" Tessa cried, alarmed. "Don't you see? He is not so eager to hit you! He wants to seize your ship. You can fight him, or you can outrun him!"

"Mademoiselle, you will go below!" he roared again, shaking his head. *"Mon Dieu* and *Dios mio!"* he muttered, combining his Spanish and his French. "I warned your papa that you had been in *English* schools too long!"

"Outrun him!" Tessa demanded. "Else, dear Captain, you will be saying much more to my father!"

For a moment it seemed that Don Diego could not decide if he was more afraid of the pirate or of Tessa's father, not merely the Comte de la Verre, but a man among the Sun King's favorites.

"Go below, I beg of you," he pleaded, "and I will do my best to outrun this English menace!"

"Come, my lady, please!" Anna Maria begged, tugging now on her arm.

Tessa remained on deck for a moment, feeling the touch of the breeze, the sea spray upon her cheeks. She didn't want to go below. But Anna Maria was pulling at her arm and Don Diego was still staring at her, a mute and desperate plea now in his eyes.

She allowed Anna Maria to hurry her along. They ran quickly down the narrow stairway to the quarters below the topside deck, and then down the hall to the captain's cabin, given over to Tessa for this long voyage from the Old World to the New. Small paned windows looked out from the bow of the cabin, and as Anna Maria closed the door after they entered, Tessa hurried to the broad bunk that sat at the right side of the cabin and stared out the glass at the sea beyond it.

Her heart shuddered hard again. Perhaps she was a fool. She didn't mean to cast a death sentence upon all the men who sailed the *Mademoiselle*. The pirate ship had come closer upon them, so very close, and with such tremendous speed that Tessa was frightened to death. She was a bigger sloop than the *Mademoiselle,* and Tessa could count thirty guns just on her starboard side.

Now she could hear the shouts from above decks, Don Diego, calling out in his mixture of Spanish and French for his mixture of a crew. He had said that he would try to outrun the pirate ship, and he would.

He had very little chance, and Tessa knew it.

"He must surrender!" she said suddenly, with a sinking heart. She pushed away from the bunk, swinging around on Anna Maria. Anna Maria was tall and slim and just beginning to gray. Her face was very lean, her eyes very big and brown. She was dressed in a gray gown, her only thought to fashion at all the hoop beneath her skirt— the revival of the farthingale. Poor woman! She had led her life caring for Tessa's little half-brothers, and she had never experienced a moment's violence in her life. She was in definite dismay now, and though she had irritated Tessa since they had met, Tessa now felt sorry for her.

"I have to get by, Anna Maria."

But Anna Maria was backed against the door, ashen, frozen. She finally managed to shake her head. "You mustn't go out there. Pirates are coming! And what a pirate might do with such a young beauty as yourself—"

"Not so young," Tessa corrected her quickly, and with bitterness in her heart. Her father had been exceptionally anxious for this marriage because she was over twenty now, very old to him, since he had wed her mother when he had been but sixteen and his bride a full year younger. "Practically decaying, as my father would tell you," Tessa said, trying to smile. "Anna Maria, you must let me out now. I have all but damned these poor men, and I must change things."

Anna Maria stood her ground, too frozen to move, but Tessa was determined. She strode to the door and gently but firmly removed the slim woman from the doorway, all but lifting her aside.

"You are in my care, I am to watch over you!" Anna Maria called in dismay, but Tessa had no time to answer her, for she was already hurrying back down the hallway to the narrow stairs. She had nearly reached them when the ship shuddered violently. She staggered against the paneled wall, fighting to regain her balance while panic filled her. They had been broadsided. The pirate ship had reached the *Mademoiselle* and rammed her hard.

She pressed her hands over her ears, crouching to her knees, hearing the screams and the shouts and the wild cries of panic. Then she leaped up, determined to right what she felt she had put wrong with her reckless demands.

She raced up the steps, and coming onto the deck, nearly smacked headlong into a slim, dark-haired pirate with a knife between his teeth and an unsheathed cutlass in his hands. He froze when he realized he faced an unarmed woman.

Terrified, Tessa took a wild swing at the man. She caught him in the jaw and winced, clutching her hand as he fell. Her knuckles seemed to explode in pain. She shook her hand, staring in disbelief at the man she had felled.

She crouched down beside him, looking up, and saw that more men were hurrying toward her. "Take care! The woman is dangerous. Look what she did to Wily Fred!"

Once again, it was not courage but rather simple panic that brought about her actions. The men were rushing at her. She had to have some defense, and so she grabbed up the fallen pirate's sword and waved it menacingly at the half-dozen English privateers who suddenly rushed toward her. They all stopped out of range of her wild swipes and looked at her warily. She looked from one man to the next; they weren't quite what she had expected. They were certainly well-dressed for pirates, all wearing hugging breeches that came just below the knee, silk stockings or none at all, and bare feet. Their shirts were white linen, oddly clean. One pirate was very tall, gray-haired, gray-eyed, and lean; three were younger, one a redhead, two blond; and two were middle-aged fellows, white-wigged despite the battle they had enjoined.

She wanted to shout out in English, to tell them that the ship would surrender, to demand mercy for all the men, but she wasn't given a chance. A deep, rich voice suddenly boomed out, and before she could speak, the men parted ways before her, and she was silenced by her first glimpse of *him.*

He was tall, shirtless beneath the sun, with broad shoulders that glistened a deep bronze color. He was in high boots and crimson breeches that seemed to cling to his hips and the hard columns of his thighs. He moved like a great cat, smooth, sleek, silent. When he stood before her, he seemed almost like some pagan god. He was heedless of his half-nakedness, steady upon his booted feet, his pirate's cutlass hanging idly for the moment from his right hand. He seemed intrigued only by her, and stared openly with yellow-green eyes, like a cat's, set deep in a bronzed face—a face of startling appeal with high cheeks, clean-arched brows, long straight nose, and full, curling, very sensual lips. His hair was a very deep, rich auburn, a full head of it, cropped just below his neck, as if such a style might keep it from being bothersome. There was something about him, perhaps merely the power with which he seemed to move, which instantly alerted her that he was the captain, the wretched pirate Red Fox.

"What have we here?" he murmured, and she was startled by the richness and refinement of his voice. It had a deep and masculine tone, one that seemed to touch her inside and out, in a way she had never felt before.

She realized that she was still standing with her stolen sword raised, meeting his cat's gaze. He didn't seem at all afraid. He seemed, in fact, so self-confident that she almost longed to run him through just to take the self-assured look from his cocky eyes.

Yet he seemed to realize everything that went on in her mind, and he bowed deeply. "Mademoiselle, I will take the sword."

She shook her head. He had spoken to her in French, and she gave him a simple answer in the same language.

"Non!"

Muscled shoulders rippled. Hands on hips, he seemed to straighten to an even greater height. Again, he spoke to her in French. "Mademoiselle, you are the Lady Tessa Dousseau, daughter of the infamous Comte de la Verre, and soon to be bride of the despicable Comte Raoul Flambert, heinous governor of the French colony Dejere."

She remained very straight, saying nothing, staring into his green-gold eyes with her stolen sword aimed at his throat. She inhaled and managed to speak her demand in swift, angry French. "You, sir, are the very wretched pirate Red Fox. And you must swear now that these men, who have done you no harm, will receive none in return!"

A smile curled ever deeper into his mouth. Then suddenly she gasped, for he lifted his idle sword, struck hers from her grasp, and brought the point of his own to circle lightly just inches away from her throat.

"The business of death does not pleasure me, my lady, while that of besting Spaniards and Frenchmen—and acquiring great treasure along the way—does." His voice, low and soft, suddenly rose to a thunderous level once again and he called out, still in French, "Drop your weapons now! You will not be put to death, or tortured or abused, if you surrender your weapons now!"

There was an instant clatter of swords upon the deck.

Tessa had wanted the crew to surrender. They simply had not needed to do so with such humiliating speed.

"And now you, *ma cherie*," he said pleasantly, "will accompany me aboard the *Golden Wind,* serene in the knowledge that no man will die on your behalf!"

He was laughing at her, she thought, and she longed to reach out and slap his handsome face, but his sword remained too close to her throat for comfort, and she managed to remain still.

"I don't care to change ships," she told him loftily.

"You what?" he inquired, arching a brow.

"I do not care to accompany you to your ship, or anywhere, you filthy pirate!" she said, still replying mechanically in French, for it was the language he spoke.

"Filthy?" He turned to the tall, gray-haired pirate, now near his back. "Don't I bathe more commonly than most men, Thibault?" he asked.

"Most commonly!" Thibault assured him eagerly in English.

"Nod!" the Red Fox told him. "Our mademoiselle is Français, and probably understands little English, and I would surely have her understand you now!"

The Englishman smiled and nodded strenuously. The Red Fox turned back to Tessa, arching a brow.

"Monsieur," Tessa said, "the body is but the shell of our existence, and the dirt with which you live rests most heavily upon your soul!"

"Indeed?" he inquired. He had kept smiling, but now those cool gold-green eyes were narrowed, and she thought that she had angered him as well. Alas, she thought angrily, such a small price for his piracy!

"As I said, Monsieur le Pirate! I will accompany you nowhere!" she charged him.

"Is that so?" he asked softly.

And then, before she could say more, she found herself swept off her feet, crying out as she was tossed over his shoulder. She felt his naked flesh, burning hot, against her cheek. She felt his heartbeat, felt his breath.

"Bastard!" she charged him, trying to rise, but to no avail. She could only struggle up and slam her fists against his shoulders.

An effort surely wasted, for he did not seem to notice her ferocity at all. Again, he moved like a cat. As swift as a panther in a New World jungle, striding across the deck, leaping atop the rails of the joined ships.

"Wait, *si'l vous plait!*" she heard Don Diego calling out in distress.

On his own ship, still heedless of the woman pounding upon his shoulders, the pirate Red Fox spun around.

"What is it?" he demanded irritably.

"What—what will you do with her?" Don Diego asked breathlessly.

"What will I do with her?" The question seemed to puzzle him. Then he laughed softly. "Why, I will ransom her, of course."

"The Comte Raoul Flambert will pay for her—for her safety! For her—her innocence—her chastity!" Don Diego cried swiftly.

"Will he?"

Tessa found herself going still suddenly at the strange tone in his voice, one that was very bitter.

"He will pay whatever price you demand!" Don Diego cried out eagerly.

"Oh, indeed, he will pay!" the pirate Red Fox called out. "Indeed, he will pay."

"You will ransom her quickly!"

"I will ransom her," the pirate answered softly, "when I have finished with her!" And with that, he spun around, and Tessa heard herself scream with rage and dread, pounding furiously against his hard-muscled shoulders again as he began to stride across his own deck.

Heading for his own captain's cabin.

Chapter 2

So this was to be her answer! Tessa thought as they burst through the cabin door, and she found herself flung down hard on a huge bunk, covered with a richly embroidered—*French!*—spread. She landed hard and breathlessly upon a deep pile of down pillows, and she stared in a wild fear and fury at the man who had brought her there.

He seemed amused once again. Leaning back against the door to his cabin, he smiled and made no move, yet watched her as she struggled to sit up, to settle her wayward skirts and petticoats, to gather some dignity.

And to seek some defense.

He made no move toward her, yet she could not stop thinking that he was, indeed, like a New World jungle cat, playing with her, teasing her, aye, yes! A cat playing with its food—right before devouring it whole. He smiled, yet there was a look of sheer danger about the man. He was young, agile, striking—and quite deadly, Tessa was certain. Any minute now, he would be upon her...

This, *this,* was her answer.

She had prayed—day and night—to be rescued, and now here she was, the prisoner of a pirate captain. Not, it seemed, to find escape in execution—he meant to spare even the captain and all the crew of her own ship. No! She wasn't even to be used and abused and released—she was to be used and abused...

And sold to Raoul once again!

It wasn't fair—she simply wouldn't have it! This wretched privateer was not going to seize her father's ship, seek to frighten her to tears, debase and molest her—and get away with it!

"You... bastard!" she hissed, the words very low, husky, tense, and filled with venom. "You will not get away with this! Flambert will slice and dice you, rip you to ribbons! He will slit you from the gullet down to the toes!"

He arched a brow to her. He leaned against the door, his head somewhat cocked, his arms crossed over his broad chest. "He'll do all that?" he inquired.

"More!" she promised.

"Ah! I am a-tremble!" he told her, eyes wide with mockery, then his smile faded and he pushed away from the door. "Flambert, my lady, will not challenge me. No, I am afraid, *ma belle,* that your elegant comte will make no effort to come to your rescue—he will pay the price asked under any circumstances, and then, only then, will you be returned to the waiting arms of your lover."

"In the best of condition, I do assume!" she said, eyes narrowing, breasts heaving.

Again, the bright light of amusement lit his eyes. "Hmm. I shall have to think on that. I utterly despise the man, so it will not be out of consideration for a worthy enemy that I would spare you. Of course, it has been rumored that he wouldn't consider anything but the sweetest innocent for a bride, and since you have come all this way... Well, perhaps it is your own good behavior which will determine the condition of the goods I offer for ransom."

Outraged, she found herself standing, staring at him incredulously. "Pompous English... ass!" she found herself calling him. They were still speaking French, and for the first time in her life, she was finding herself in sympathy with her father's people and determined to speak their language. "You mustn't be too sure, counting your own magnificent courage—preying upon ships carrying women!—against that of a decent man such as the Comte Flambert!"

"Decent! Ha!" he exclaimed, shaking his head. "My lady, it might be every mercy I have offered you, for each hour I hold you keeps you from the hell you will find with that heinous creature. But then perhaps you have as yet to meet your fiancé. His face is not so monstrous, but I promise you, his soul is."

"That from a pirate!" she said sweetly. "And you are mistaken. I *have* met my fiancé."

"Have you, then? Tell me, was my mistake in thinking that you had not met him—or that you were not aware that the man is a monster?"

"English pirate, you should dive straight to hell!"

"Does that mean you know him to be a monster?"

"It means nothing of the kind!" she lied swiftly.

"Oh." Did some flicker of disappointment touch his eyes? He seemed to tire of the game between them.

"Since you do not find him to be so loathsome, you will write him a letter, and do so immediately. You will assure him that you are my prisoner, awaiting his rescue. His monetary rescue. And you will enclose a lock of that beautiful blonde hair to assure him that I do indeed hold a treasure he has been joyously contemplating. My desk sits yonder. I will leave you, and you may begin now. Oh, you may also assure him that—as of this moment—you remain as chaste a maid as you boarded my ship, but you might want to suggest that he hurry, that we are impatient men, too long at sea. And ravaging monsters ourselves, of course."

"I will say nothing of the kind," Tessa informed him regally.

He stiffened, staring at her. "Your pardon, my lady?"

"I will do nothing of the kind."

"I have told you—"

"And I have told you. I will not aid in your raiding and thievery! I will not write a word down on paper! If you must convince Comte Flambert that you are holding me, then you will do so on your own!"

"You do not know what you risk!" he charged her harshly.

"And you do not fully comprehend—I do not care!" she assured him, but despite her brave facade, she heard her voice trembling, just a bit, at the end. Did he too hear that slight tone of fear, of uncertainty?

He bowed to her, suddenly, deeply. "My lady, I will leave you for the moment. Your courage and bravado are most stirring—but hardly temperate or intelligent, under the circumstances. I would prefer not to harm you. But I do have a fierce and personal hatred for Flambert, and as he is a coward I am most unlikely to meet again at sea, it will not take much to persuade me to deny him anything that he might prize. My lady..."

And again, he bowed.

In the same swift movement he turned, threw open the door, and with a single long stride exited the cabin, slamming the door hard behind him.

Shaking, Tessa sank back down to sit upon the pirate's bunk. It seemed as if the waters of a rushing stream swept through her as she lay upon the bed, clutching the pirate's plump down-stuffed pillow, resting her head upon it as she stared at the door, stunned by all that he had said...

And her own responses.

This was not what she had intended when she had prayed for rescue...

For just one miracle. One little Christmas miracle. And it seemed that she invited disaster down upon them all instead!

She did not want to marry Comte Raoul Flambert. This pirate certainly could not know her feelings, and she most certainly dared not give them away. But she had met Flambert five years ago when he had come to England with her father. She had been in school in Oxford, the nuns had been in an absolute tizzy, and she had been in something of a wild mood herself—she had not seen her father since she had been a child of three. Her mother had died that year. Her grandfather, the lofty English Lord Simmons, had swooped down on her father's estate just outside Paris and assured Comte de la Verre that Tessa must be carefully, gently raised, and the raising of such a gentle young creature was best done in England. She never knew exactly why her father had agreed, except that, as she grew, she had learned that he had been very young and extremely handsome, and though he had loved his English wife dearly enough, with her passing he was once again a most eligible man within the marriage market, and there were fine estates for a man to gain through marriage. So Tessa had gone to England, and she had dearly loved both her grandparents, and she had even liked the school they had chosen for her, and the kindly, if sometimes far too naive, nuns who had taught her there. When her father had arrived with Flambert, Sister Mary Margaret had brought Tessa down to meet the men, and although Mary Margaret was nearing sixty—if she was a day—she didn't seem to fathom a thing about her father's friend—which Tessa did. Age, apparently, did not guarantee either wisdom or instinct.

Flambert was striking, a handsome man like her father, thin-featured, with rich, long, chestnut curls; a slender mustache; and small, perfectly curled beard. His eyes were dark and sparkled with a most unnerving light as they slid up and down Tessa's length. Tessa had scarcely recognized her own father, but then it had been well over a decade since she had seen him, so her memories were very vague. He had remarried twice since then, and busied himself with the sons from his second and third marriages. Tessa had somewhat assumed that he had forgotten her existence, which was quite fine. She liked her life, and she didn't want her father back in it.

But he had come, and with Raoul Flambert. And Tessa had noted with deep disdain that the man had stripped the younger nuns with his eyes, just as he had seemed to devour her. He had been polite, courteous, and entirely proper. He hadn't spoken a word of English, though he was a guest in a hostile land, for England was on the brink of war with Spain and France. "A pretty creature, eh, *mon ami?"* Tessa's father had queried his friend—after inspecting Tessa himself. And Flambert had allowed a curl to slip into his lips. "Ah, *tres jolie,* Comte de la Verre. A beautiful young woman indeed." Tessa's father had frowned for a minute there. "Very young," he had informed Flambert. "Ah, but youth is beauty, is it not?" Flambert had asked, and Tessa had found herself filled with unease and revulsion. Once again, Flambert's eyes flicked up and down the length of her. She felt like shrinking within herself. But it was not long after that the men departed, and in the months that followed, Tessa, much to her relief, heard no more from her father. She loved England. She loved her vacations on her grandfather's estates just outside London, and she adored London itself, and the wonderful days when she went to serve the Princess Anne, heiress now to the crown of England upon the death of William III. Anne was gentle, devoted to her husband, kind to those around her, and eternally a romantic.

Her father meant nothing to her. Tessa had imagined that life could go on for her as it always had. She would reside with her grandparents, serve the princess who would one day be queen, and flirt with the very handsome young lords and gentlemen who served William, but also realized that one day Anne would be queen. They amused Tessa. She was happy to listen to their sonnets and songs. Yet worldly matters did not much please her. A woman would soon sit on the throne of England, but it seemed that women were in little control of their lives, that despite this age of enlightenment, women were still all but bought and sold by their guardians—men—in the marriage game. Thanks to her delightfully temperate and gentle grandfather, Tessa was spared concern regarding the marital field. She and her grandfather had a wonderful, unspoken agreement on the subject.

But then Charles II of Spain died, leaving no heir. Tessa had never imagined that such a thing could so direly affect her own life.

It was to change it completely.

Charles II had willed as his successor a grandson of Louis XIV of France. It was more than England and her allied enemies against the Sun King—Holland, Austria, Prussia, Sweden and Denmark—could tolerate. France had tremendous might, and a union of Spain and France created a threat that simply could not be tolerated by the neighboring nations. The French king was supporting the Pretender to the English throne, and not only that, but levying ruinous taxes on English goods. For months, Tessa trod carefully about the Princess Anne, watching with fear every evolvement in the rising tensions.

On the very eve of war, the Comte de la Verre arrived with a large French delegation, going straight to King William and demanding the return of his daughter, since hostilities would so soon commence between the nations.

Tessa was aware that her life could have little meaning to King William, and yet she threw herself on Anne's mercy to remain in England. The Princess Anne cried with her, but it was decided that when a nobleman—French, English, or other—demanded the return of a child, in the interests of all concerned, the child must be returned.

Tessa soon found herself heavily escorted by her father's men—who surely knew she longed for nothing more than escape—and bade farewell to those who had so gently raised her.

True realization of her fate touched her just as she was about to board the ship which would take her across the channel with a perfect stranger—her father. She turned, ready to bolt, and found herself facing several of his armed men again, and she knew that she would board the ship willingly—or tied and trussed.

Although she hated her father then, she later discovered that Christian de la Verre was not a cruel man, but a man in the old mode of nobles, who considered himself gifted and superior by birth. He was lord of all that was his—including his children. He had three sons for whom to provide, and the one daughter, Tessa. Her father's current wife, Jeanne Louise, was not many years older than Tessa and seemed to despise her, no matter how often she granted Tessa her forced smile.

Tessa kept out of her way.

She begged her father to allow her to return to England, but events conspired to make that impossible.

King William III died; the Princess Anne became Queen Anne, and her gentle husband became prince regent. In September 1702 Queen Anne began to give out commissions for piracy.

Her father became incensed with the English. There wasn't a prayer that he would return Tessa to the place she considered home.

After she had been with him for one year, he had summoned her to his desk, where he was seated with a number of his letters, and had informed her in a cool and distant tone that he had made a most advantageous marriage arrangement for her. Raoul Flambert, titled, wealthy, a noble with impeccable family lineage, an old friend of her father's and one well-favored by the king, had asked for her. Her father was now eager to see that she arrived upon his doorstep for a wedding to take place before Christmas, so Raoul might find his holiday enriched with the warmth of newfound love and marital bliss.

There had been several long seconds when Tessa had simply stared at her father, unable to speak. Then she had, of course, spoken too swiftly. She had told her father that she wouldn't even think about marrying Flambert, that she considered the man old and disgusting and his interest in young girls completely unseemly. In saying that, she managed to completely offend her father, who was near Flambert's age, and did not consider himself at all old. Any chance of her talking her way out of the situation ended then and there.

But her determination *not* to marry Flambert did not end there. She made a plan to escape her father's mansion and return to England, which she still considered home, only to find herself physically returned by her father's servants, two giant peasant men who apologized profusely, yet needed their work with her father, and must therefore obey him.

She had been absolutely humiliated when her father told her that children—daughters, most especially—must obey. And he had ordered her strapped to a chair and given her twenty harsh lashes himself upon her bare back. She had hated him then, and she had willed herself not to cry, no matter how great the pain.

And when he had finished, she had assured him that she didn't think what he had dealt out would hold a candle to the misery of life with Flambert, and once again, her father had been deeply offended. In her room alone at last, she had cried again. And there she had begun to pray. "Don't let it happen, please, God! Send a miracle, I beg you! Let Father see the truth of his friend!"

The more Tessa argued, the more her father insisted she needed to be wed, and wed to a strong man such as Raoul Flambert, one who could keep a firm and steady hand upon a young bride. Tessa had then assured her father that she would be miserable and wretched, and Flambert would not want to marry her. Flambert, her father assured her, had been warned, and did not care. He was ready to meet the challenge of such a young bride, and he would carefully tend as guardian, teacher, and mentor as well. There was nothing to fear.

"But there will be a great deal to fear, Father!" Tessa had assured him. "For I will not say the marriage vows!"

"Alas, my dear, I think, when the time comes, you will do so."

"I will humiliate you with my tantrums, sire, I do so swear it!"

"Then as your guardian and betrothed husband, Flambert will see that you are duly chastised." Then her father had slammed his fist upon the arm of his chair. "It is the English who have done this to you! A daughter's duty is to obey! You are nothing but an Anglo wildcat, Tessa, and I will be greatly pleased to visit in a few years and discover you to be a good and quiet wife to such a fine noble as Flambert!"

"You will find me dead, like as not!" Tessa shouted back. His own too-young third wife walked into the room then, and Tessa's father slammed his fist down upon the arm of his chair once again. "Madam!" he told his wife. "Provide me with no more daughters!"

And with an oath, he left them both. But it seemed he realized just how determined she was that she would not marry Flambert. When the day came for her to sail, she carefully planned to appear to board the ship, and then escape it and make her way back to England. The dream was a sweet one. Her grandfather would provide for her, ask nothing of her in return, and she would love and serve him dearly. But even as she sipped her morning coffee, she felt a strange lethargy stealing over her, and right before her head landed on the snowy white cloth of the breakfast table, she realized that her father had drugged her. No sodden, teary goodbyes for his only daughter. Pick her up, pack her aboard, and have done with her.

When she awoke, they were well under sail. And bleakly, she began to pray once again. "Do something, please, dear Lord! Stop this, just grant me one little miracle..."

And here she was, in this wretched position, the prisoner of a domineering English pirate, threatened from one side right up the other! The Red Fox was interested in one thing only—gold. She would be duly handed over to Flambert. Indeed, the wretch thought that *she* would write her own ransom letter!

He was mad.

She would certainly do no such thing.

She bit her lip suddenly, sitting up.

At least she had been delayed. She would certainly do nothing to aid this English pirate...

And she would begin to plot out her chances for escape.

The door suddenly slammed open.

He had returned. Once again, he was there, the Red Fox, the English scourge of the seas! A silhouette that dominated the doorway, he stood now with his hands on his hips, his booted feet spread wide apart, his legs solid and shapely. A well-defined brow shot up in a high arc as he surveyed her with cool disdain, a smile curving into the fullness of the man's sensual lips.

"Well, my lady?" he asked, and the question was surprisingly soft. "Have you determined to write your betrothed as yet?"

She stood, her own hands upon her hips, her stance every bit as solid and determined, her head high, her throat arched back. Her eyes sizzled into his.

"Hell will freeze over, my lord pirate, before I do anything whatsoever that *you* command!"

His smile deepened. He stepped into the room, closing the door quietly behind him.

"If the fires of hell will not freeze over, my lady, then they will begin to burn like an inferno, here and now!"

He took a stride toward her, and the courage she had summoned nearly failed her.

For then he took another step...

And another.

Chapter 3

Sweet Jesu, what was it with the woman? Didn't she have any sense within her at all? Here he was, the infamous Red Fox, striking terror into the hearts of many a stalwart French and Spanish sailor, and this little bit of baggage with her headful of golden hair and her wide azure eyes was defying him with complete confidence.

He had thought once that he might want to hurt her. Hurt her as that wretch Flambert had hurt sweet young Jane. Perhaps it wasn't in him to be quite so ruthless, or perhaps, now that the time had come, he had been too startled by Flambert's beautiful young fiancée. From the moment he had first seen her, the defiant creature in her elegant blue linen and velvet, her hair golden against it, her eyes matching the tempest of the sea, he had been at a disadvantage. Even when she had held her steel against him, when he had knocked aside her blade, he had been at the disadvantage. She was not what he had expected.

That she wasn't angered him all the more. Flambert did not deserve such a girl. Not someone so beautiful, not someone with so much courage. Not someone with such a wild and reckless will, so boldly determined that she would neither buckle nor bend!

So what? What did he do now? Now that he was walking toward her, the threat in his eyes if not in his heart—and yet all the desires and infernos of hell seeming to awake within him? She would rant, she would turn, she would beg, she would plead, she would somehow break before him now!

But she did not. He stood directly in front of her, and she did not back away. Those endlessly sea-blue eyes stared into his with a wild rage and fury, her slim hands and long, delicate fingers remained planted firmly upon her hips. He touched her chin, lifting it. And then, giving in to the fiercest temptation ever to touch his soul, he kissed her. No cruel, biting, pirate's kiss. He touched his lips to hers, fascinated, tasting, testing, breathing in her sweet fragrance, feeling the burst of heat that seemed to emanate from her, feeling the insatiable seduction of that very simple touch...

Then she was in his arms. She stiffened, yet it seemed for only seconds, and then he was feeling the softness of her, the full pressure of her breasts, the silk of her flesh, the honey-sweet taste of her mouth. *Well, I have threatened to rape and ravage,* he thought as his tongue delved more and more deeply, and his fingers wove into the velvet of her hair, and the fires built within his groin. *Ah, yes! I could well be the pirate she thinks me, I could do things I had imagined myself, I could strip her, have her here, now, for I am certainly the stronger, and the pirate, and in all my life, I have wanted no woman more...*

A groan escaped him, rumbling between their lips, and suddenly he found that he was holding her still, his hands now digging into her shoulders as he stared into her eyes, even more beautiful now, for they were touched with a tinge of dampness, as were his slightly swollen lips.

"Girl, you have no sense!" he all but roared at her. He gritted his teeth, and suddenly grabbed her and threw her down atop his bunk. He pointed a finger at her. "You will learn to obey me, or you will pay the consequences!"

To his amazement, she was instantly up once again, and stalking him. She walked to within a foot of him, blonde hair now spilling erotically down the length of her back. She stared at him, and suddenly, with no warning, sent her hand cracking hard against his face.

Stunned, he caught her wrist and wrenched her to him. "Never again, *ma belle!*" he warned softly. "Never, never again!"

"And what will you do?" she demanded heatedly, and despite his anger, he felt something inside him twist and groan, for he was certain that, despite her words and actions, she was close to tears. "Beat me, sir? Drown me? Throw me overboard, perhaps? Feed me to the sharks?"

"It would most assuredly give the sharks tremendous indigestion!" he swore. He thrust her a distance from him by the wrist, then released her, and bowed deeply once again. "Will you join us in the officers' quarters for dinner, my lady? Or would you prefer your meal brought here?"

"I do not dine with pirates," she informed him icily.

He smiled once again, determined that he would strip away her haughty assurance before some uncontrollable disaster came upon them. "Fine, my lady, you will not dine with pirates! But tonight, *ma belle amie,* you will sleep with one!"

With those words he turned again, nearly desperate to escape her.

Out on the deck, his fingers gripped fiercely around the railing, he looked out across the sea in the blood-red light of dusk. He could see the *Mademoiselle,* steered now by his own men, following their course across the waves. The sun was falling, the moon was rising. He had heard there would be a gale this morning, but they had sailed it out, and now the waves just rose and fell with a rhythmic beauty. The night was calm, the salt air was sweet, the breeze was cooling.

He still felt as if her hellfires swept through him. *Never.* Never in all of his life had he wanted something so very much. Never had he touched a woman and felt such an agony of desire...

He groaned out loud to the wind. Behind him, Billy Bowe, a wizened little old scrap of a man who had signed aboard as his personal servant, cleared his throat. "Captain, what will the lady's pleasure be? Shall I bring her a morsel to your cabin?"

The Red Fox—better known as Steven Mallory to his few close friends—leaned against the rail, now staring at Billy Bowe. What could the man know? Yet Billy seemed to be looking at him with sorrowful eyes, as if he sensed something wrong, though he knew not what.

"Aye, give her a morsel of something!" Steven muttered raggedly, shaking his head in frustration. Billy was an intuitive man. He had advised Steven often on what ships to take, he had known who sailed upon them, and he had been able to weigh what each Spanish and French captain might carry as cargo—he had the ability to read men, and thus had served Steven very well. Their commission, of course, came straight from Queen Anne, and it was true that they might be called privateers, but they were pirates, and that was that. Of course they only preyed upon the ships of England's enemies, but it made no difference. It was a harsh life, and one Steven had chosen only because of Jane.

Only because it might one day provide him with a way to have his revenge upon Raoul Flambert.

Steven had always loved the sea. His family home was near Bristol and his father was Lord Malcolm Mallory, who had long served high in the British navy. He fought first against the Dutch with Charles II, held fast to his command during the brief reign of James II, served William and Mary, and then William alone, and retired from the sea only with the death of King William, when he had determined that he had already outlived several monarchs and wanted to spend time with his family. Of course, by then his sons and daughters were grown, but his wife was glad to have him home, and Steven was still happy to visit the family estate when he was in England. But though he had determined not to join the Royal Navy himself, Steven had sailed all his life. He was fascinated by the countries and islands of the New World. He loved New York, the old "New Amsterdam" they had wrested from the Dutch, and he was in love with the rolling blue and green hills of the Virginia Colony. The Caribbean islands were places of lulling beauty, places with white sand; hot, shimmering suns; gracefully waving palms; and exotic plants and flowers. He had sailed for various monarchs himself on private ventures; he had grown rich in trade, and by the time the war broke out, he had acquired a handpicked, hearty, talented, and loyal crew. And still...

He would have battled any enemy ship with all his power, but he had not chosen to fight for the queen's cause until he had learned about Jane.

They had grown up together near Bristol. She was his third cousin, sweet, and yet with a lighthearted spirit for fun and adventure. Just as the hostilities had broken out, she had been sailing with her older brother in the Caribbean, quite near the island of Dejere. A French ship had attacked their merchant sloop. Jane's brother had been killed in the fighting, and Jane had been taken to Dejere.

He had never learned exactly what had happened to her there; she had cried every time he tried to talk to her about it. But she had been sold back to her father by Flambert after months of furious negotiations. No matter how the very pious Queen Anne had tried to intervene, there was nothing she could do to speed up the process. Jane had been with Comte Raoul Flambert for months before the French king finally demanded that his subject return her for the ransom agreed. Steven had sailed up the James River and into the new capital of the Virginia Colony, Williamsburg, just days after Jane had been returned there. Her brother was gone; he was all that she had. Steven was ready to bring her back to her family in England, but

Jane would not go. She had been engaged to Sir Ralph Lawston, a brilliant solicitor rising high in British politics, but she begged that Steven bring Ralph her letter severing the engagement. She would never marry, she assured Steven. She planned to remain in Virginia and bring Christianity westward in the colony to the Indians.

It was a noble enough cause, but Steven feared not only for her life, but for her sanity. Ralph had dearly loved her and would be heartbroken; her parents would be bereft.

Jane was staying in the Virginia manor of a mutual friend, when Steven first arrived after her return. He paced the length of the drawing room as he sought vainly for the right words to say to her. Jane, ever the lady, would never say that Flambert had raped her; when Steven suggested such a thing her lip would tremble and she would demand that he not make her talk about it. Frustrated, he paced the room like an angry lion. "I'll kill him, I swear, Jane, I will kill him for this. You mustn't throw your life away for him!"

"I cannot marry; I will never marry."

"All men are not Flambert!"

"But I will never—oh, Steven, you do not know!" she whispered.

"I want to know, I want to help you—"

"Then leave me in peace."

"I will marry you."

"Steven, don't be a fool, you do not love me."

"I have always loved you."

"As a good, dear friend. No, I will not marry you, and I will not go home. I must build my own soul again, Steven, please understand!"

At length, with no choice, he had left her.

Three weeks later, she died of a fever. He brought her home to England in a coffin, before which he sat morosely day after day of the long trip. When he reached England, he had taken a commission from the queen as a privateer in the War of the Spanish Succession. Within months, he had gained a reputation as one of the most dangerous pirates at sea. He was known among the enemy by his ship and by the name the Spanish had given him—Red Fox. *Red* for his hair, *fox* for his ability to come upon them out of nowhere and to slip away into banks of fog whenever it seemed he might be outnumbered or outgunned.

He had already taken a total of twenty-three Spanish ships and fourteen French.

But he had never been quite so anxious to take a ship as the *Mademoiselle*. Rumor had gone swiftly through the islands that Raoul Flambert, governor of the French colonial island of Dejere, was expecting a bride. She was the young and innocent daughter of a wealthy French aristocrat, very beautiful—a Christmas gift he was avidly awaiting from his old friend, the girl's father. And she would be aboard the *Mademoiselle*.

Steven hadn't given a whit if there had been a single piece of gold upon the ship. He would have died to have taken it—just to steal Flambert's bride.

Well, he had her. And now that he had her...?

He realized that Billy Bowe remained before him, waiting. Steven frowned.

"She's not willing to take her meal in the room with the officers, eh, Captain?" Billy said.

"She doesn't think of any of us as officers, Billy. To her we are pirates," he said irritably. "Besides, she probably speaks no English, and she would be most uncomfortable there."

"Perhaps we should have brought her maid aboard this ship, for company," Billy suggested.

"Perhaps you should stick to my laundry!" Steven said with a scowl, but Billy merely tried to hide a smile.

"What will it be, Captain? Do I bring her a decent meal, or bread and water?"

Steven's eyes narrowed and his features darkened further, but Billy pretended not to notice his captain's raw temper. "She's quite something, eh, your little French sprite!" He shook his head in admiration. Then he spat over the bow. "And to think! You are going to give her back to the likes of Flambert!"

Steven stiffened against the bow. "What would you have me do with her—pitch her overboard?" He hesitated just a moment, then felt some of the tension ease from his muscles. "The girl is not guilty of any crime; Flambert is the monster. If she is so determined on marrying him, I will see that she is returned to him. For a price that will break him, I swear it, and only when he believes that she has suffered as he has caused others to suffer."

"So... she will suffer, or she will not suffer?" Billy asked, and the trace of a smile remained at the corners of his lips.

"Will you attend to your tasks in the galley, man?" Steven demanded, aggravated.

"Aye, Captain, right away!" Billy agreed. He started away, then turned back. "Sir, shall I have some other quarters prepared for you, since the hostage remains in your own?"

"Aye—" Steven began, then he paused, remembering his promise to the girl. She would not eat with pirates.

But would sleep with one.

He thought again of Jane...

And gave little heed to the agony twisting inside him. "No, Billy. I will be sleeping in my own quarters tonight. If our guest finds herself uncomfortable... well, it is a risk one takes when sailing these waters!" he assured Billy. "Now out of my way, Mr. Bowe. I must see to our course!"

He stepped around Billy, determined to get the girl out of his mind. Steven had decided on the island where he would take his captured ship—and Flambert's captive fiancée. It was a very small island in the Caribbean, not far from Flambert's own Dejere, yet it was all but unknown, and those who did see it were usually wrecked upon the surrounding reefs, unaware of the deep channel that gave clear access—if you could find it. The sands were brilliantly white there, the sea the most extraordinary shade of aquamarine. The cliffs protected the harbor, there was a good supply of fresh water, and they had found harbor on the island often enough to have left behind some of the comforts of home. Steven and his men had built wood and thatch houses there and brought ashore cooking implements, sheets, blankets, basins, salt, rum, ale, and even such luxuries as stolen French soaps, perfumes, and fine vintage wines.

From there he would send out his negotiations with Flambert and begin to strip his captured ship to be refitted as an *English* vessel of war.

He walked on toward the helm.

* * *

Billy Bowe watched his captain leave, and sighed. Steven Mallory was a fine captain for whom to sail—and despite the Frenchies' and Spaniards' natural loathing of such a talented enemy, he was also an extraordinary man. They always placed tremendous importance on all human life when they fought—first on the lives of their own men, and then Captain Mallory was determined they should fight in a way that brought them the greatest riches and cost the fewest enemy lives as well. And they had done well. Their mate in the crow's nest had an eye like a hawk, and he could see ships at a tremendous distance, determine their names, and—from the continual rumor and gossip they picked up at their ports of call—calculate what their strengths were, and what their booty.

Indeed, the captain was a good man...

And long a tormented one!

Ah, well, now the time had come. Revenge lay in Steven Mallory's grasp. What would come of it all?

Billy Bowe started to whistle. He made haste to the galley, and with the cook's help, prepared a tray for their prisoner that was quite outstanding for shipboard. There was a fine Chablis to fill a delicate silver cup, there were fresh-caught, lemon-seasoned grouper; dark bread; bananas from their last port of call, and coffee with cream— Bessie, their one milk cow down in the hold, never failed to provide for them. With his tray in his hands, Billy paid his first visit to their lovely French captive.

He tapped on the captain's door and received no answer. He tapped again and heard a slightly guilty *"Entre!"* He pushed open the door with the tray—even a flower upon it—in his other hand.

He found the Lady Tessa seated at the captain's desk, the captain's log lying closed atop it, a plume, ink, and sheets of writing paper near it, yet untouched. She had been reading the log, Billy thought. Clever young miss. Plotting her own escape.

He came to the desk, sweeping up the log. "I shall take this out of your way, mademoiselle," he told her. An uneducated seaman, Billy had still learned to speak fluent French, Spanish, Dutch, Italian, and Portuguese, as well as his own Liverpool-accented English. "And *voila!*" he said, taking the cover from her plate. She looked from the tray to him, studying his wizened face, and then his slim, bowlegged body. He gave her a gamin grin and she smiled back, perhaps surprising herself by doing so.

"Merci," she told him. "It is lovely. I am not very hungry, I am afraid—"

"Oh, but you must be!" he told her gravely. "This is a ship at sea, my lady. You must keep your strength up since you—since you never know which way the wind might blow, and what opportunity might come your way."

She had started to reach for her wineglass, but she stared at Billy again. He'd never seen such eyes, he thought. They were exquisite. More beautiful than the exotic blue-green of any Caribbean waters. And her hair. It seemed like gold. There was nothing pale about it; it burned with the light of the sun.

"Opportunities..." she said softly. Then she suddenly reached for his hand. "You seem like a kind man," she told him swiftly. "If you would be willing to help me in any way with an escape, I would reward your richly, I swear it!"

Billy pulled his hand away in dismay. "Mademoiselle, I am so sorry! I—I cannot help you. I serve a good master—"

"A good master! One who kidnaps innocent women!" she charged him.

"My lady, I can only say again, I serve a good master. Take care with him. Speak gently, and he will see that you are quickly given to your fiancé—"

"Indeed!" she cried out, angry and disturbed. She picked up her wineglass and sipped at its contents, then drank more deeply. She drank until the glass was drained, then set it back down again.

"If there is anything that I can get you, my lady, it will be my greatest pleasure."

"Will you get me out of here?" she asked softly.

He shook his head sadly.

"Then there is nothing that you can do," she told him.

"'Til—I'll leave the tray," he told her, the logbook still in his hand. She watched him, half smiling, her eye on the book. She hadn't wanted him to take it.

Mallory would hang him if he didn't!

Billy Bowe left their captive, closing the door to the captain's cabin behind him. He leaned against it, hugging the logbook to his chest.

Ah, but it was going to be an interesting Christmas season! He stepped lightly then, about his business, not at all sure why he felt that the captain's dark mood might soon be disappearing to the wind....

* * *

Steven sat at the head of the table in the officers' mess, large by shipboard standards. The cabin, far down the length of the ship from the captain's private quarters at the bow, was handsomely appointed, with the paneled walls beautifully carved, the table and chairs in rich mahogany, their dishes fine china, their glasses Italian crystal. Sipping wine from his goblet, Steven mused that this pirating business did have its special benefits, for there was little that he and his men lacked in the matter of small extravagances.

"So we go to the Hidden Isle," his first mate, Walt Shelby, said to him, speaking low, and keeping the words, for now, between just the two of them.

"Aye, we'll see that the *Mademoiselle* is stripped there," Steven replied, speaking softly in kind. He shrugged. "Perhaps we can put her own crew to work transforming her into an English ship—now that I will enjoy! But when it is finished, I want the crewmen released to the French—only the girl stays behind."

"What of the girl's maid?" Walt asked him.

"I haven't given the woman much thought," Steven told him. "Perhaps... well, I will ask the Lady Tessa what her preference will be."

"Surely the girl will want her maid!" Walt said.

"Aye, surely. And therefore, perhaps, she will become a little bit more agreeable!" Steven said. "We'll see on the question of the maid, but I think the girl will be more manageable without her."

"She has yet to write of her position to Flambert?" Walt asked him.

Steven poured himself more wine. "No," he said after a moment.

"Sweet Jesu, remind her that she can be in her lover's arms before Christmas if she will but cooperate!" Will said. He was a good family man himself, a father with daughters. He was not pleased to be holding their captive, yet had heard enough about Flambert to be quite willing to strip the man of every treasure on Dejere.

He suddenly pointed a finger at Steven. "You must become more threatening toward her!"

"More threatening!" Steven protested. "They say the Spaniards quake when they hear I am near; men throw down their arms when I step aboard their ships. I *have* threatened her, I assure you. Besides, it does not matter. I will continue to urge her to write, but I will send Flambert my demands with a lock of her hair. With or without her compliance, I will see that our demands are met. Now, if you will excuse me, gentlemen...?" He rose and looked from Walt to Ned, the bo'sun, and to Thomas, their chief gunner. "Good night, my friends."

"Captain,'tis a night for celebration!" Thomas, a handsome youth, informed him with a wide smile. "You are the finest English pirate on the seas! All this time, we've lost but two men, and scoured the sea of enemy ships! Today we have bested that wretched Frenchie Flambert! Sir, you should stay with us awhile, and have a bellyful of good rotgut rum!"

Steven paused, shaking his head with a half smile. He stared down at Walt. "Alas, not tonight, my friends."

"Where are you off to?" Ned asked.

"To be a fiercer pirate!" Steven said, and left them.

Steven walked out on deck, feeling the wind against his cheeks for several minutes. Well, what was he, a man or a mouse? With a bitter amusement, he left the salty night air of the open sea and headed for his cabin again with long, sure strides.

Billy, bless him, had taken care with their captive, sliding the bolt across the door. When he'd walked out on her himself, he had been too aggravated to take such a precaution. Yet would she have escaped his quarters? Dangerous men stalked these decks, or so, surely, she must think!

Yet it was irritatingly true—she did not scare easily.

He paused before the door for just a moment. Then, not giving himself much time to think, he slid the bolt, entered the cabin, and slammed the door in his wake once again.

She was there, still fully dressed, her blue leather slippers still on her feet, peeking out from beneath the hem of her elegant skirt. She sat at the chair before his desk, but she was not writing any form of letter. She was using plume and ink—but only to sketch a likeness of Billy Bowe, a very good one. Billy's face was all there in the ink sketch, the wizened wrinkles from all his years in the hot sun, his gamin's smile. More. There was a look of kindness about his eyes. The sketch was very good. It had captured something of the spirit of the man.

She stared at him, saying nothing, as he entered the cabin and came her way. He sat at the foot of the bunk, reaching out for the sketch. He studied it again, then met her eyes. "This is excellent," he told her.

She didn't reply. He was quite certain that she wouldn't dine with a pirate by choice—and neither would she thank one. Steven gazed from the picture to her eyes. "I wonder what a sketch you were to do of me would resemble!" he said.

"A dragon," she said flatly.

"A dragon?"

"A monster, certainly."

He laughed softly. "Ah, well. Such is life. Where is my letter for your dear fiancé?"

"I have assured you that I will write no such letter."

"There is always tomorrow."

"What will be different tomorrow?" she demanded coolly.

He felt his smile deepen. *Become more threatening!* Walt had told him.

"Why, my lady. Come tomorrow, you will have spent your first night in the arms of a monstrous pirate!"

She stared at him again. So cool, so remote. So untouched by any threat...

And then she bolted. She threw herself up, slammed her fists against his chest, and raced for the door.

But he was there before her. Capturing her wrist. Spinning her back around.

And indeed...

She was in his arms.

Chapter 4

Her hands lay upon his chest. His white shirt was half opened, and she could feel his flesh, hot as molten lead, vibrant, muscled, covered with crisp dark red spirals of hair. He held her close, so close that she thought she would pass out as the breath left her body, and none seemed to return. Those eyes stared down into hers, green-gold, so masculine, they seemed to pierce through her, and condemn her.

"Let me go!" she demanded, dismayed that the words were nothing but a whisper.

"I am trying to let you go. You will not help me do so."

"I cannot help you!"

"Then, my lady, you will pay the price."

"You are all what they say you are. Ravaging beasts, scavengers, monsters—"

"Write the letter. Then I will leave you be."

Her lips were dry. The oddest spirals of heat were ripping through her, tormenting her. Write the letter. Escape this moment! she told herself.

But into Flambert's arms... No!

She found herself studying the man again. He was a good captain, the little gnome who had brought her dinner had told her. A good man.

He was a young one. Five to ten years her senior, she thought. Handsome, striking. The feel of his flesh beneath her fingers was incredibly exhilarating. The ripple of his muscles was both frightening and exciting.

She was losing her mind, she told herself. She was so desperate to escape Flambert that she was finding a pirate appealing.

But he *was* appealing. His face was both rugged and handsome, his mouth alluring, seductive. His eyes were compelling; even the sound of his voice was enticing...

"I—I will not write the letter," she told him.

"Then you'll sleep with me," he said flatly.

She cried out when he spun her around and started upon the tiny hooks and eyes of her gown. She tried to twist back to face him, to stop him, but his hands were firmly on her shoulders and his whisper touched her earlobe with both threat and promise. "Only the gown and the wicked petticoats; they would pierce flesh, my lady! Yet if you would fight with any greater menace, I could find myself ripping far more than intended!"

Her heart thundered against her chest. For the moment, she went still. One by one. Down her back. She felt the brush of his fingers, and with each accidental caress, she nearly cried out. Finished with the delicate task of undoing hooks and eyes, he took her gown and dragged it over her shoulders. Her boned petticoats and corset remained over her pantalettes and chemise. She stepped away from him quickly, but her fingers were trembling so that she couldn't untie the ribbon that held her petticoats around her waist. She found herself dragged back against him, now very aware of each little hair on his chest as it rubbed her back. His fingers made deft work of the ribbon, and she stepped away from him again, and out of the pile of petticoats. Across the room from him she spun around again, shoulders and breasts half-bared. She still tried to stand tall, to meet his eyes with a sizzle in her own. "Enough?" she demanded.

His eyes moved over her. Slowly. He smiled. She felt as if a hot fever were rising within her, coloring her flesh bloodred. "Not nearly enough, but for tonight..." He shrugged. "I will not be stabbed accidentally by bone."

"If—or perhaps *when*—I manage to stab you, monsieur, it will not be by accident!" she assured him.

"Then I will take the gravest care with you, my lady!" he promised, but she thought that he was laughing, and if so, he might just be laughing at them both, for his voice had a bitter note once again. He sat at the foot of the bed and drew off his boots, then pulled his white shirt over his head. Muscle glistened like gold in the candlelight.

Hugging herself slightly, Tessa moved back from the bed again. She thought that he was about to strip off his breeches, but she let out a little gasping sound and he turned to look at her. He arched a brow and reminded her softly, "My lady, this is your choice."

"Hardly my choice."

"You could write—"

"I shall take the left side of the bunk!" she told him haughtily, and crawled in, pulling the covers to her chin and all but falling from the space she allowed herself.

A moment later, he snuffed out the candle and crawled in beside her. And she cried out softly again when she felt the expanse of his fingers on her belly, pulling her in from the edge. She trembled, yet was surprised by the soft sound of the voice that touched her in the darkness. "My lady, I am seeking only to save you from a nasty fall. Come into the center of the bed."

"I—"

"You are safe, my lady, this night."

She went still. She felt him settle beside her, his arm remaining around her. He did not sleep, but he did not move. He had told her that she would be safe this night...

She sighed, the air escaping her. She closed her eyes, amazed to realize that she was exhausted. And then she found herself wondering again about the man beside her. There was a pleasant scent to him, masculine, clean, touched by the sea. He was beautifully built, strongly built, supple, lean, powerful. She liked his eyes, his rich, full head of unpowdered hair. She liked the length of him, the sound of his voice...

He was a pirate, demanding a ransom for her. And she was lying beside him, wishing...

Wishing that she could be with him, instead of with a man like Raoul Flambert.

52

"Rest, my lady," he said very softly, a hand smoothing a tangle of hair from her face. There was tenderness in that touch. She felt a trembling seize her again, and she knew that it was not from fear.

It had come from a sudden longing...

"Truly, I have no desire to harm you, my lady. Think on this. If you cooperate at all, you will be with your betrothed, a sweet bride by Christmas. Dream of what you may ask your rich noble to grant you as a Christmas gift!"

She stirred slightly on the bed. "There is only one thing that I want for Christmas!" she murmured.

It was dark, very dark. She couldn't see his face, but she sensed that he had risen on an elbow to look down at her. He could probably see in this darkness. "What is that?" he asked her, his tone very serious.

She moistened her lips. "My freedom!" she told him.

"Your freedom? From me? But I have told you—you can achieve that easily enough—"

"Just freedom!"

"Ah, from all men," he said, and there was amusement and mockery in his voice. "But, lady, I can scarcely demand a massive ransom from your betrothed if I do not plan to return you to him."

"Will you leave me be?" she demanded angrily.

But he was silent again. She knew that he watched her still. After a moment he said, "Raoul Flambert is to slice and dice me for this indignity, *ma belle*, remember?"

"Indeed! Now, if you intend to set me upon the rack or—or—"

"Rape you?"

"Yes, if you intend to, please get on with it! And if you don't, if you've nothing more to torment me with tonight, I pray you, leave me be."

"Ah, but I lie here in such torment!" he murmured, and there was a rich, tremulous sound to his voice, no mockery, no bitterness.

A simple truth, she thought.

She closed her eyes tightly.

She prayed to sleep.

Eventually she did. And she dreamed. Sweet dreams in which the world was different, so very different! It was a world in which her father had not intruded, had not imposed. One in which she was not sailing across the sea to face a man like Raoul Flambert, nor was she a prisoner of any pirate. She was simply loved. Strong arms held her. She lay warm and comfortable and secure against all evil. A gentle mist surrounded her and her sleeping lover, and she was free to bask in his masculine excellence, his strength, face against his bronze chest, nose teased by the tickling of the short dark hairs there...

She awoke, and for a moment she did not know where she was. Her nose *was* being tickled by the hairs on a very masculine, hard-muscled chest. Her hand lay atop it too. She was stretched beside him—no, half atop him!—and all the warmth was very real, growing wickedly now as she realized her position. She looked up slowly to his face and realized that he had been awake some time, that he had known she slept there, that he had let her sleep so, his fingers moving gently through her hair all the while.

She bolted away from him, dismayed. The bastard was a pirate, only interested in selling her back to Raoul, and keeping his hands off her because she would be worth more undefiled!

Those green-gold, glittering hazel eyes of his had been studying her with a surprising warmth, but they narrowed quickly now. "Having second thoughts about that letter, *ma belle?*" he demanded.

"No!" she told him curtly, and leaped from the bed, quickly looking for her clothing. She stepped into the pile of her petticoats, pulling them up rapidly. He watched her silently as she dressed, and she found herself more alarmed, more afraid of him than she had ever been. Oh, what an idiot! She was coming to care for him, making comparisons between him and the man whose arms awaited her on Dejere.

A two-foot hunchback would have been preferable to Raoul! she told herself, so thinking that this pirate was more appealing was certainly no real compliment. And yet she *was* thinking that. Even if she were to be forced to spend her life with Raoul, she would give almost anything to know what it would be like...

To be loved. No, not love; for sure, it was only a lost illusion. Maybe then the illusion was what she craved, just once perhaps, just for a night...

She was struggling to do her own hooks when she felt him at her back, ably redoing what he had undone last night. "We'll get your things from the other ship today," he told her. "We've a tub on board, if you wish to bathe. Anything that we can provide, we will—"

She spun on him, not caring that all her hooks were not in place. "Air!" she told him. "I—I want some air. Please—I just need air!" With that she spun again and headed for the door to the cabin. It was unlocked. She swung it open and stepped outside, hurrying to the wooden rail at the bow of the ship.

In the distance, there was an island. A beautiful island. Cliffs abounded around it; rich greenery grew there. Sweet Jesu, but it would be a dangerous place, she thought. Surrounded by outcrops of rock...

* * *

In the cabin, Steven winced as she tore from his presence. Well, what in God's name did the woman want? He had left her to fall asleep in peace last night.

He had lain awake until the coming of the dawn, fighting the heat and agony that had burned through him all those wretched hours. She had been so determined to keep her distance—he should have let her. So what if she would have fallen to the floor! She wouldn't have been in half the agony the night had caused him.

He spoke her language; he tried to be polite. But when she had awakened, she had wanted anything but to be near him!

Even as he tugged on his shirt and boots, he was astounded to hear a startled cry from the deck—and the sound of a splash. He went tearing out of the cabin, only to discover that his crew was staring at him as if he'd grown horns and cloven hooves overnight.

"She's jumped!" Thomas cried in dismay.

"What in God's name did you do to her?" Walt demanded.

"Nothing! Not a damned thing!" Steven replied briefly, hopping up and down as he stripped off the boots he had just donned, leaped to the edge of the rail, and dived cleanly into the water.

He hit the warm Caribbean sea easily, pitching downward until his strong kicks stopped the impetus of his motion. He surfaced, sweeping his hair back, looking out to study the horizon. There! She was ahead of him, swimming strongly toward the island. She must have imagined it as a refuge; perhaps she hadn't realized that there was a channel and that their ship was seeking the island as its own haven.

She had merely wanted freedom, wanted to escape...

And again, perhaps she hadn't realized her distance from it, for as he swam harder, catching up with her, he could hear the ragged way she was inhaling. She was surprisingly enough a very good swimmer, but she had pitched over the bow fully clothed, and her skirts and petticoats were weighing her down heavily. Even as he swam determinedly and was almost upon her, she started to go down, a small cry escaping her.

He caught her, dragging her to the surface. She coughed and sputtered—and turned her energies toward fighting him. "Let me go, you rogue!"

"You're drowning, little fool!" he charged her.

"I'm not drowning, I swim very well, I'm just—" She broke off with a startled cry as she saw him take his knife from the sheath at his calf and direct it toward her.

"Hold still!" he ordered fiercely, chopping away at the heavy skirt that was about to drag them both down to a watery death.

"I can do this myself—" she gasped out, fully aware that her clothes were very near to killing them both.

"So you weren't trying to kill yourself!"

"Kill myself?" she demanded. "Over you? I can swim exceptionally well, I'll have you know—" she began, but her head was suddenly under water as he tugged at her skirt, dragging its weight away from her, and letting it fall to the bottom of the sea. She struggled back up. "As I was saying, I swim exceptionally well— unless someone is trying to drown me!"

"It's a long way to the island, my lady!" he told her.

She trod water as she stared at it, then looked back at him. Her skirts were gone now. Perhaps she was debating, wondering if she might just possibly swim away from him, straight to her freedom, once again.

"You might make the island. And if you did, my crew and I would be joining you shortly."

"What?"

"It's my island. Well, all right, it isn't mine, but I consider it so. It's on very few maps, and to most men, it is unapproachable."

"But not to such an experienced pirate!" she charged him.

"It's very comfortable," he assured her, still treading water as his crew stared on, wondering what could possibly be going on between them. "We've built houses, we've—"

"You can't have!" she cried in dismay.

"But we have," he told her softly. "Shall we sail there?" he asked her softly. "It is a very long swim!"

Defeat touched her eyes just briefly. She closed them, then they flew open once again, and she began to swim strongly past him.

In seconds, she was back at the ship. Billy Bowe was there, ready to throw the rope ladder over for her and Steven to board, ready also with a blanket to wrap her in. The sea water had been warm enough, but the breeze this morning was cool.

Steven felt it himself as he crawled up the ladder to the deck. She stood there, wrapped in her blanket, staring at him. Then she swung around, wet hair sending out a spray, and marched back to his cabin.

She slammed the door hard. He started after her, but then stopped and smiled. Witch.

He followed her but didn't enter his cabin.

He slid the bolt, loudly and securely, on the door.

Chapter 5

Steven made it a point not to return to his cabin. When they were safe within the harbor and the anchor had been cast, he boarded the first small boat for the island, still fuming from his latest encounter with his hostage. His crew had continued to give him dire looks, and to the last man, they were wondering what he had done to the girl to make her willing to throw herself overboard. It was hard to explain that she probably swam much better than the majority of them, especially since half of them were, oddly enough, afraid of water, period. Then he decided he just wasn't giving anybody any explanations; they could think what they damned well pleased.

Coming to his own home on the isle, he found that it had been kept clean in his absence and made ready for his return by Judith, the widowed, elderly matron who had sailed with him long ago from England for the Virginia Colony, only to discover when they stopped by the island that she loved it; she loved the sun, the sea, the easy, soft breeze, the lazy feel of it all. Tall and thin, with iron-gray hair and a very handsome face still, perpetually clothed in black, Judith was happy enough to fend for him when he was there, and to care for his home in his absence. She had her own little house on the isle, and liked living in it alone. When he arrived on the beach, he looked up the cliff to his own home, and was glad he had left his captive behind.

Damn her. He was going to write his *own* letter to Monsieur le Comte Raoul Flambert. And he was going to do it before his little wildcat was brought to him. She was exceptionally distracting.

Walking from the beach to his house, he waved to a few more of those who called the Hidden Isle home; Miles and Jake, fishermen who pirated with him on occasion; John Hill, the feisty little Irishman who governed the small community in Steven's absence and arranged for the coming and going of captured ships at Steven's command; Bill Whaley, who kept their local tavern supplied; and Rachel and Louise, John Hill's two young daughters, who were playing by the surf, kicking up sea and sand.

He burst into his own little house which was simply composed of two rooms separated by a central hall, the bedroom to the left, and the main room where he entered. The main room was quite large, with a huge fireplace and cooking hearth spread across the far wall, a large dining table before it, heavy, carved of oak, and to the other side of the room, a handsome set of Tudor chairs and chaises, all set comfortably around the room with a small cherrywood table in the center.

Steven's attention was instantly drawn to the table, for it seemed that Judith had been quite busy in his absence, setting the house up for Christmas. While there were no holly leaves with which to decorate here on the island, nevertheless, Judith had set up a fine crèche in the midst of wild island leaves and fragrant flowers, all displayed in the center of the cherrywood table.

Steven paused to pick up one of the handsomely crafted figures.

The crèche was Spanish; he could remember the ship they had gotten it from. Holding the tiny Christ figure he'd taken from its cradle of hay, Steven mused over the beauty of the piece someone had so patiently carved. Someone had created an angelic, peaceful face for the infant Jesus. He hoped that the workman had been well rewarded for his efforts, and he might have been sorry to have stolen such a piece, but then it had merely been meant for the marketplace in some Spanish port, and he was certain that he would give the beautiful crèche as fine a home as anyone else might. He found it extraordinary, yet even as he held it, he felt a wave of guilt washing over him.

The girl had been a Christmas gift for Flambert. Not that he could feel any guilt where Flambert was concerned, but...

She would be free soon enough. With or without her participation.

He firmly set the little piece down and turned his back on it. He felt as if the figure's eyes were following him. Mary was probably giving him a most condemning look, and even Joseph might have his eyes boring into Steven's back!

"No harm will come to her!" he muttered out loud. "I've just got to get her off this island as swiftly as I can!"

He strode into his bedroom and went to the large captain's desk near the window, sitting down in the swivel chair. He drew writing paper, his quill, and ink from the desk, and with bold determination, he began to write his ransom letter to Flambert:

Monsieur le Comte Flambert, if rumor has served you well, you will already be aware that the Red Fox has taken your Christmas gift, your bride. May I compliment you, sir, on the exquisite beauty of your fiancée.

He ceased writing for just a moment. Then it seemed that his quill began to fly across the page.

The lady has the softest skin, alabaster in its perfection, silk to touch. Her hair is like a spill of radiant sunlight, her eyes rival the aquamarine of the seas around me. She is pure fire and spirit as well, and I shall be loath to return her to you at any price, but then, Monsieur le Comte, I will be eagerly awaiting word on just what you will pay. I suggest all haste. My fascination for the demoiselle grows by the hour.

He stopped writing again.

Sweet Lord, but writing the letter had gone quickly. Describing his hostage had been an easy effort. He stared at the words he had written, feeling a growing irritation with himself. Well, it was done. It could be sent. The girl was so determined to be free of Steven, let her have Flambert. She would discover herself what Flambert was like.

Ah, and there the rub! Yet how could Steven be the one to pirate her ship, abduct her—and then tell her that *Flambert* was the despicable rodent?

Impatiently, he folded his letter, dropped hot wax upon it to seal it, and stamped it with the insignia from the ring on his little finger, a baying fox. It was only then that he sensed something behind him. He spun the chair around.

She was there. Standing near the foot of the bed, her hair cascading down her back in endless sun-touched waves, her eyes burning into his now like blue fire. She had shed her chopped and soaked clothing, and was gowned now in elegant emerald-green with full sweeping sleeves and a soft beige underskirt.

She was... breathtaking. So much so that he felt an instant tightening in his groin and a swift, irrational rise of his temper to go along with it.

He was especially irritated that he hadn't heard her come in. He could usually hear the fall of a sparrow's feather! But then, he had been deep in concentration, describing her to Flambert, trying to make Flambert realize just what he was holding.

"What are you doing there?" he snapped.

"I was delivered here," she returned icily.

"Delivered—to stand behind me?" he demanded.

"Delivered to your doorstep, ushered into your house. And I just came in here and—and saw that you were writing."

Had she been reading over his shoulder? But he had written to Flambert in English. She couldn't know what he had said in his taunting demand.

"So?" he inquired.

She spun around on her heel, exiting the room. He heard her walking through the broad main hall of the house, toward the door. He leaped up and followed her quickly.

"Where are you going?" he demanded.

Her lashes fell over her eyes for a moment. "I had thought I was—to stay here. If not, I shall see to myself—"

"Get back in here, my lady. You *are* to stay here. You're a pirate's captive, remember? You are to see to my things, cook for me, clean for me."

She arched an elegant brow. "Oh, I do not think so!" she assured him.

It hadn't been what he had meant to say, but her cool refusal left his temper flaring.

"I like my coffee strong, hot, and plain, my lady. And I like it very much when I first awaken."

She arched an eyebrow in response.

There was a knock on the door. Without awaiting a reply, Billy Bowe shoved it open, and Steven quickly saw why. Poor Billy was laboring beneath the weight of a heavy trunk, and all but got it through the doorway before giving out and sighing. "Captain, I beg your pardon there, but..."

"Leave it, Billy, leave it!" he said in English.

Billy nodded. "Well, if I'm free, Cap'n, I'm headed into the tavern, am I."

Steven started to nod, then shook his head. "*A* moment, Billy," he said, still speaking English. "I've written the ransom note for the girl. The Frenchman must know we've got her by now, and since she'll not take up a quill herself, I've sent him a message warning him that his bride is a tempting morsel. Indeed, bring it to Patrick, and have him get it to a neutral ship and into Flambert's hands as swiftly as possible. I swear if I do not hear from him in twenty-four hours, 'tis like as not I'll have wrung her neck!"

Billy arched a brow high. "Captain—"

"All right, Billy, so perhaps I'll not wring her neck, but by God, Flambert will not have her returned in the same shape she came aboard my ship, I do so swear it!" He stared at his hostile captive, and left them both for a moment to retrieve his letter, and then thrust it into Billy's hands.

Billy looked at the girl unhappily. "Captain, I—"

"What?"

Billy sighed. "I'll see it reaches a neutral ship," Billy said, and departed, and Steven found himself alone again with his beautiful hostage.

He bowed deeply, mockingly. "Make yourself at home, my lady."

She lifted her chin very high and pointed to the doorway between the rooms of the house. "Is that to be my prison?" she asked.

"You're not in prison—"

"The room will do. You will, of course, stay out of it now?"

He crossed his arms over his chest. "No, I will not. And you are not in prison in this house."

"Merely on this island."

He grated his teeth together with impatience. "Aye, then, you're a prisoner on this island! And if that's the way you'd have it, you'll *be* prisoner in this house! You'd be trying to swim away, I imagine, were I to let you free to roam the place!"

"Indeed, I would do *anything* to escape you!" she hissed.

Freshly infuriated with her, he strode out of the house, slamming the door in his wake. Outside the house, a number of the crew awaited him, and he called out a sharp order. "See that she doesn't move! Two men on duty; spell yourselves, two hours on, two off, until I return!"

Scowling in a fury, he headed for the tavern himself. He was ready for a good pint of pirated rum!

* * *

He spent the afternoon drinking with his crew, able to throw some caution to the wind, since John Hill would be keeping a sane and sober eye on the island. Walt was there, drinking in the tavern as well, yet Steven was quite certain that the whole lot of them could instantly sober themselves should it become necessary. There was little danger here. Even if an enemy ship came upon the island, there were guns positioned upon the cliffs to the harbor, and most any ship would rip up on the coral before coming close enough to offer them any real threat.

Rose and Sarah, two free-spirited tavern girls, kept the rum flowing, the food coming, and a high level of entertainment going; singing, dancing, and carrying on all the way around. Steven tried to throw himself into the festivities of coming to a home port after such a successful capture. But it seemed he smiled too hard, laughed too easily.

Falsely.

He wanted nothing more than to return to his house.

Why? he mocked himself. To torture himself longing for another man's Christmas present? Ah, it wasn't that. He didn't give a damn for Flambert, it was just that...

Sweet Jesu, if he could be the wretch she thought him for just one night!

Finally he wearied of trying to laugh and jest with his fellows. He left the tavern behind and made his way to his own house, not nearly as drunk as he had longed to be, plagued much more by a headache instead.

He passed one of his men dozing on the porch, nodded, and entered the house to hear splashing sounds. Puzzled, he made his way across the main hall to the bedroom door, and paused there.

She was bathing. Someone had seen to it that the massive wooden hip tub had been brought in to her. They had taken it off a French ship about six months prior and it was quite an elegant piece of extravagance, with hammered gold lions interlaced with the bronze trim. The tub was fashioned almost like a lady's chaise, with a high back and nearly enough room to completely stretch the legs out in front.

Hers were not stretched out. They were hugged to her chest as she leaned back, her eyes closed. Her water still steamed, and smelled subtly and sweetly of some bath oil. Her eyes did not open as he stood there. Her hair was up high, coiled and pinned to the top of her head. Her throat seemed incredibly long. Standing there, watching her, he ached as he could not remember aching in all of his life.

Her eyes opened suddenly, glistening aquamarine, glittering by firelight.

"How dare you!" she whispered furiously. "You could knock; you've no right to just stand there!"

"Pirates do not knock," he told her.

"Out!" she demanded.

He didn't leave. He strode to the tub and knelt down beside it. He dangled his fingers into the hot water, feeling as if the steam infused him.

"Get away from me!" she demanded again, but her words were tremulous, and when he met her eyes again, it seemed that they were now tormented with an unhappiness that tore at his heart. "You smell like the whole of the tavern!" she told him, and added softly, "and like every strumpet within it!"

"Pirates do not knock," he told her, "nor do they explain themselves, my lady."

With a sudden angry motion she slashed her hand through the water, dousing his head and shirt. Startled and infuriated, he rose, shaking off the water, reaching into the tub for his captive. Before he quite knew what he had done, he had taken her naked and dripping from the tub and carried her across the room.

"Don't you—"

"My lady, you do not seem to understand the situation here!" he told her angrily, his own voice shaking. What the hell was he doing? He now had her in his arms, all of her, and all of her naked perfection. Slim, she seemed nothing heavier than a feather to carry.

Yet every inch of that slimness had been curved and molded into something incredibly beautiful and exotic and sensual, full breasts with crimson crests, the peaks as tight as pebbles, tempting his touch, his lips, his caress. Hips that flared provocatively, legs that were exquisitely long and shapely, slim waist, silken flesh, the scent of her sending a pounding torture straight to his head and heart.

Before he knew it he was down upon the bed with her, tasting that flesh, palms exploring the wild beauty of each shape and curve.

"Don't you dare! Get off me, leave me!"

She pounded against him in sheer fury, but something within him had seemed to explode with the longing she had elicited. "Pirates don't ask permission, my lady!" he assured her. "And you have been duly warned..." he whispered, his lips touching her throat.

She whispered softly to him then. "Please, not like this, not when you've been drinking so much, please..."

Oh, she was good!

A ragged groan tore through the entire length of him. He didn't know if he cried it out loud, or if it silently tore him asunder. He must have stiffened there for endless minutes, then he fell to his side. After a moment, he touched her cheeks. The dampness there was not from the steam of her bath, but from the tears which had touched them. Again he groaned, and fighting the agony in his groin, he slipped an arm around her and pulled her close. "It's all right. I'm not going to hurt you," he said softly.

She didn't fight him, didn't move, didn't whisper a single word.

Thank God for the rum blurring his senses, blurring the pain. After a time, it even made him sleep.

* * *

When he awoke, he panicked to realize his captive was gone.

He leaped out of his bed and raced out to the main hall. Billy Bowe sat at the dining table, sipping coffee.

"Where is she?" Steven demanded heatedly.

"The waterfall," Billy said.

"The waterfall?" Steven roared. "Alone?"

"Now honestly, Captain, how's the girl to escape the isle? She awoke and asked if she might just feel the morning's breeze, and I told her about the stream and the waterfall. No one will disturb her there, and the lass couldn't just be kept pacing the confines of this room again and again, eh, sir?"

"If the French ever get their hands on us, *we'll* be pacing much smaller spaces!" Steven assured him angrily. "You can't trust her! You dare not trust her; she knows every little twist of manipulation. If I don't find her, Billy Bowe, you'll discover just what it's like to pace small spaces!"

"She's getting to you, eh, Captain?"

Steven swore softly and slammed his way out of the house, praying that he would find her, that she had not disappeared somehow.

He had slept late and the sun was already rising high. He followed the trail upward along the cliff and through the foliage quickly, nearly at a run, as if he could make up for lost time. He broke into the ragged piece of land where the big palm grew on a spit overlooking the clear freshwater spring below. He leaned against the tree, gasping for breath, and looked below.

She was there. Naked. Beneath the place where the water fell in sheer cascades. Her head was back, and the cool, clear water rushed over her face and hair.

"You wretched little witch!" he raged down at her.

She wasn't startled; she wasn't at all surprised to see him. Her eyes opened on his, her chin remained high, a delicate brow hiked just a little.

"What now, Monsieur le Pirate?" she inquired.

"What did you do, walk out stark naked in front of Billy Bowe and strut through the village so?"

A smile curved her lips. "My clothes are hanging on the branch just yonder," she told him.

He wanted to look to the branch but couldn't tear his eyes away from her.

She was more beautiful in the daylight—and through sober eyes—than even he had realized. Everything about her elegant, slim, haunting, perfect.

"Damn it, if you think that you can continue to play me like a fool, my lady, you are mistaken! You beckon, you tease, and then you cry foul! Well, lady, bear this in mind! I am a pirate, and our very purpose in life is to raid and ravage——"

"Threats!" she cried to him, striding out from the waterfall, naked, golden, her hands on her hips, her eyes alight with pure defiance. "Threats, threats, threats! Well, are you a pirate, or aren't you?"

"Ah, dammit, lady, that I am!"

And once again, before he knew what he was doing, he was in motion.

From the cliff he dived into the clear cool waters below, and even as the water enwrapped him, he knew that this time, when he touched her, he would not let her go.

Chapter 6

Just what in God's name had she been doing? Tessa wondered with a moment's panic. There would be no turning back now. She knew that from the look in his eyes, right before he had plunged from the cliff and into the water.

But even as he emerged from the crystal-clear water, fully dressed and drenched, she felt the fierce pounding begin in her heart again, and she realized that she knew exactly what she had been doing. She had weighed *life,* or at least her life, and had decided that there was every likelihood that she would be forced to spend year after endless year with Raoul Flambert. And if that was eventually to be the case...

Then she wanted this first. So he was a pirate. So he had captured her ship, and intended to sell her back to Raoul. He hated Raoul—that she didn't fully understand. But it had become surprisingly clear to her in the time that had passed between them now that the Red Fox was a gentleman pirate. And he was striking, muscled like steel, with a smile that compelled and haunted, like the deep, rich tones of his voice. If the rest of her life was to be with Flambert, then this would be hers first. Her time with this man. She liked him, she admired him, she found him fascinating, no matter what these outrageous circumstances. Far beneath the pirate facade, he was an exceptional man. She might have done a lot of fighting, teasing, taunting... and walked away from him. Last night they had come so close...

But just as she had discovered that she longed for him, she longed for the little piece of paradise she intended to touch to be just that. She didn't want him awakening with a rum-soaked headache, not remembering a thing about her when it would be one of the most momentous occasions of her life. She wanted to awaken knowing that he...

That he had touched something special as well.

Ah, well, so now she had done this! And he had risen in the water to come striding toward her, and the gold in his eyes seemed to glisten like pure fire, and the length of her seemed alive with the waiting. Again, the stirrings of panic seized her as he neared. What would he remember of her? She had so very little idea of what she was doing here. She only knew that he had touched her as no one had before, awakened a strange, exciting heat in her blood. Indeed, he had done something quite miraculous to her, for how else could she stand here, waiting...

He paused directly in front of her, fists clenched at his sides, his soaked clothing hiding nothing of the tension, or ardor, within his body. She tried very hard to keep her eyes level with his, and not let them fall to the bulge in his slick wet trousers. "Lady, you tempt beyond mercy—" he warned her.

"Are you afraid of me, pirate?" she demanded breathlessly. She fought for control. She tried to accost him with such a tremendous bravado when she was beginning to shake like a leaf in the wind. But she soon ceased to shake as she was drawn into his arms with a harsh jerk, and she was achingly aware of the pounding of his heart too as she felt her nakedness crushed to him. Fire seemed to burst from within him, warming her as his hands ravaged her hair, his lips and tongue her mouth. She clung to him, savoring every bit of wild, sweet sensation, finding that she shook anew, that she could barely stand, and yet she wasn't in the very least cold; indeed, despite the cool water, she was afire.

She started to fall in earnest, but he slipped his arms beneath her, lifting her, his eyes blazing, face tense, as he carried her from the cool fresh water to the on the soft grassy bank beyond. The breeze whispered softly and gently, tree branches danced and fell and made shadows on the earth and water. She scarcely saw the day, and she was aware of every sensation, the feel of the earth at the back, the slick dampness of the water droplets that clung to their flesh...

She felt his fingers in her hair again, his lips upon hers, his hands... all upon her nakedness. She wanted to undo his shirt, to touch his flesh, yet she hadn't quite the confidence to do it, and in seconds, it didn't matter. He had stripped off his shirt and stood again, casting off boots and breeches, and for a moment, staring at his bare, bold splendor, she felt again as if the earth itself were shaking, as if she were slipping from it. But then he was down with her again, and the feel of his flesh against her own was a new, exciting fire, and the tempest of his touch swiftly grew wild and demanding. She met his kiss, twisted to his touch, and caught her breath when she suddenly found her limbs parted and the weight of his body between them. He cradled her in his arms, and she fought the sudden, searing pain that wracked her, biting her lower lip, and willing herself not to cry out. But hot, dazed tears stung her eyes and she wound her arms very tightly around him, burying her face against his neck and shoulders so that he wouldn't sense her sudden agony. Yet he went very still, groaning softly. And then his words, whispered in French, touched her earlobes. "Sweet Lord, but why did you tempt me so? Now it is all too late. I would not have hurt you, *ma belle*, yet now I fear that I cannot leave you!"

"Don't leave me!" she managed to whisper, holding close to him.

"Tessa..." Her name on his lips was so soft, so tender. But then it seemed that his mind was made up, that he had come this far...

And there was nothing to be gained by stopping here.

He caught her chin, bringing her eyes to his. He kissed her eyelids, and her lips, and he began to move within her again, so slowly at first that she discovered, as the pain ebbed, she was rocking to meet his thrust before it came, and once again the feeling of longing, of hunger, of intense craving came sweeping back into her. Each magical second then seemed to bring some sweeter hunger, a greater need. She reached and stretched, and did not even know what she sought...

Until it cascaded down upon her. Beautiful little silver rivulets of ecstasy seemed to encompass her; the world was black except for those silver explosions. She was only dimly aware of him, her pirate, the man who had brought her to this shimmering glory, and she was vaguely aware that he too seemed to reach that wickedly sweet pinnacle, to become as tense as a bow, and to bring a new heat like molten mercury to sweep within her...

Damp, breathless, fighting for reason once again, Tessa lay still as he fell beside her, silent as well, staring up at the sky. Then, after a long moment, he groaned and sat up, staring down at her with his features rigid and hard. Her heart seemed to leap inside her, and she bit into her lower lip again, wondering why he should be so damned angry when she was the captive here.

"You couldn't just behave, eh, my lady?" he demanded. "You'll be no man's chaste Christmas bride as it now stands! God knows, lady, your wretched betrothed may deny you now—"

"Ah! And you'll not get your ransom!" she cried, sitting up as well, tears stinging her eyes as she crossed her arms over her chest, feeling foolish and ashamed. She had wanted him so badly. She had wanted him to want her, she had longed for the magic, and now...

Now she knew that what had been momentous for her had not been for him—he wasn't such a gentleman, he was merely determined to sell her for the highest price!

She flew at him in a sudden fury, fists flying, seriously trying to do him harm. He grunted as she belted him in the chest, but he caught her wrists then, dragging her down and beneath him.

"You little fool!" he berated her. "Don't you understand, my argument was with your wretched fiancé, not you! I never wanted to hurt you! Jesu, but you are driving me insane! Last night you cry out, today you stand naked in a stream and taunt me until I cannot bear it! And when I am dismayed that I might have ruined your life—"

"You didn't ruin my life!" she snapped out. He paused, handsome features still very tense, gold eyes wary and angry.

"If you had just—" he began.

"Oh, you dolt!" she charged him. "I do not want to marry Flambert; I despise him as well, you fool! My father arranged this wretched marriage, so determined that I would be Flambert's Christmas bride."

She had said too much. She went very silent, and very still, staring up at him, swallowing hard.

"Ah..." he said after a moment. "What an amazing creature you are, my lady. First you were as feisty as a chained panther, then as innocent and outraged as a nun! Next you are the most amazing seductress... Yet now I understand. It was not personal in the least. You seduced me in the hopes of escaping him!"

No, she hadn't. But against his anger, it seemed the best defense. She narrowed her eyes and spat out, "Aye, and why not? You're supposed to be a pirate; I've surely but added to your most wondrous reputation!"

"Comte Flambert and I have both been taken, my lady! By a little minx who wants nothing for Christmas... but freedom."

"Is that so horrid a thing to want?" she whispered.

After a moment, he shook his head. Some of the anger and tension seemed to leave his rugged features, yet the gold still blazed in his eyes. She thought that he would rise, release her then. But he did not. He lowered his head, touched her lips again. He kissed her very slowly, tasting, savoring. She tried to twist her head away, yet he held her to his kiss, and after a moment she no longer had the will to leave him; she could feel the fantastic warmth, the hunger, the longing building within her once again.

And the memory of the magic he had brought still remained so vividly fresh, so sweet within her...

"What are you doing?" she whispered desperately when his face rose above hers again.

"Well, *ma belle,* we have come this far. It matters not now how much further we tread."

She trembled beneath him. "It matters!" she whispered. "It matters because..."

"Because?"

"You have to want me!" she managed to say.

"Oh, lady! I do want you!" he said harshly. "Dear Lord, but I do want you. Indeed, Tessa, what Flambert has been denied, I will take to heart as my own incredible Christmas gift!"

His lips touched hers again. His hands crafted their magic upon her flesh.

And she touched him. Stroked the muscles of his shoulders, planted her lips against the burning vibrance of his flesh. The world rocked anew, and she was lost in the passion and desire, sweeter, higher, this time, for there was no pain. Only the absolute wonder, the ecstasy. And when it was over, she noted that the sun had moved downward, that the shadows had deepened. He held her in silence for the longest time, then sighed. "We must go back. Before we are missed, and others come to find us."

She said nothing, but rose and found her clothing. She was startled when he insisted on helping her with her hooks, and somehow touched by the intimate feel of his fingers at her back. He took her hand then, leading her along the trail that would bring them back to his house in this paradise.

"What are you going to do now?" she asked him softly.

"Pirates do not answer such questions from their captives," he told her briefly.

"But—"

"All right, my lady. *Right now?* I am famished. I am going to hope that Judith has been to the house, and that she has spent the day cooking something remarkable."

"Judith?" Tessa demanded breathlessly, trying to keep up with him. "Judith?" she repeated.

There was a glitter in his eyes as they fell on her. "My woman here," he told her.

She tried to wrench free from his hold upon her, but he caught her close instead, holding her even while she struggled. "Well, Lady Tessa? What if I did have a woman, a wife, a mistress? Didn't you assume I'd spent last evening in the company of harlots? Tell me, did you assume that a pirate had waited his whole life to be seduced by you?"

"Let me go—" she demanded.

"I cannot let you go because you determined on this course!" he warned her. He turned suddenly, walking again with his long strides and dragging her along.

"Stop it, pirate!" she insisted.

He did stop, swinging back to her again. "Pirate? Eh? But then, that's right! You don't even know my name."

"I didn't need to know your name!" she cried out. "I just needed to know..."

"What?" he demanded.

Her eyes fell for a moment. *"You,"* she said softly.

He sighed softly. "I was a better offering for a first experience than Flambert, is that it, my lady?"

"Yes," she whispered.

His fingers curled around hers again. "Judith is sixty," he told her. "You'll like her very much, and she's a wonderful cook." He was silent for a moment. "And my name is Steven."

He started walking again, her hand still in his. She followed him with no further comment. Billy Bowe was sitting on the little veranda to the captain's house, whittling. He offered her his gnome's smile. "Stew's on inside," he said in French. "Since the two of you have been gone some time, you must be starved." He rose, looking at Steven, then switching his words to a soft-spoken English, assuming that Tessa would not understand.

"We've heard from Flambert already. He heard that you seized his bride's ship almost immediately, and he has written that he will pay any ransom and take his bride back—in any condition—and begs that you merely speed up the negotiations."

Tessa froze, fighting to control her expression, determined that they not realize that she spoke fluent English. There was so much more that she could learn this way.

Even if she hated what she learned.

"What are we going to do?" Billy Bowe asked Steven.

Steven scowled, glancing at Tessa. "We will make arrangements later," he said curtly. He urged Tessa into the house ahead of him. In the dim light, it took her a moment to see the woman standing by the hearth.

Indeed, if this was Judith, she *was* an older woman, yet somehow a fascinating, very attractive one. She had slim, elegant features and was dressed from head to toe in a black, old-fashioned gown with slim skirts. Her hair was gray, swept into a chignon at the nape. Her eyes were gray as well, curious, appraising—and somewhat condemning as they fell upon Steven.

"Ah, but it smells wonderful in here!" Steven said in English.

"Aye, and I'll feed you now, my lord Steven, but we'll be having a good discussion before I do so again!" Judith said.

"Now, what—" Steven began.

"You're a pirate commissioned by the queen, preying upon the enemies of the crown, and that's well and fine. But you've yet to abduct a prisoner and bring her to your bed! My lord, I am stunned!"

"You'd be much more stunned if you knew the half of it!" Steven told her wearily.

Judith sniffed and walked on past him, taking Tessa's arm and leading her to the table. "She speaks no English, eh?" Judith said. "And my French is so poor... ah, well, let me think, *Avez-vous faim?*"

"*Oui, J'ai faim,*" Tessa assured her, taking the seat offered to her at the table. She was hungry. Starving. Judith quickly set a bowl of stew before her, and Tessa thanked her, listening carefully to what was said—and not said—between the two.

"I shall take her to my house," Judith said firmly.

"No, you won't," Steven argued. "Don't be deceived by that angel's face. She'll escape you."

"And where will she go?"

"Judith, may I have some stew as well, please?" he asked irritably.

"I should make you get it yourself!" Judith murmured, but it seemed that Steven did have his authority on the island, or else Judith was more fond of him than she intended to let on under the circumstances, for she gave him a bowl of stew and a pint of ale, yet stayed there before him, pursuing her course.

"Steven—"

"She's not going with you, Judith."

"But—"

He sighed. "Judith, it would be locking the stables with the horse long gone."

"Really, Steven—"

"Don't worry! She'll not be on the island that long!" Steven said firmly.

Judith pursed her lips together. "Hmph!" she sniffed. "Well, then, my French is too poor to talk to the girl, and I've no desire to talk to you!" She stalked to the door and departed. Steven sat back in his chair, watching her go, then looked at Tessa.

She wouldn't be on the island long. Raoul had already promised to pay anything for her—no matter what. Steven was going to give her back...

She bit her lip, determined that she would give nothing away. She had to find some means to escape—soon. Before she could be given to Raoul.

"She's angry with me," he told Tessa.

"Why?"

"Because I've violated you."

A blush touched her cheeks.

"She wants to take you to her home."

"Oh."

"Do you want to go?" he asked her.

She lowered her eyes. Then she met his again, her expression touched with all the innocence she could muster. "It would be closing the stall door with the horse gone, *mais oui?*"

"Something like that," he said, his eyes narrowing. They remained on her face. "Not that it matters. I will not let you go there. Not now," he said very quietly.

He ate another bite of his stew, then finished it hurriedly. He stood suddenly. "Billy Bowe is at the door, and I have told him, no more roaming the isle for you. I have to... discuss some matters with my men. I will return shortly."

"Will you be discussing my return to Raoul?" she demanded.

He shook his head. "Don't forget, he may no longer want you," he said.

Liar! she almost cried out. She managed not to do so. She waited until he was gone, then she jumped up from the table and nervously began to pace the pleasant living room. She saw the crèche on the table in the center of the room, and she walked over to it. She sat down, studying the very beautiful little figures. She picked up the Christ child. *"You* were the miracle!" she whispered softly. "Faith and forgiveness, peace... Oh, dear Lord, I prayed for a miracle myself, and this is what you've given me! Please, dear Lord, send me a miracle, if it is Your will. And if it is not—"

She broke off. Well, she had spent the day seducing a pirate, and the nuns back at school would hardly call that behavior worthy of a miracle—especially a Christmas miracle. But she wasn't sorry. She didn't know her pirate all that well—certainly much better now than she had before—and yet she wasn't sorry. She had told him the truth. Even if she had grown angry later, she felt that she had known him.

And the day had been beautiful, and something she would remember all of her life.

She leaped up. God, she had been told, helped those who helped themselves. And it was time for her to get started.

She opened the door a crack and looked out to see Billy Bowe whittling on the veranda. She could slip around him, she was certain, and disappear up the cliff toward the waterfall and freshwater river. Then she could double back to the shore...

And take one of the small boats out to sea.

Then what? She could perish there...

No! With God's mercy, a ship would find her. And with that same mercy, it would be an English ship.

She waited at the door, watching Billy Bowe. He was very intensely working on his piece of wood, and she chose a moment when his back was completely to her to slip from behind him, and tiptoe against the wall until she reached the end of the house. She slipped beneath the wood rail then and held her breath while she tried to pass silently through the foliage to the trail.

He did not see her. She ran.

* * *

She wasn't going to Flambert. Steven met with his officers and most of the crew in the tavern, and he told them frankly that he had learned their captive despised Flambert just as they did. "I cannot send her to him, for any price," he said simply. "I will, though, make up her ransom to you all with shares of other booty we have taken, and I will pay my due to the queen as well."

There was silence in the room at first. Then Walt raised his ale pint and called out, "Yahoo, my lord captain! We're agreed here, to a man, I think!" Then he paused. "What *will* you do with her?"

Steven shrugged. "I don't know. Somehow, I'd like to give her her Christmas wish. Freedom. I can't send her home to her father; her father will merely send her back to Flambert."

"You could make an honest woman of the girl and infuriate Flambert beyond all measure. Marry her," Walt suggested.

Steven smiled. "She doesn't want marriage. She wants her freedom. I will have to figure out the best way to give it to her."

He drank with his men, laughing, talking, yet inwardly trying to solve his problem of what to do with Tessa. Perhaps he could bring her to New York, or Virginia, and she would be safe there. But that held problems as well, for she was a noblewoman, the daughter of a comte, and she was accustomed to a life-style far different from that in the Colonies. So what did he do...

Hold her here, he told himself. Hold her, love her, sleep with her, wake up to see those glorious aqua eyes, that delicate face, hear her whispers, touch her, make love to her. Spend Christmas in paradise...

Weary, he returned to his house, determined that he would decide on a ship for her, one with a strong captain he trusted, and send her to Williamsburg for the time being. He had many good friends there, friends who would help her, at his behest.

He stepped by Billy Bowe, and by the gamin's smile, he could tell that the man had heard they would not be turning their captive over to Flambert.

"She's here, Billy, I assume?" he asked.

"Aye, Captain, that she is!" Billy assured him.

Steven stepped by him. He threw open the door, startled by the silence within. Was she sleeping? Weeping somewhere? "Tessa?" he called. He strode across the hall to his bedroom, and discovered that she wasn't there.

Angry, he hurried out to Billy. "She's gone!"

Billy's startled look assured him that the little man knew nothing of the hostage's departure.

"She must be there—"

"She's not! Dear God, it is all but dark, and this island can be dangerous in the night. Get Walter and the others; tell them she has to be found before something happens to her!"

With that said, he tore from the house himself, desperate to find her.

* * *

Escape had been incredibly easy. She had taken the path to the cliff, crossed the river where it was nothing more than a trickle, made her way back down toward the beach, and there paused, staring at the small boats pulled up on the sand. Sailors were there, talking, chatting, some pulling in fish, some scrubbing barnacles from their small crafts. Yet, as darkness began to fall, they left their tasks, pulled in their cleaned catches, and headed up cliffside.

There were men on guard always, Tessa thought. She could see the figure of a man silhouetted on one of the high rocks that overlooked the harbor entrance.

But he would be looking for large enemy ships. He might not see a small boat just drifting out into the sea lanes. Still she waited. She waited so long she wondered if she didn't want to be caught. It was true enough that she didn't want to leave him. She loved the isle with its beaches and beautiful freshwater stream, the waterfall, the foliage. A hostage here, she had still been happier than she had been since...

Since her father had come to England for her. Then she had truly been a prisoner. Now...

Now she was a captive still. And she could dream about going back to all that she wanted, about sleeping in his arms again, and it would mean nothing because he was busy, even now, making arrangements for her to go back to Raoul.

She stiffened her spine. And when the last of the men had been gone a good while, she slipped from her cover of shrubs and swiftly made for one of the small boats.

It took far more effort than she had imagined to push it from the sand. And once she was seated within it, she found that rowing was not all that easy either. Yet she persisted, pulling hard, pulling until her arms ached and she was ready to cry out.

She was just moving into the center of the harbor when the first bolt of lightning streaked across the sky. The tiny boat began to heave and toss.

Seconds later, the rain began. Then the wind rose, whipping the water and her boat wildly and cruelly. She cried out as her left oar was all but ripped out of her hand and the small boat suddenly began to spin. She could no longer control it. The rain pelted her, the wind bit into her. It seemed that the entire world was black, except when those lightning slashes lit the sky.

She dragged in the oars, screaming and ducking when the wind plucked up the tiny boat again, careening it in a wild circle, all but capsizing her. So this was to be her miracle! A watery death!

She screamed again as the boat began to tip and tilt, the bow almost buckling into the sea. Then she gasped, too terrified to scream, for it seemed that something was rising out of the sea.

Not something, someone...

"Where are the oars!" he roared over the rip of the waves and the cry of the wind. "Little fool, where are the damned oars! We'll smash on the reef any second!"

She fumbled for the oars with frozen fingers as he climbed into the boat and took the oars from her hands. His hair looked ink-black, sodden against his flesh. His clothing clung to his body. He was barefoot, and she vaguely realized that he had shed his boots to swim after her. In this. In this awful storm.

"What in God's name made you come out in this?" he demanded. "Was I so wretched to you?" he asked, deep emotion in his voice.

"No," she choked out.

"Then—"

"You intended to get me off the island and to Raoul as quickly as possible. I told you—I hate him! I will not marry him, I—"

"What made you think that I was sending you to Raoul?"

"I heard what Billy told you; I heard what you told Judith—"

"You understand English?" he said slowly.

"Of course I understand it!" she gasped out in that language. The wind whipped up again. She was thrown heavily against him.

"You're about to kill us both!" he cried, trying to catch her and hold the oars and the craft steady.

"I didn't—"

"You speak English?" he roared.

"I *am* English!" she flared to him. "If you'd ever cared to find out—I grew up in England, my mother was English, and I lived under the care of my English grandfather most of my life. My father brought me to France right before the war broke out. He must have intended to give me to Flambert when he came for me, but he didn't tell me then."

"You little witch!" he accused her. "You've heard everything that we've said, that I've said—"

"And I knew what you meant to do!" she whispered.

"Hop out!" he cried suddenly. "We've hit the beach."

He leaped over the edge of the boat himself, shoving it onto the beach with far greater ease than she had managed to dislodge it. Tessa sprang out, staggering through the wind and water to the sand. She gasped for breath, shivering against the pelting rain. She staggered again when a gust seized hold of her, but as she sought her balance, she suddenly found herself swept up in his arms again.

They were both soaked and freezing cold from head to toe. She wrapped her arms around his neck, holding close to him. He started to walk, shouting that he had found her. Men hurried around him, calling out their relief in turn, and shouting to others in the wretched storm, letting them know that their hostage had been found.

Alone, Steven continued to carry her up the path to his house. She felt his eyes on her and looked up into them.

"You were wrong," he said very softly. "I would never have given you to Flambert once I knew you weren't longing to get to him. I had my hesitations even before that, but when I seized your ship... It's a long story. I didn't leave you to make any plans to return you for the ransom. I went to tell my men that I would make good for the money myself."

"Oh!" she gasped.

The door to his house burst open. Judith, in her black, was awaiting them.

"Poor lass, and look what ye did to her, Steven Mallory! Bring her in; I've a steaming tub waiting. She'll catch her death of cold!"

Steven grinned, stepping onto the veranda where the rain no longer pelted down upon them—they merely dripped all that which had already fallen.

"Then she's going to want to take you home with her," Steven whispered in Tessa's ear.

"But I'm *your* captive," Tessa protested loudly.

"Why, she does speak English!" Judith exclaimed.

"Quite perfectly," Steven said ruefully. "And you heard her, she's my captive. Bathe her and clothe her, Judith, but she stays here!"

He set Tessa down and disappeared out into the rain once again, making sure that the word was out that she had been found.

Indeed. His captive would-be Christmas bride was back.

Chapter 7

"It was always my favorite time of year," Tessa said two weeks later, curled into his arms in his room, clean and warm, and far more content than she should be with an English privateer in his island bed. But once she had realized that she was not going to be delivered to Flambert, she had allowed herself the luxury of caring about nothing more than the fact that she had received her one little miracle. And she had received it at Steven's hands.

And she was falling very deeply and intimately in love with her pirate.

It was so easy to be with him. Talking idly after they had made love, encircled by his arms, feeling so serene and secure with his strength about her. Tonight she had confessed to him that she had been praying for a Christmas miracle, and though perhaps it had taken her some time to realize it, he had, in truth, been that miracle.

"Christmas is when magic can happen," she said softly. He was silent for a moment, and she continued, "I used to love my grandfather's mansion at Christmas. The hall was covered with leaves and boughs and there was always a tremendous Christmas feast. Snow lay on the ground, and we'd light many candles against the cold and dark. We always started the day in the chapel. My grandfather is a very good man, and he carried on tradition, so the poor people were all invited in and we washed their feet and gave them coins. Christmas music is so beautiful, and it's truly the season for brotherly love and—"

"And?" he asked her, after she had suddenly broken off.

"I could not believe that I was going to be Raoul Flambert's bride for Christmas!" she told him, shivering.

"All that you wanted for Christmas was your freedom," he said softly. "Freedom you will have. Rest assured, I will never let you go to Flambert," he promised, passion in his voice.

"Not for Christmas?"

"Never for Christmas. And certainly not ever!"

She thought that her heart shook within her chest at the sheer happiness that filled her when he pulled her into his arms once again, when his lips touched hers. She was in love with him, she realized, falling more deeply in love with him as each hour in his presence passed by...

The night was bliss, yet it seemed that he was insatiable. Nor did he have much need for sleep. When Tessa finally drifted to sleep to stay, she slept very deeply, and when she woke, she could hear the chirping of birds and feel the brightness of the light beyond the windows. It was very late morning, perhaps nearly noon. She didn't think that she had ever slept so late.

She jumped up and washed and dressed quickly, coming out into the main room, certain that she would discover herself alone, that Steven had gone to see to business with his men.

But she wasn't alone. She was startled to find Steven and another well-dressed, properly white-wigged gentleman. They both stood quickly when she came out.

"Captain Tyler," Steven said, "may I introduce the lady in question, Tessa Dousseau. Tessa, Captain Henry Tyler, in her majesty's service—and yours."

"I—beg your pardon?" Tessa said.

"He has come to take you home. To England. To your grandfather's house," Steven said, eyes emotionless as he stared at her.

"Oh!" she gasped. She gripped the doorframe, praying that she would not betray her dismay. He was sending her away. She had been falling in love, living in a fool's paradise, in a dream...

Well, indeed, she *had* been the fool. She had seduced a pirate, lived with him, loved him. And the pirate had remained a gentleman, not betraying her, even for a fantastic ransom. But he was sending her away.

She lifted her chin. "Captain Tyler," she acknowledged politely. "Sir, when do we leave?"

"With the tide," he told her. "You've perhaps an hour or so to gather your things. Of course, the men will see that your trunks are brought down to the small boat, and we will see to them from there. You will, of course, have the use of my cabin."

"Thank you, sir."

"My greatest pleasure, my lady."

"You can get your things," Steven said rather curtly. "I have other business with Captain Tyler."

"Indeed, we've other business!" Captain Tyler said. He came to Tessa, bowed, and kissed her hand, a warm, courteous man with fine eyes. She smiled in turn, feeling weak.

The men left. She walked back into the bedroom and sank down to the foot of the bed. Men! He had talked to her about Christmas, about freedom. He had held her through the night.

He had made her fall in love with him.

And now...

She had thrown herself at him, it was true. She had never thought to wonder if there might be a mistress somewhere, a woman, a lover...

Perhaps there were many.

She fought tears. She had what she wanted. Her Christmas miracle. She might not make it in time for the holiday, but she would be back with her grandfather soon enough, and they would celebrate Christmas all over again. The minstrels would play the times, the snow would still fall, the hall would be filled with the lush smells, and the world would be...

Empty.

It would be what she made it! She chastised herself. She was leaving.

When they returned, she was ready. She had donned one of her best gowns; she had carefully tended her hair. She was as distant and regal as she could manage.

She nearly snatched her hand away when Steven took it to escort her down the path and to the small boat. When they reached it, she was ready to step quickly away, so very close to tears. But he caught her hands, pulling her back as the captain's other men stepped into the small boat.

"Godspeed you to England, to freedom," he told her.

She nodded, not trusting herself to speak. Then she moistened her lips and told him, "Thank you. Freedom was a wonderful gift."

"Love is a greater one," he told her. He kissed her hand, seemingly reluctant to let her go.

"We're about to lose the tide!" Captain Tyler called.

Steven stepped back, dark, tall, muscled, and splendid in his high black boots, breeches, and simple white cotton shirt. "Think of me, my lady, at Christmas!" he called to her.

She nodded again and stepped into the small boat, her back to him. The men began to row them from the beach.

She dared not look back.

Far ahead, resting just inside the harbor, was Captain Tyler's ship, the *Marianne*. She kept her gaze upon it.

And she did not burst into tears until she was alone in the Captain's cabin.

* * *

How had he let her go? Steven wondered, sitting alone in his house, slumped in one of the chairs, staring at the fire.

He should have kept her a prisoner. It had not been so bleak for her—she had laughed, she had smiled. Her eyes had dazzled him with their light, and she had held him, touched him, made love to him, as surely as he had loved her...

It had been Christmas. Damn Christmas! When she had talked about her grandfather, and the snow, and the wonders of the season. And all he could remember was that she had said she wanted one thing.

Freedom.

And so he had let her go, even if it felt that his heart had been gouged right out by a sword. He suddenly realized that up to the last minute, he had been hoping. He had been hoping that she would turn to him and tell him that she didn't want to go. That she didn't give a damn about anything else, that she was in love with him...

He stared at the little crèche and smiled. "That's what I want for Christmas!" he said softly. "But I've been a privateer, serving my country; doing so with mercy, so I always thought! I've not been perfect, by any means, yet as it is the season for forgiveness..." his voice trailed away for a moment. "One little miracle, dear God. Bring her back," he said softly.

The door suddenly burst open, but it was not Tessa, not his miracle, that had arrived.

Billy Bowe stood there, face drawn and tense. "They've been attacked! The Frenchie sailed a ship just out beyond the inlet for the

Hidden Isle. He's surely been searching for her since he heard his bride was abducted, her ship seized. For the love of God, Captain, they're bombarding Tyler's ship, with Lady Tessa aboard!"

Steven bolted out of his chair. Before Billy could say another word, he was out of the house, heading down toward the small boat, roaring out orders to anyone within hearing distance that they were to sail immediately. Billy was quickly behind him, with members of his crew following just as swiftly. When he reached the beach, he leaped into the first boat, followed by Billy, Walt, and two of his stalwart crewmen out of Galway Bay.

Steven rowed the small boat himself, cutting through the water at incredible speed. He had scarcely crawled aboard his ship when he was roaring orders again, and she was setting to sail even as the last of the crew who had managed to join him dangled from the rope ladder to reach the ship itself.

Within thirty minutes they reached the spot where a pitched battle was now taking place. The mast was blown to bits on Captain Tyler's *Marianne,* but the floundering ship was still returning fire for fire with the French sloop, *Aurora.* The *Aurora,* however, was shifting in the wind, ready to make the last sweep down upon the *Marianne,* and take her prisoner with grappling hooks and irons.

"Bring her around!" Steven called to Walter at the helm. "Gunners to your stations. Aim your cannons quickly; light and fire at will!"

His guns began to roar, three shots falling short, but the fourth and fifth tearing into the French ship, one ripping her rigging asunder, the next barreling into her bow. The ship floundered, but even as she listed, the clank of hooks could be heard, and she brought herself hard against Captain Tyler's *Marianne*.

"Sweet Jesu, Walt, get us to her! Men, taper the sails, bring us hard about her bow side!"

The sea was calm, in strange contrast to the scene of chaos before them. The French ship had come outfitted for war; dozens of men fell from her rigging upon the crippled English vessel. The minutes that it took Steven's crew to bring his ship about seemed endless, yet even as the first hook was thrown to bring his ship against the *Marianne*, leaving her pinioned between his own vessel and the French sloop, he had climbed the rigging himself and prepared to leap to the deck.

The ships came together with a fierce shudder. Steven leaped into the fighting taking place on the *Marianne's* deck. Men hurled themselves toward him, swords raised. Pistols were fired, smoke rose. He gave little heed to those who tried to waylay him; he sought only one man, one enemy, and he thrashed his way through the others, praying that he was not too late.

He was still searching for Flambert when he heard a scream.

Tessa.

He leaped over a coil of rope and balanced his way swiftly across the fallen mast. When he came to the bow where carved doors gave entrance to the captain's cabin, he saw her there, her arm held in the rigid grip of a brocade-clad Frenchman, well-dressed even for this occasion. A darkly handsome man with a cruel curve to his smile as he saw Steven.

"Ah, so it is the Red Fox. We meet at last, sir!"

"Indeed. Let go of the English girl if you value your life at all."

"French girl, monsieur! My betrothed, with contracts signed by her father."

"We do not live in the Dark Ages, sir. The lady has no wish to marry. She considers herself English, and England is her home of choice."

"Do you insult my country?"

"Ah, France!" Steven murmured, trying not to meet Tessa's eyes for the moment. He thought of what he might say to stall the Frenchman, giving his crew time to board the *Marianne*. His men, with Tyler's, could take the ship, no doubt.

Yet the Frenchman had Tessa. And a rapier-sharp sword. And Steven was quite sure this man knew how to use it.

"I do not insult your country, Comte, even though I am at war with it. Paris is the most beguiling city, the countryside is *magnifique, non?* Her women are beautiful, French wine superb. Yet, sir, even from such a wondrous country, monsters do come forth. Let her go. Now."

Raoul Flambert moved with lightning speed. Tessa cried out softly as the Frenchman's sword touched her throat, held there against the vein as Flambert stared tauntingly at Steven. "I suggest, Monsieur le Pirate, that you drop your weapon. And stand aside.

Then, sir, you shall order your ship given over to me, and if you wish to live, you will have to swim ashore from this rotting hulk!"

"Steven, don't! He'll kill you in a second, I know it!" Tessa cried.

Steven smiled at her. "I've no choice!" he told her.

"What rubbish!" Flambert snickered. "What a fool! You'd have been a rich pirate, had you but accepted my offer for the girl. Now you shall be a dead one."

"You've caused enough death," Steven assured him heatedly.

"Ah, so that's it! Revenge for the English girl! What I did was no worse, pirate. I had her; I set her free. It's not my fault the fool girl went on to die in the English Colonies!"

"What?" Tessa cried, staring from him to Steven.

"Ah, you see, dear girl! The pirate was not so interested in loving you as in hating me. He sought revenge for some silly dalliance I had with one of his friends."

Those aquamarine eyes that he had stared into for the last few weeks turned on Steven. His heart shuddered in his chest as he prayed she would not falter because of Flambert's taunts.

"You're wrong, Flambert!" she said after a moment.

"Had he thought of revenge, I would have been dealt with cruelly. He but gave me freedom."

Steven, watching her, smiled slowly, feeling the message of pride and sympathy she sent with her eyes.

"None of this matters!" Flambert roared. "I will give up my Christmas wish for no one, English bastard."

"Neither will I!" Steven said softly, staring at Tessa. He lowered his arm and hunched down, setting his blade upon the deck and staring at Tessa. Her eyes widened with alarm, and for all their danger, he felt a thrilling in his heart. She did care for him, he thought. Indeed, it was almost as if she... loved him.

"Now, your ship!" Flambert said as he lowered his blade—just an inch, but enough. Steven leaped at him like a tiger, catching the man with his full weight and bringing the two of them down hard together to roll on the deck, fiercely locked into a life-or-death struggle. Steven heard Tessa scream, but could only think, *She is free*.

Flambert sent his elbow slamming into Steven's throat. With a tremendous burst of energy, Steven rolled again, bringing Flambert beneath him. Flambert tried to rip his knife from the sheath at his calf. Before he could do so, Steven sent his fist smashing into Flambert's jaw. The Frenchman let out a startled groan and went silent. Steven drew back his arm to strike him again, but a sudden cry and the curl of feminine fingers upon his arm stopped him. "He's unconscious, Steven. Such revenge will not ease the pain he has caused you. He's no threat to us. Let them take him back to England to stand trial for all our ships he has seized. Steven, please!"

He drew a deep breath. She was right. He had spent years wanting to slay this man with his bare hands, but justice would be served—before an English court of law. And that was all that mattered.

He allowed Tessa to pull him to his feet. Steven looked into her eyes for a long moment, then took her into his arms.

"She was a friend," he said softly.

Tessa smiled. "And still, you were never able to hurt me. Threats, threats! I had to do all the ravaging myself. You pretend to be a good pirate, Steven, and you do it very well. But what you are is a very good man."

He kissed her lips, savoring the taste and feel, holding her as if he would never let her go.

"Captain! We've secured the ship, sir!" Walt called to him. "What orders, sir?"

"Survivors aboard our ship, my friend, for these vessels will sink together. Salvage what we may. We'll outfit Captain Tyler anew from the isle for his trip home." He looked down at Flambert. "He must stand trial in England. I will entrust him to Tyler, for I cannot entrust him to myself!"

Tessa looked up at him and smiled slowly. "It will take a while to outfit a new ship, won't it?"

"As long as I can make it take," he told her.

"One little miracle," she murmured.

"What?"

"My Christmas miracle," she said softly. "I am truly free from Flambert. And..."

"And?" he asked her.

"I will have Christmas with you."

His breath seemed to catch in his throat. *One little miracle.* "If you spend Christmas with me, my lady, you'll not be as free as you desired."

Her smile deepened. "Freedom is choice, Captain Red Fox. I choose to be with you."

"A Christmas bride?" he asked huskily.

"Well, it *was* what my father intended," she said.

He started to laugh. Then he picked her up and swirled her around, and he was certain that all the seamen looking on, French and English, all surely thought that he had lost his mind.

He ignored them, carrying her across the floundering ship, grabbing hold of a rope tossed to him to bring them both swinging back aboard. Billy Bowe was there, waiting for him.

"We've got her back, Billy," Steven said.

"Aye, Captain!"

"She wants me for Christmas, Billy!" he told his man.

"Aye, sir!" Billy said, with little surprise. In fact, he was smiling as if he had arranged it all.

Steven took Tessa in his arms one more time and kissed her deeply as his crew looked on, cheering loudly. He lifted his lips from hers and whispered softly, "Say it, Tessa!"

Her eyes were shimmering with their sea-green beauty. "I love you!" she said softly. "You are my Christmas miracle, and not so little a one at that!"

He smiled. "Home!" he roared to his crew. "Home," he said again, more softly to her. He wrapped his arms around her as the ship moved with the flow of the wind.

"There will be no snow," he told her. "And we've no holly boughs for the house. We've not too much music, but we can do our best—"

"Christmas, my love, is not a place. Christmas is within us all."

"Ah, lady," he told her humbly. "I am not the miracle, but one exists. It is one that always comes with Christmas."

"And that is?" she queried.

"Love!" he said softly, and kissed her again.

Epilogue

Christmas Day dawned warm and balmy. They were not so deprived of amenities on the island as Steven had described, Tessa decided. The English pirates—privateers! she reminded herself—had a jolly priest living on the island with them, sanctioning marriages, carrying out baptisms, and, of course, conducting Mass in a palm-covered chapel.

The chapel itself was a beautiful place, alive with the scent of wildflowers. Tessa stood in front of the priest on the day they were married, surrounded by the sweet scent of tropical flowers, and by her new friends. Judith stood as Tessa's witness, Walt as Steven's.

The service was not without music. They hadn't too much in the way of instruments, but a number of the men could play flutes beautifully, and the islanders were happy to sing Christmas songs. They had a huge feast, roasting their food before open fires on the beach, and everyone who resided on the island attended the ceremony.

GIFTS OF LOVE

Prologue

Twenty-four...

Kaitlin carefully scratched the number into the hide of the teepee. Twenty-four. It followed her other numbers, a series that began with the number three, and was arranged like the numbered days of a calendar.

As she finished scratching out the number, tears sprang to her eyes. She wiped at them furiously. She hadn't cried when she'd scratched out all of the other numbers, but this one was different. Twenty-four. The month was December. It was Christmas Eve. And tomorrow would be Christmas. At home, in their small town, people would be caroling in the streets. For the first time in her life, she would have celebrated Christmas in her own home.

Shane had given her that.

She would have decorated the house with evergreen boughs and holly, just as she had promised Francesca she would. She could still remember the little girl's eyes growing round with wonder when she had told her about Santa Claus.

"Well, he is really Saint Nicholas, you see," Kaitlin 99 had told her with a wink, as they had shaken out a bed sheet. "He was a bishop hundreds and hundreds of years ago and he was kind and generous, the patron saint of children, and he loved to give out gifts. To the Dutch people who came to live in New York, he was 'Sinter Klaas.' So for us now, he is Santa Claus! And he comes every Christmas to bring gifts. A minister named Mr. Moore described him in a poem back in 1823—before I was even born—and he is wonderful, Francesca, truly wonderful! He dresses in a red suit with white trim, and he is this huge roly-poly bear of a man, so kind, so very wonderful."

And she could still remember looking up to see that Shane was watching her from the hallway, his gaze speculative and curiously soft. He'd caught her arm when she would have fled. "Thank you."

"For what?"

"For giving her Christmas."

And she had nodded, needing to flee the warmth of his touch. She'd given him so little. He'd given her so much. But she had built the walls that lay between them, and Shane had seemed more than determined to stay on his own side of them. He could be so hard. Their battles, perhaps her survival, depended on his being that way.

But then he had touched her cheek. So gently. "You're just like her, you know. A child deprived of Christmas." And his voice was soft, so soft. "This year, we will have Christmas. We'll drink mulled wine before the fire. I'll chop down a fir tree and we'll decorate it with angels and stars. And we'll all put gifts beneath the tree. You will have Christmas, Kaitlin."

She'd had to pull away. Knots had tied within her stomach, her heart had seemed to lodge tight within her throat. How did he know her so easily, so well? How could he touch upon those places in her heart that were the most vulnerable?

"I have no money of my own," she had told him. "I shall have no gift for you."

That glittering gaze of his, hot, too-knowing, taunting, wicked, and wise, had come sweeping over her and she had heard the sound of his laughter, a sound that touched her up and down the spine. "Oh, but, my love, think of it, you do, you do."

Her cheeks had grown hot. She wanted to slap him then and there.

She wanted to fall into his arms...

She'd had a chance to do neither. He had pulled her close to him. Yet for all the rough carelessness of his touch, there had been a note of true and painful longing in his voice when he spoke. "A son, Kaitlin, give me my son."

And she had pulled away from him once again. "You'll have to speak to God on that, sir, since I seem to have no choice in the matter."

"But you do. You run. You fight me," he told her. His voice was too soft. His eyes too searching. He was coming so very close to the child who had always missed Christmas, to the woman who was still so terribly afraid.

"I don't seem to run fast enough," she informed him primly, which brought laughter to his lips, but something else to his eyes. He wanted things from her. Things she couldn't give.

Things she was too afraid to give.

"What is it, Shane? Is something wrong?" Francesca asked worriedly. Poor little thing. She was just ten, and she sometimes seemed very old. Life had given her a too-acute awareness. She had been passed from relative to relative, and now she was concerned that she might be the cause of the troubles that lay between them.

"Wrong?" Shane said to his niece, lifting the little girl into his arms. "When I live with two of the most beautiful women in the West? Never! We were just discussing Christmas, Kaitlin and I. And Santa Claus is coming this year."

"He never came before," Francesca said.

"Well, he's coming this year. Right down the chimney."

"He'll singe his rump!" Kaitlin advised.

"Never. Santa Claus is invulnerable to fire."

Francesca laughed. "Will he come for us both, for Kaitlin and me?"

His eyes had touched Kaitlin with a curious light of understanding as he answered Francesca. "Oh, yes. Santa will come for you. And for Kaitlin."

But Santa could not come. Not here, to this teepee in the wilderness where all those who surrounded her did not believe in Christmas.

The tears grew hot behind her lashes. She blinked hard, not willing to let the first one fall.

She hadn't cried yet. No matter how frightened she had been, no matter how despairing, she had never given way to tears. She was strong, her will was strong, her spirit was strong. Shane had said so. It was one of the things that he admired about her. Watching her with that cool expression in his eyes, his hands on his hips, his head just slightly cocked at an angle, he had said so. She could still remember the deep timbre of his voice as he had spoken to her after the first Indian raid. "Well, you've courage, my love. And a will of steel."

Perhaps the implication had been there that she was lacking other things, but she did have courage.

Kaitlin leaned back against the tough hide of the teepee, closing her eyes, continuing to fight the overwhelming urge to cry.

You were wrong, Shane! she thought. So very wrong. Some of the other things were there. I did love you, but I was lacking the courage to tell you.

She had almost told him. She had almost done so on that fateful day when she had etched her first number into the hide of the teepee. A three... for December third, 1869.

That was the day when they had fought so furiously because she had disobeyed him.

Genevieve had disappeared into the far north field. She was a small, part-Arabian, part-wild horse, and she was precious to Kaitlin. She wasn't just the only horse Kaitlin had ever owned, she was fine and beautiful, and so affectionate. She gave Kaitlin so much love.

So when she had disappeared, Kaitlin had gone after her, riding old Henry, the plow horse. She hadn't found Genevieve but Shane had found her. And he'd very nearly dragged her back, calling her a fool over and over again, and warning her that he didn't have time to keep going after her. It was going to prove to be a brutal winter for those living at the foot of the Black Hills.

"I didn't do anything—"

"Tell it to the Blackfeet when they find you the next time!"

"I'm not worried about the Indians. Chancey told me that they're a distance away."

"They're right on our border!"

"Living their lives. While we live ours—"

"Don't fool yourself, Kaitlin! The Blackfeet were the most warlike tribe in the area!"

"Yes, and they killed a lot of whites, and the whites killed them. But that's because the whites were infringing on their fur trade. And now we *buy* the furs from them and—"

"And that's supposed to make everything all better?"

"But the Indians don't come in this close—"

"The hell they don't! Ever since that fool trapper disappeared with Black Eagle's boy, the Blackfeet have been coming in closer and closer. All kinds of rumors are going around, of Indian war, real, horrible, disastrous war. Damn you, Kaitlin, I know Black Eagle! I know him well. You stay the hell out of the north field and the north woods!"

"But Genevieve—"

"Genevieve is an Indian pony now. There aren't any finer horse thieves in the world than the Blackfeet. If only you'd really cared for any living thing around you, she might not have disappeared!"

To Kaitlin, that had been it. She had promptly assured him that he was the only living thing around her that she didn't care about.

"I pulled you out of a New Orleans sewer. Maybe that's where you belong!"

She struck him. And suddenly she was being dragged across their room, and tossed on their bed. "I've seen the fire in you," Shane said angrily. "I've seen you smile, and laugh. By God, it's there. It was there for Daniel Newton."

"Daniel's a gentleman—"

"And a half-assed fool. And he isn't for you. But damn you, Kaitlin, the fire is there. Within you."

"Maybe you haven't the spark to light any fire within me!" she replied furiously.

And he had gone still. Dead still. "Oh, but I do," he had assured her. "Oh, but I do!"

She had leapt up, suddenly feeling very afraid. But she was determined that he not see it.

She wanted to run—she couldn't. He had planted his hands on his hips, blocking the doorway. "Well, you've courage, my love. And a will of steel. But that won't help you now. Not one bit. Whether I wooed you or won you, Kaitlin, I made you my wife. And you agreed to the terms. And I'll be damned if I'll let you try to cast me out one minute longer. You want a spark, Mrs. McAuliffe? I'll light a boxful of matches, and so help me, we will find the fire within you."

His voice had thundered, deep, harsh, determined. Sitting in the teepee, Kaitlin could still hear the thunder of it in her mind. Remembering, she felt a trembling in her fingers, and the trembling seemed to spread. She couldn't forget what had followed. She had relived it time and time again, here in desolate captivity in the wilderness.

There had been more that afternoon. So much more.

Even now, the thought of all that had happened could bring a crimson flush to her cheeks. There had been so much more...

There had been his hand on her arm and the startling iron-hard grip of his fingers. She had gazed at that hand detaining her, and some sharp retort had sprung to her lips. But then she had met his eyes. Hazel eyes, with sparks of glimmering gold. Eyes that commanded, eyes that held her fast. Eyes hotter than the glitter of the sun, alive with anger, with determination, with fire...

And with desire.

Oh, yes, there had been more. The violent force of his kiss, the rent and tear of fabric. Her fists had flown in protest, pummeling against him. And then...

Then there had been the magic. Things whispered in shadows of their bedroom. Intimate things. A touch, a brush, his hands, his caress, so knowing. Demanding here, so tender there. The feel of his naked flesh against her, and a burst of the fire-hot gold of his eyes entering her so that a flame was ignited within her, stirring her, arousing her, taking her places she had never been before, until showers of ecstasy had burst upon her like a honeyed rain from heaven...

She'd been tempted to cry then, too. For the words should have come. She should have whispered them, she should have made him believe. She should have had the courage to risk ridicule; she should have been able to give to him at last.

But she had been so afraid that he would shove that gift aside...

And so she hadn't spoken, and he had risen, and she had turned her back on him. "I'm sorry, Kaitlin. No, damn you, I'm not sorry. You're my wife. And I want you to be more than a cook. I'll not be stopping at Nelly Grier's when I've a black-haired beauty at home, even if she has emerald eyes flashing nothing but hatred my way."

Kaitlin didn't respond. If he hadn't been so fond of the industrious Nelly Grier, she might not have longed to be the ice princess he liked to call her.

"Black-haired, and black-hearted," Shane whispered softly, and it was then that she spun on him.

"No! No! It's not me, Shane MacAuliffe. You prove time and time again that you prefer the company at Nelly's to that at home—"

"Damn! I prefer a spark of warmth!"

What had she just given him, she wondered, feeling lost. And why did he seem more violent and furious now than ever before? She had thrown the pillow at him in a sudden fury herself, and she had cried out that she hated him...

And he had stared at her. Hard. He had almost spoken, but he had not. He had turned on his heel, and left her, slamming the door behind him.

"No, no, that was a lie!" she whispered, but she spoke to a closed door. "I love you, Shane." And she did love *him*. Not the beautiful home that he had given her. Not the closet full of dresses. None of the things that she had married to possess really meant anything at all, not when she compared them to that look in his eyes when she had insisted that she hated him.

She had to tell him. And she had to make him believe in her.

And so she washed quickly and hurried out of the house. She ran to the stables he had built on the edge of the wilderness. Chancey, Shane's old sidekick and now master-of-all-trades, was there, whistling as he rubbed oil into a harness. "Chancey, where's Shane?"

"Why, I think he rode off to the north field. Said there was supposed to be some good hunting up that way."

Forgetting everything Shane had said to her about the north field and disregarding all of Chancey's protests, she had saddled old Henry. "I have to find Shane," she'd said urgently.

And she had ridden out.

And she quickly learned just how wrong she had been, for she had barely reached the north woods before she had heard the cries. She had turned, terrified to see them. A war party. They were in winter gear, dressed in fringed deer hides, beaded jackets, and fringed breeches. Feathers had danced from the bands at their heads.

Their cries, their whoops and calls, had sent panic spiraling through her.

She might have made it safely back to the ranch on Genevieve, but not on old Henry.

She had tried to run the horse. But she had barely started off before the first of the warriors had come upon her.

She waited to feel an arrow or a tomahawk pierce her back. Strong arms wrapped around her instead. She was drawn onto the Indian's mount. The wild ride that followed was almost as frightening as the first sight of the Indians.

But she hadn't cried. She'd refused to be cowed.

Even when the Indian had pushed her from his horse to the ground.

Even when she had realized that the Indians seemed to think that old Henry was a greater prize than she was herself.

Perhaps not, for she quickly realized that she was to be the property of that first warrior, who had led the party and swept her from her horse.

He was tall, nearly as tall as Shane, and had long, straight, ink-black hair. His face was deeply bronzed, with hard, high cheekbones and deeply set dark eyes. If she weren't so terrified, she might have said that it was a noble face.

She could not think of it as a noble face for long because when night fell the Indian came to the teepee where she had been brought. Quickly she had realized that he meant to have white property indeed, for he had barely finished the meal provided for him by an Indian woman before he had reached for her.

She had fought. Valiantly, she thought. But there had never been any contest. The Indian had laughed, finding her struggles amusing. He had wrested her to the floor, his dark eyes claiming her, his lips curled into a smile. Then suddenly his fingers had moved over her ring.

Her wedding ring. There had been no proper band of gold when Shane had wed her. Her wedding ring was his signet pinkie ring, set upon her middle finger, made to fit her with long lines of thread.

Ah her struggles had done nothing.

One look at that ring, and the Indian had drawn away.

Then she discovered that the Indian she had been calling all manner of names spoke English, and spoke it very well.

"This is MacAuliffe's ring. What are you doing with it?"

"I am MacAuliffe's wife," she had said, her heart seeming to have ceased to beat.

And that had been that. The Indian had risen. "MacAuliffe's wife."

He had walked out of the teepee.

And Kaitlin had scratched the number three into the hide of her curious prison.

December third...

So long ago now! And she hadn't been hurt. They had dragged her back when she had tried to escape, but other than that, they had been kind enough to her.

Shane had told her that he knew Black Eagle. Knew him well. She didn't know how, but apparently, there was some kind of bond between them, for the Blackfoot chief respected her husband. Why, she wasn't sure.

Yes, she was. Because Shane was always honest; he kept his word. Because he was determined, and honorable. Because he was brave. Because he respected his Indian neighbors; because he saw them as human.

There were so many wonderful things about Shane.

And she had just discovered them too late. She'd been so wrapped up in her desperate need to find happiness that she had let it slip right through her fingers.

And now it was nearly Christmas. How foolish her pride had been. Now that it meant so little, she could so easily have thrown it all away. She closed her eyes tightly. She should have been home. With the fir branches and the holly. With the decorated tree. With the mulled wine before the fire...

No, the decorations didn't really mean anything. Shane meant everything. She should have been with him. She should have been able to sit on his lap, put her arms around his neck, and whisper into his ear. *"Shane, I have a gift for you..."*

But Christmas would come and go. Christmas would be the number twenty-five etched into the hide of the teepee. There could be no help for it. Black Eagle's tribe of Blood Blackfeet so far outnumbered the white settlers in the region that no one could come to her rescue. As Shane had said of Genevieve, "She is an Indian pony now," so they must all be saying of her, "She is an Indian's woman now." If they assumed that she was still alive.

No great posse could come riding to her rescue. No one could ride to her rescue. No one at all.

Kaitlin started suddenly as the teepee flap, closed against the cold of the season, was suddenly thrown open. Black Eagle, tall and menacing in his buckskins and winter furs, stood before her.

He reached down a hand. "Get up, Kaitlin."

She stared at him uneasily. She had been here for what seemed like a very long time now. She felt that she knew Black Eagle fairly well herself, for she had talked with him many times.

But he had never come to her like this, demanding that she come with him. Not on a day when the winter snows piled up high outside and a vicious wind swept down upon them.

"Kaitlin, get up!" he repeated.

She didn't dare to refuse him. She let him take her hand and pull her to her feet.

He threw a heavy fur over her shoulders and led her out where the wind blew strong and wickedly and snowflakes swept wildly through the village of teepees.

And then she saw him.

No one could come to her rescue. Any white man who rode into Black Eagle's camp now had to be mad, for Black Eagle was furious with the whites, and the Blood Blackfeet were known for their skill at warfare, torture, and death.

But Shane had ridden in.

He was mounted on Diablo, the fine black stallion that had taken him safely through years of war, wandering, and peace. He was very tall in his saddle, just as he had been the day she first met him back in New Orleans.

He was clad against the severe cold in his high hunting boots, a black wool cape with shirted shoulders, black leather gloves, and a low-brimmed hat. Wisps of his sand-colored hair escaped the hat in the wind. Beneath the brim of his hat, she thought that she saw the glitter of his eyes. Gold, challenging, never wavering as they met the coal-dark stare of Black Eagle.

Kaitlin's heart seemed to slam against her chest. He could not be there, not really. She had been thinking of him so poignantly that she had caused this mirage to appear. This was not really happening...

But it was.

"This is your wife?" Black Eagle asked, holding tightly to Kaitlin.

"Yes, that's her," Shane replied easily enough.

"Then we will talk," Black Eagle said. His grip remained tight on Kaitlin's shoulders. As Shane dismounted from Diablo, Black Eagle spoke softly to Kaitlin. "MacAuliffe is a brave man. We will see how brave. Perhaps he will leave with you. Perhaps he will die at the end of my hunting knife."

Her knees were trembling. She was going to fall.

"Go back to the teepee," Black Eagle commanded. "I will meet with him elsewhere."

She shook her head ferociously. "No! I—"

"I will talk with him elsewhere!" Black Eagle repeated.

Once again she shook her head. "Please, just a moment!"

She didn't wait for an answer. She didn't believe that Shane had come here, that he had risked nearly certain death.

For her. She had to tell him to go.

She broke free from Black Eagle's hold and started to run. The snow was deep on the ground and she had to flounder through it.

"Kaitlin, stop! Go back to him!" Shane ordered.

But she didn't obey him, she couldn't. She had nearly reached him and she stumbled through the last of the snow, vaulting into his arms.

He felt so good. She raised her eyes to his. God, they were so gold. As gleaming as the sun. As startling, as powerful.

She had never expected to see him again. The handsome, hard-chiseled features of his face. That jaw that could clench so determinedly. She had never expected to feel his arms around her, feel the soaring heat within their protection.

"Shane! Go!" she said, her lips trembling, her teeth chattering. "Go, while you can. He likes you, you know. He admires you. If you just leave him alone and go home, back to Francesca—"

"MacAuliffe!" Black Eagle thundered.

Shane shook her. "Stop it, Kaitlin, now! Go back to him, and leave me to talk."

"He could kill you!"

"It's a gamble," Shane admitted.

"Then—"

His lips twisted in a wry grin. "Ah, but it always seems to be a gamble, doesn't it, Kaitlin? It was a gamble that we met, the flip of a card that we wed. Well, I am a gambling man. Leave me to play the game."

Black Eagle was nearly beside them. Shane was going to hand her back, until they played this game of chance between them, whatever it might be. It filled Kaitlin with dread.

"Shane, I love you!" she cried out suddenly, passionately.

His arms tightened around her. They were nearly brutal. "Damn you, Kaitlin, don't say things like that just because I've come here for you!"

"No, it's true!" she whispered urgently.

His eyes, fierce and golden, met hers. I have loved you for such a long time, really! she thought. But she couldn't tell him that now. She couldn't begin to explain it.

"Don't gamble your life!" she pleaded.

But his eyes left hers and met Black Eagle's. He shoved her back to the Blackfoot chief.

"You are a fool, or an extremely courageous man," Black Eagle told him.

"It's nearly Christmas," Shane said. "A very great holiday for my people. We exchange gifts on that day. I've come to ask for my wife back for Christmas. She would be your gift to me."

"I am not white but I know all about Christmas. Why should I give you such a gift?"

"Because I have a gift for you," Shane said. "If you will just come with me...?"

"Alone? Why should I trust you?"

"Why should you not? When have I ever betrayed a trust?"

"If I am not pleased with your gift, I will kill you, no matter how well I know you," Black Eagle told Shane.

"You will try. I will defend myself," Shane said.

Black Eagle smiled. "It will be as you say." Abruptly he turned to Kaitlin. "Go back to the teepee as I have commanded, or I will call the women to be sure that you do so. You will be one man's gift this night, either mine or his. For if he is slain, I need not, by any man's honor, respect his wedding vows."

Her knees were buckling again. She meant to obey him, though, for she knew that the Blackfoot women could be far worse than the men when they took hold of a hostage.

But Shane was still there... with his blazing eyes upon her, filled with some emotion. Passion, hatred, love?

She knew not which.

"Please...!" she whispered.

And Shane moved. Against his own better judgment he took a step through the deep pile of snow. He took her into his arms for a moment, and his kiss seared her lips with a startling force and heat. She would fall because of the fierce pounding of her heart... because of the way her blood was streaming through her veins.

"Go back," he told her.

"Shane—"

"It's a gamble, Kaitlin." He touched her cheek, smoothed back her hair. His breath was a cloud against the cold of the day. "And I'm a gambling man. You know that well."

He turned, thrusting her away from him, leaving her. Kaitlin felt the tears stinging her eyes with a vengeance now. She started to stumble back to the teepee through the snow. There was nothing that she could do.

But wait.

She fell to her knees in the teepee. Tears flooded her eyes.

She looked up and saw the numbers she'd scratched on the hide of the teepee.

The last number.

Twenty-four.

It was Christmas Eve. The last day she might ever see Shane.

She closed her eyes again.

And suddenly, all she could do was remember the first day she had seen him, the very first.

Funny.

It had nearly been Christmas then, too.

Chapter 1

Christmastide 1868
Vieux Carree—the French Quarter
New Orleans, Louisiana

Kaitlin stood in the smoke-shrouded hallway of Madame de Bonnet's Wine and Ale House, staring blankly at the man named Jack Leroux.

He was seated at one of the tables. His game tonight was poker.

Thank God for poker.

The game had taken Leroux's attention from her, and if she could just gather her wits about her, she could find a way to escape Leroux. Did she really need to escape him? She hadn't yet legally committed herself to him; he had no right to hold her!

But from the moment he had seen her at the station, he had begun to laugh, a laugh of pure pleasure.

The last thing she had felt like doing was laughing. The fear that had consumed her on her journey all the way from eastern Georgia swiftly became horror.

Whatever had possessed her to answer an ad for a mail-order bride?

Life, she reminded herself bleakly. Not that it had ever been really good. Her father—God rest his soul—had been a drunkard. Once, he had done well enough with his gambling to acquire an attractive spit of land. Enough to convince her aristocratic mother's folks that he would be a fine catch.

But the land he had acquired was slowly sold off acre by acre. Kaitlin's mother had died when she was barely five, leaving behind a beautiful portrait of herself and nothing more. There had been years of struggling to get enough to eat, to make ends meet. And there had been Jemmy, her brother, a year younger than her, her only salvation.

But the war had come. And the war had taken Jemmy. And when it was over, the war had taken even the meager roof over her head.

She had tried. She had tried so hard. Although he'd been a drunkard, she'd loved her father, and she was the only one left to care for him. She'd taught children to read and to write, but the war had taken the money from the aristocrats, too, and left behind the carpetbaggers and a world that was merely a ghost of what it once had been.

Then last year Pa had finally died and she had looked around at the devastation of Georgia, and she suddenly decided that it was time to leave. In the West, in Montana and Arizona and South Dakota, there were new worlds. Worlds unravaged by Sherman and his troops. Worlds where little children didn't go hungry.

She had wanted a taste of that world.

And so she had begun to read the papers, and at long last, she had found the perfect advertisement. A Mr. Jack Leroux was seeking a bride. He was a businessman of means, French by descent. He was tall, young, handsome, and amiable, and seeking a lovely young lady to brighten up his days.

He had sent her a picture of himself, and asked for one in return. She had sent him one, and soon after, she had received the passage money.

It was a wild idea. But there was nothing left for her at home, and the idea of meeting this Frenchman in New Orleans was exciting. His property was in Montana, but he often traveled to New Orleans. It would be a fine place to meet and marry a bride.

From the first moment she had seen him—awaiting her in his carriage—she knew that she had made a dreadful and horribly naive mistake.

He didn't begin to resemble his picture. The tintype had shown the slender face of a lean young man with dark hair and a luxuriant mustache.

Well, this Jack did have dark hair and a mustache, but that was where any similarity ended. Jack Leroux was a big man, broad in the shoulders, paunchy at the middle. Kaitlin didn't care about that. She hadn't expected to fall in love. All that she wanted was something tangible out of life. A house with a good roof. Clothing that wasn't mended on top of the mends. Food other than onions and potatoes.

Simple things really. And the man in the letter had promised so much more. Silks and satins and so forth.

What horrified her about Jack Leroux was his eyes. They were nearly jet black and small.

And they were evil.

She had barely felt his fingertips on her own when she realized what a fool she had been. What a naive fool. Jack Leroux had not been looking for a wife. Or perhaps he was—perhaps he married many women. But she knew—knew!—as soon as his gaze raked over her assessingly that he had other plans for her that didn't involve any homestead in the West.

She tried to keep her smile in place as his hands touched hers. She excused herself discreetly, saying that she needed to look for her luggage.

And then she had tried to run. She didn't know where to go. Or how she would manage once she got there. She had spent Leroux's money on the passage. Did that mean that she was indebted to him? Did he have a legal claim to her?

She was afraid, even, of the law, for Reconstruction had brought with it a horde of procurers, and thieves and scalawags, and it didn't seem to matter if there was a title before a man's name or not.

It didn't matter because as she tried to run away she wasn't caught by the law. She was caught by two of Leroux's thugs, who promptly returned her to their boss. He had rudely informed her that he had a game to attend, and that she might as well spend her first night in New Orleans getting accustomed to her new station in life.

According to Jack, she was indebted to him. To the tune of fifty dollars in gold.

"You can't force me to marry you!" she had told him, as the carriage lurched forward.

When he had laughed she had known that he didn't care in the least about marriage.

"You'll get used to your new life soon enough, my precious. But you are a beauty, quite a prize! You'll pay me back in no time."

"I'll not!"

"I hope you're not thinking of trying to run away from me again, my dear."

"And I'll not do anything for you, either!"

"I know men who like a feisty woman."

"I'll manage to kill you somehow, I will."

That had sent him into further gales of laughter. "Another Rebel boast! Well, Miss High and Mighty, your side lost the war, remember?"

She spat at him. He pulled out his snow-white handkerchief and mopped his face. "I'll see that you pay for that later, *ma cherie*. Right now, open your eyes. Take a look around. You've the beauty to make money. Real money. Think about it."

When the carriage stopped in front of the alehouse, Leroux and his thugs had forcibly escorted her inside. Then Leroux had walked away, leaving her in the hallway. It didn't matter. The place was filled with his people. He was confident that there was no way that she could run.

But she had to, somehow!

And it was nearly Christmas. The season of peace, of good will toward man!

There were decent folk in New Orleans, Kaitlin was convinced of it. War or no war, carpetbaggers or no. If she could just manage to elude Jack and his men.

The poker game seemed a godsend. Jack was seated at a table, leaning back in his chair. The lights were very dim, and the smoke was heavy. There were other women in the place. Blondes, brunettes, and redheads in strange, scanty outfits. They moved about with various parts of their indecently exposed bodies jiggling as they served drinks to the men.

The players were drinking straight whisky.

The stakes were high.

With nothing else to keep her panic at bay, Kaitlin began to study the players. Beside Jack there was another big fellow. He was as round as a cherub with a little bow mouth and a clean, bald head. He must have been very wealthy, for he threw gold piece after gold piece on the table. Beside him, in contrast, was a reed-thin fellow with sallow dark cheeks and long stringy hair.

Next to him was a younger man. He wore a low-brimmed hat, even at the table. He would probably be tall when he stood, Kaitlin thought, and he was built well, with fine broad shoulders and a narrow waist. He was clad in a long railway frock coat, and he appeared to be a friend of the fellow sitting to his right.

That fellow was a young man who had caught Kaitlin's attention.

He had beautiful blue eyes. Soft as clouds. Kaitlin knew because he had looked right at her as she stood in the hallway. His features were very fine, and his hair was so light that it was nearly a platinum color. He smiled at her, and she felt her heart thud against her chest. He was wonderful. If only he had been the man to advertise for a bride...

But surely, such a man would have his pick of respectable young women. He wouldn't need to advertise. She had been such a fool.

At his side, his friend nudged him. The blond man said something, and his neighbor looked up at Kaitlin.

And she saw his face clearly.

Brilliant eyes, hazel eyes that gleamed like gold, fixed on hers with amusement and speculation. He chewed idly upon a straw and looked her up and down in a fashion that seemed to make her blood steam. She wanted to crawl beneath the table.

It's not my fault that I'm here, and I'm not that kind of woman! she wanted to scream. Damn him. There was so much mockery in his golden gaze. So much speculation. Something cold, and something hard. And something so curious, too.

She gritted her teeth. He was a very handsome man—lean, taut, and bronzed, at once both rugged and elegant. But his manner disturbed her and she stared at his friend again.

Hope was suddenly born in her chest. When the time seemed right, she would throw herself on the mercy of the blond man. Surely, he could not be part of Jack Leroux's party!

"Come on, Leroux, put your money on the table!" the blond said.

"And don't pull out another ace," the man with the golden eyes warned.

"You're accusing me of cheating!" Leroux was suddenly on his feet.

"I'm not accusing anyone of anything," the man said. He was calm, he was smooth. Those gold eyes assessed Leroux. "I'm just suggesting that you don't pull out another ace."

"Why, you—" Leroux began, and from behind him, two men appeared with guns.

There was the roar of a firing gun. Kaitlin was certain that she cried out.

The man with the golden eyes had pulled out his guns and disarmed the men who had aimed at him.

He hadn't killed them. He had shot them both in the hands. The gun hands.

"Jesu!" someone gasped.

"You want to put your money on the table?" the reed-thin man asked Leroux.

Leroux sat very still, staring at his cards. Then he stared at the pile of gold on the table.

"I haven't got any more gold."

"Then you're out of it," the man with the gold eyes said.

"No, no, I'm not." Leroux grinned broadly. "I've got something better than gold. A Christmas gift, gentlemen."

Suddenly he pushed back his chair and rose. Turning, dramatically, he swept an arm in Kaitlin's direction. "A prize far greater than gold, gentlemen. Miss Kaitlin Grant, my fiancée." He drew papers from his pocket. "Her indebtedness to me, gentlemen. She can be yours." He threw the papers down on the table.

Kaitlin gasped. She stared at the men seated at the table. The thin man had a lean, hungry look about him. It was not reassuring.

The fat man looked at her as if she were a steak and mashed potatoes and apple pie, all rolled into one.

"But I'm not property!" Kaitlin protested.

Jack Leroux ignored her. "Are we on, gentlemen?"

The handsome blond man with the blue eyes and his golden-eyed friend were both watching her, too.

The blond, kindly.

The golden-eyed man—more speculatively than ever. Well, she belonged to Jack Leroux, it seemed. She must appear to be a whore.

"I am *not* property! I don't owe anything to any man! I'm trying to get hold of a sheriff or a constable or the law in some shape or form—"

"Shut up!" Jack said, walking toward her. "Shut up, or I'll see you black and blue—"

"The lady's fate is on the table," a voice interrupted sharply. It belonged to the man with the golden eyes. "Don't touch her. Show your hand."

Jack swore in bastardized French. But his two henchmen were still moaning about their bullet-torn hands, and he didn't seem to relish the idea of testing the fast-drawing stranger again. He sat down and flipped over his cards.

Kaitlin couldn't see them. She was afraid to breathe.

Quickly, one by one, the rest of the men flipped over their cards.

The handsome blond gave a glad cry. Jack swore again, partly in English, partly in French. The fat man looked deflated.

The stranger with the golden eyes shrugged. "Seems to me like you're done, Leroux."

Kaitlin heard no more, for the blond man was up and out of his seat, hurrying toward her. Before she knew it she was picked up and spun about. Then, laughing with a wonderful boyish humor, he set her down again.

"You're saved, princess!"

She smiled in return, certain that he had won the game.

"Let me introduce myself. I'm Daniel—"

"Daniel, watch out!"

Daniel turned, sweeping her with him, just in time. Jack Leroux had risen, a small but razor-sharp knife glittering in his hand. But before he could use it, the sound of a shot exploded in the room. Leroux screamed, the knife clattering to the floor.

The man with the golden eyes had made another perfect shot.

"Maybe we'd best take our winnings and get out of here, Shane," Daniel said.

"I think I agree."

The golden-eyed man, the one called Shane, was on his feet, having collected the gold from the table. He was wary, his eyes on every man there as he backed toward the hallway.

"Bastard!" Jack hissed at him.

"We're leaving, Leroux. Don't let anyone lift a hand to stop us. Next time, I'll shoot to kill. And I'll be aiming right at your heart."

Kaitlin looped her hand around Daniel's arm, following as he led the way out. The man named Shane stayed behind, covering their exit.

A minute later they were out in the street. A breeze was wafting in off the Mississippi. It lifted Kaitlin's hair, and seemed to caress her cheek. Excitement was bringing a flush to her cheeks; relief was making her giddy.

Don't be a fool! she tried to warn herself. She had trusted in Leroux's letters enough to endure a rough journey through several states only to find out he'd wanted to turn her into a waterfront harlot.

And there had to be something to the mail-order debt. The men had all been willing to play for it.

Or for her.

But this Daniel...

He was so good-looking, and so very kind. She couldn't help but laugh with him, couldn't help but feel wonder in his presence.

"We took him!" Daniel exclaimed. "We took that Frenchie bastard, Shane!"

"Yes," the one named Shane said, his hat brim pulled even lower now. Still, Kaitlin felt his eyes. She couldn't really see them on her, she just felt them. Watching her. Wondering about her.

Condemning her?

They had found her with Leroux.

"Instead of standing around here cackling, I think that we'd best get a move on," Shane said. "We're too close to the river here, and not a good section of it."

Daniel mentioned the name of a hotel. "It's very proper, we can make arrangements for our princess here—Kaitlin. Kaitlin Grant. That's what he said your name is, right?"

She opened her mouth to reply.

Shane answered for her. "If he was giving us your real name."

"What other name would I use?" Kaitlin demanded. If she had hackles, they would be rising. Just like those on any hunting dog when it knew that a dangerous beast was nearby.

Maybe not a beast quite so wicked as Leroux, but dangerous nonetheless.

"I don't know," he said bluntly. He shoved back his hat, and those golden eyes studied her from head to foot. "What exactly were you doing with him? How long have you been with him? Were you making big money for him?"

Kaitlin gasped.

Not even Yankees spoke like that!

Quick as a trigger, she reached out to strike him.

He was quicker, catching her arm.

"Shane!" Daniel protested, distressed. "Shane, look at her dress! It's obvious that she's a lady. Let's hear her out!"

He still held her arm. Her teeth were gritted, her eyes were blazing. "Get your hands off me!"

The sound of her voice was cutting. She had lost her mother years ago, but she had never, never forgotten her. Never forgotten the things that a lady should do, the way that a lady should act. She knew very well how to don a cloak of dignity that few people could breach.

Nevertheless, she was somewhat surprised when this man released her.

However, she still didn't like the mocking smile on his face.

"Perhaps we bested Leroux. Perhaps she's besting us."

Kaitlin wasn't even going to speak with him any longer. She turned to Daniel. "Every member of my family is dead," she said softly. "My brother died in the war, my father just a year ago. There was nothing left. I had to get out. I had to. If you could see the way that they're running the place—"

"The Yankees?"

She hesitated. "I met a few Yankees who weren't so bad," she went on quietly. "They tried to leave me something of a roof, and something to eat. They were tired soldiers when they came through, just like my brother might have been a tired soldier up in the North. It wasn't soldiers who came in afterwards. It was trash like Leroux. So I had to get out."

"So you sold yourself to a man like Leroux," Shane interjected dryly.

"No! Yes! I didn't think that—oh, never mind! You won't understand no matter what I say!"

Shane grunted noncommittally. Daniel took her arm. "Come on, Shane. She's shivering something awful. Let's go to the hotel and have some dinner."

Shane shrugged. "But I've got to head back in the morning. No matter what."

"I don't—" Kaitlin began.

Daniel tugged lightly on her arm. "Please let's go to the hotel," he said.

They walked quickly through the streets. There were sailors out, and probably thieves, pickpockets, and whores. Daniel had thrust her between himself and Shane as they moved along the street. She swallowed hard, aware of the hard body of the man on her left. She didn't want to allow him any grace at all, he was so cutting and so rude. But to his credit, she realized, he had no intention of letting anything happen to her.

And she couldn't forget just how quickly he could make the pistols in his gun belt blaze.

As they walked, the atmosphere of the city gradually changed. Not so many sailors seemed to roam the streets. Handsome carriages began to roll by.

The women had a different look, and a different air.

Then Daniel paused before a set of heavy wooden doors with the words "The Saint Francis" emblazoned above them. He opened the door and ushered her in.

The hotel was beautiful. Kaitlin didn't think that she'd ever seen anything like it, even before the war. Dark, rich velvets covered an array of chairs and love seats. Brass chandeliers with glittering crystals hung from the ceilings. The lobby was papered in an elegant beige with barely discernible embossed white flowers. The reception stand was made out of the deepest, darkest wood.

"I'll make arrangements," Shane said, leaving Kaitlin with Daniel in the center of the lobby where a circular seat was set beneath one of the grand chandeliers.

"Why is he so mean?" Kaitlin asked Daniel.

"Shane? Well, he's not exactly mean. I guess he's just not too trusting of folks anymore, that's all." He wasn't going to offer more. He seemed more perplexed with Kaitlin and the circumstances in which she found herself.

"You've no home to go to?" he said.

She shook her head. "And I'm sure that you've won my indebtedness. I can make it up to you, I promise. I teach. I can teach almost anything. Reading, geography, history, piano."

"But you intended to be a mail-order bride?"

She nodded, feeling color seep into her cheeks again. Did this man intend to marry her? Excitement rippled through her veins. It would be just right. He was so attractive, and so kind. She could easily manage marriage to him. She didn't love him, of course; she barely knew him. But she hadn't been expecting love any more than she had been expecting white-trash vermin like Jack Leroux.

People were watching them, she realized suddenly. She had drawn the attention of any number of masculine eyes. No one walked into the room without glancing her way. It made her uncomfortable.

"Well?" Daniel persisted. "Are you still willing to be a bride?"

Was he asking her to marry him? "Yes," she said softly.

"And you teach? Can you cook?" he asked.

She glanced into his eyes. He had such a beautiful smile. She nodded, smiling, too. "Yes. Rather well, actually."

"You'd be so good for Francesca."

She frowned, but then she realized that he wasn't really talking to her.

The man named Shane had come up behind her. She didn't know how long he had been there, or how long he had been listening. She didn't really care.

Shane grunted.

Daniel went on talking as if she wasn't there anymore. "She has to be the most beautiful creature I've seen in my entire life. She cooks and cleans and teaches—"

"So she says. Maybe her true talents lie in those eyes, or maybe even when she's on her back—"

"And just how bad would that be?" Daniel demanded.

"That is it!" Kaitlin exclaimed.

Daniel caught her arm. "Please! I apologize for him! He hasn't met a lady in so long he just doesn't know how to behave!"

Shane ignored him. "You think she should be a bride?"

"What could be lost?"

Then Shane was staring at her with those gold eyes of his. They seemed to blaze right through her. They seemed to undress her, right there in the lobby.

Then he smiled again, mockingly, but the mockery was addressed somehow toward himself. "Hell, yes, you're right, just what could be lost! Well, Miss Kaitlin Grant, there could be no love match here. But let's hear it from your lips. Are you ready to face a land that's nearly raw wilderness? The Indians still think that it's theirs. You'd get a house and a home. And a fair amount of riches, I think. But there are terms to a marriage like this. The wilderness can also offer a hard life. And a house must be taken care of. It's a lonely place at times. And a husband has to be taken care of, too, Miss Grant, if you understand my meaning, which I'm quite certain that you do."

She felt a spark of fire racing to her cheeks again. If she could just hit him really hard, just once, she would feel so much better.

But she couldn't, not standing in the elegant lobby, not with the very kind and gentle Daniel awaiting her answer.

Why was he letting this Shane ask all of these questions? Well, when she married Daniel, she wouldn't let Shane run his life a minute longer.

"Leroux was right about one thing, sir," she said tightly. "You certainly are a—a *bastard*."

"Those are the terms, lady."

146

"Your terms."

"My terms," he echoed flatly. "Oh, yes. You do appear to be a very beautiful woman, Miss Grant. There's nothing beneath the fabric that would mar that beauty, some fault we should know about?"

"Shane!" Daniel protested.

The nerve of the man! He should know, didn't he have her practically undressed with his eyes, right there in the lobby?

"No faults, sir," she snapped.

"Well, do you agree to the terms?"

She gazed at Daniel. He wanted to make things so much easier for her, she could see it. She swallowed hard. The intimate part of marriage was going to be hard no matter what. But she had accepted that when she had agreed to Leroux's proposal.

"I understand the bargain, sir," she said coldly to Shane.

"Then maybe we can solve this now. Tonight," Daniel said gleefully.

"Why not?" Shane said. "Excuse me. I'll see if they can help us at the desk."

Once again, Shane walked away. Kaitlin felt numb. So much had occurred in one day.

She turned and looked around the beautiful hotel. Someone had laced the windows with holly branches and the tiny red beads of holly were bright and beautiful. A string of brightly colored Christmas angels hung over the paneling behind the desk, where Shane now stood.

It was nearly Christmas. How wonderful. For Christmas, she'd be receiving a husband—Daniel.

"I imagine we could go up to the suite," Daniel said, smiling. "Ah, here comes Shane now!"

He was striding toward them again, so tall in that long railway frock coat of his. He should have been incongruous in the elegant lobby. But he was not. He cut an imposing figure, striking and commanding.

And mean, Kaitlin thought. She cast her eyes trustfully upon Daniel.

"I've spoken with the manager, and he was very understanding of the—er—delicacy of our situation. He'll be up immediately with a friend, a Father Green of Saint Paul's. Shall we go? Suite 204, Daniel, right up the stairs."

Kaitlin wished that those golden eyes of his wouldn't blaze so intently into her own, nor flicker with quite so much amused challenge.

Daniel took her hand, and led her up the stairs. She was startled to feel Shane's touch on her shoulders, pulling at the simple cotton fabric of her dress.

"You'll need a whole new wardrobe," he commented. "Expensive."

She swung around on him, arching a brow. "Maybe my husband will find me worth it."

He laughed softly. "Maybe."

"Ah, here's our suite!" Daniel said.

Shane fit a key into the door and pushed it open. They entered an elegant little parlor with several dark wood side tables and richly upholstered chairs. On a sideboard was a beautiful cut-glass decanter full of brandy and snifters at its side.

There were two doors in the parlor. One leading to a room on the left, and one leading to a room on the right.

"Would you like to freshen up?" Daniel asked Kaitlin. "I'm sure there's water in the bedroom—"

"We can order up a bath for her, once this thing is over," Shane said curtly. "Brandy?" he asked Daniel.

Then he looked to Kaitlin. "Miss Grant? Perhaps you feel the need for one. After all, you are about to sell your soul to the devil."

"No, thank you," Kaitlin said sweetly. "I don't feel that I'm selling my soul to the devil at all."

"No?" he replied, arching a dark honey brow. His eyes were glittering.

There was a knock at the door. Two men came in: Mr. Clemmons, the manager, and a kind-looking old white-haired soul in robes who was introduced as Father Green, an Episcopal minister.

"Well now, I understand that the circumstances here have been a bit peculiar." Gentle gray eyes looked down upon Kaitlin. "Ah, lass, a beauty is what you are, and lured into a den of thieves, as it were! Well, let's thank the Lord that this kind gentleman intends to make an honest woman of you, give you his name, and all the earthly possessions he holds. Step forward now, and hear the words of our Lord!"

Kaitlin moved forward. She closed her eyes and listened as Father Green read from his prayer book.

To have and to hold, to honor and to cherish.

She was about to be married. Legally wed. And she would leave behind all that was familiar to her, leave behind her beloved but tattered South, and travel on to a new life. She had been saved from the grasp of Jack Leroux by a wonderful man who was now making her his wife.

"Do you, Shane Patrick MacAuliffe, take this woman to be your lawfully wedded wife—"

She heard no more. Her eyes flew open and she looked to her side.

She wasn't marrying Daniel. She was marrying Shane!

"You!" she gasped, interrupting the minister.

"Well, what did you think?" Shane demanded in exasperation. "I won your debt papers."

No! she thought with dismay. No! "But I—"

He leaned close. "Daniel is married already, Miss Grant. His wife's back home in the Black Hills," he informed her in a whisper for her ears alone.

"Is something wrong?" Father Green asked.

"Everything is wrong!" Kaitlin said.

Shane drew her aside. "What difference does it make?" he said in a low voice, his face unreadable. "It's a bargain, remember? I suggested that you might be selling your soul to the devil, but you seemed willing all the way. And the devil himself might be an improvement over Leroux, and you agreed to give your life to him."

"I did not! I explained—"

"Yeah. Sure."

"Oh, how dare you—"

Father Green cleared his throat loudly. "If there is a difficulty—"

"No!" Daniel called out from the sidelines. He stepped forward. "Shane, we can't just leave her here!"

"I can make my own way—" Kaitlin began.

"Both of you, think about it!" Daniel pleaded. "You can both give each other what you need! Think of Francesca, Shane. And Kaitlin, you'll be safe!"

"Do I go on?" Father Green asked.

"Yes!" Daniel answered for them.

Shane pulled her back to their place in front of the minister. Her fingers were cold. So cold. She heard the ceremony go on. And on. Then Father Green asked her to vow that she would love, honor, and obey Shane Patrick MacAuliffe.

And she heard her own broken whisper. "I do."

He slipped a ring on her finger. It was too big, she had to clench her fingers together to keep it on. She glanced down at it. It was a signet ring with the initials SPA.

"I now pronounce you man and wife. You may now kiss the bride, Mr. MacAuliffe."

It was done.

Kaitlin didn't give Shane a chance to kiss her. She bolted for the sideboard and the brandy bottle.

He followed her, his mocking gold eyes upon her. "So you've sold your soul to the devil. Regrets already?"

"I can keep a bargain," she told him coldly.

"Can you?"

"Mr. and Mrs. MacAuliffe, there are papers to sign," Father Green reminded them.

Kaitlin signed the papers. Then she wasn't sure what happened. She was so numb. They all had brandy. Then Father Green and Mr. Clemmons were gone. A roast beef dinner had been brought up for the three of them: her, Daniel—and her husband, Shane MacAuliffe, who had ordered up a hot steaming bath for her.

And then Shane was setting down his brandy glass. "Perhaps you'd like to prepare for your bath, Mrs. MacAuliffe."

She nodded stiffly.

He swept her a courtly bow, his arm outstretched to indicate one of the doors. "Madame, to your left." He grinned sardonically. "Our room."

Her knees were buckling. She was going to fall.

No. He wanted her to fail in some way. He had married her, but he seemed to despise her.

Well, she wouldn't falter, and she wouldn't fail. She'd never fail in her duty.

But she wouldn't give him a thing more. Ever. She swore it silently to herself.

She had just been married.

She had just gone to war, she thought woefully.

Somewhere a clock chimed.

Shane started to laugh. Startled, she looked at him.

"Merry Christmas, my love," he told her. His gaze held her and he swallowed more brandy. "Oh, yes, Merry Christmas! What wonderful gifts we have given one another!"

Chapter 2

She was, Shane decided, the most beautiful woman he had ever seen.

He had thought so long before the strange twist in the poker game. From the moment he had first seen her in the hallway, standing against the wall, looking so bewildered, he had felt the most curious fascination.

Any man would find her beautiful. She had hair blacker than ebony, almost blue in its richness. Small tendrils curled about the oval frame of her face and large, gem-green eyes while the long bulk of it was drawn from her face with pins to cascade freely down the length of her back. Her mouth was generous, the lips full, promising a wealth of sensuality. Her cheekbones were classical—they might have graced a statue of Venus in a museum. Her nose was fine and straight, her ink-black brows were beautifully arched and slim. She was of medium height, but even in her worn and mended and somewhat voluminous garments, her form was anything but average. She was small, and she was slim, but there seemed to be the most extraordinary curves to her body.

But she had been with Jack Leroux. His experience with women hadn't left a trusting taste in his mouth, and he was still wondering if he hadn't been taken for the biggest fool in the Western world.

She had thought that she was getting Daniel.

The laugh was on them both, perhaps.

"Well then, Merry Christmas, Mr. MacAuliffe!" he toasted himself. He sat alone at the bar, but he had suddenly decided—just minutes after the ceremony—that he had had enough of his brand-new wife for the moment. He'd needed to escape the suite for a while. To sit by himself.

To brood?

Well, hell, yes, it was Christmas. He drummed his fingers on the fine oak paneling of the hotel's bar. He should have been at home with Francesca. She shouldn't have been left alone. She was so fragile these days. Her father, Shane's brother, had died in the first days of the war when she had been nothing but a babe in arms. Her mother had succumbed to the smallpox a year later. Francesca had gone on to spend the next few years with her mother's sister, but then Deidre, too, had died of a frightening fever.

Shane himself had been with General Kirby-Smith. They hadn't surrendered with Lee, they had fought right on into May, and it had been near November of '65 when Shane had made it home at last.

Well, to what was left of his home.

Jeannie was gone. She hadn't been killed by any accidental fire in the war, and she hadn't succumbed to any disease, unless the disease had been greed.

New Orleans had fallen quickly. And a number of the big homes outside the city had simply been taken over.

Well, from what Shane heard, Jeannie had figured that if the Yanks were taking over the place, she was going to take over the Yanks.

When he first heard about it, he had wanted to kill her. Her, and the infantry colonel she had chosen to spend her time with. He was far away fighting, though, and all that his anger managed to do was make him careless. Somewhere, in the midst of some battle, he had decided that he just wasn't angry anymore. He had some of the right connections, and he sued for a divorce.

It seemed to take the rest of the war to get his divorce, but he did. He never had to see Jeannie again. He was glad. He was afraid that he would have been tempted to strangle her and the colonel, and since the war was over, they probably would have hanged him for it, and that wouldn't have "been fair."

He'd ridden on home, a sharpshooter, or ex-sharpshooter now, who had been raised to take on the working of a major plantation. Only it seemed that there just weren't any plantations left, major or minor.

One look at what had once been his family home just north of the bayou country in southern Louisiana had convinced him that it was time to move onward. In that aspect, he'd been lucky. At Shiloh he'd managed to save the life of a man in his company, and that man had just happened to have one damned smart father—a fellow who didn't turn against the South to invest in Yankee dollars, but who had

156

managed to hold tight to his gold and holdings by dealing in Europe. He'd been determined to reward Shane, and he'd done so, gifting him with a large parcel of land out in the Black Hills of South Dakota. It was still rather raw country, and not too long ago there had been really violent Indian activity. But the Indians were being constantly forced in a westwardly direction, and there had been very little trouble in a long time now.

The nearest town was a place called Three Mills, and an amazing quantity and range of goods could be found there, along with a fair amount of society. At least, that was what Shane had been told. And as he walked among the ruins of what had once been his home, it was something he was determined to believe. The war was over. He was going north.

He'd been there a little more than a year when Francesca had arrived. She'd been sent on a steamer up the Mississippi, then she'd been shuffled onto whatever railroads were available, and brought by stage the rest of the way. He'd never seen a more forlorn creature than his little niece when he'd arrived in town to pick her up that frigidly cold afternoon in February. Her little face had been pinched, there had been tears near-frozen on her cheeks, but her chin had been high and her eyes...

Her eyes had nearly broken his heart. They were old eyes in such a young face. They were a beautiful velvety brown, but they mirrored an awful loneliness, and a worse fear of rejection. For years, people died on her. And then those who remained shunted her from place to place. The death of her grandmother on her mother's side had brought her here now. Looking at that little woebegone face, Shane had sworn that if he managed nothing else in life, he would make up to Francesca all that she had lost in her younger years. He was quick to discover that he loved the little girl very much. And though she was slow to come around, he knew that she loved him. Trusting was difficult for her, and Shane could easily understand why. Each time he thought of his niece's eyes...

Eyes.

Francesca's were a deep, rich, haunting brown. While his new wife's were that shimmering green. But like Francesca's, they seemed haunted. They drew him in. There was something so stark in them, so anguished, so... well, haunting. More than her beauty, that look in her eyes had led him to his decision to make her his wife.

Wife. What a strange word. He hadn't thought to use it again in relation to himself.

He drank down a tumbler of whisky, rolling the word around in his mind. Jeannie had been wife enough for several lifetimes. Shane had decided that anything he wanted from a woman could be obtained at Nelly Grier's. After all, Three Mills was no fly-by-night town. Nelly ran one classy establishment with lovely, talented, and vivacious little creatures who made few demands upon a man.

And he in return, expected nothing from them. Nothing but the laughter and entertainment of the moment.

What the hell had happened? Now he had a wife again. Just when things were starting to go really well. He had nearly a thousand head of cattle. Chancey, who had been with him in the war, acted as foreman to the hired hands. Francesca kept house. Well, more or less; but he'd been a soldier, and soldiers became accustomed to looking after themselves. It was a good life. He worried a bit about Francesca, and he was heartily sorry that he wasn't with her now, for Christmas, but he'd had to come to New Orleans to settle some old family disputes. Property that had been stolen was being returned, and Shane had decided that it was necessary to have his land back. He might never give a damn if he saw the East or the Old South again, but one day, Francesca would want to know where her father had come from.

He drummed his fingers on the bar. Well, at least he could tell Francesca, when he returned to Three Mills, that he had done something for her for Christmas. His fingers wound around his glass. He'd have to have a long talk with the hostile beauty upstairs. He didn't care if she regretted her bargain from this night until the day she died, but she was going to make life pleasant for Francesca. She had said that she could cook. Dinners were going to become far better. She could keep house. Well, his clothes had best be kept clean and neat, his parlor in shape.

But none of those things really mattered. There was only one thing his new acquisition needed to do, and that was to care for Francesca in a manner that Shane could not himself.

He glanced toward the stairway. Had he just been taken in by one of Jack Leroux's best whores?

And did it even matter? As long as she had a heart, heart enough for Francesca?

He tossed a coin on the bar and stood, looking toward the stairs. It was Christmas, and he now had a wife. A woman who was exceptionally beautiful, and one who had married him agreeing to his terms.

Maybe it was time he found out just a little more about her.

He took the stairs two at a time, suddenly feeling a hot surge of both anger and desire shoot through him like volcanic lava. He burst through the doorway to the suite and found the parlor empty.

Where the hell was Daniel? Were he and the new Mrs. MacAuliffe together somewhere?

He ground his teeth, wondering why he was allowing his thoughts of her to make him mistrust a good friend. Still, the question remained with him. He strode silently across the parlor to the door on the left side of the room and quietly opened it.

She was there. Alone. Stretched out in a big tin bathtub. Her eyes were closed, her head was tilted back, the luxurious length of her hair lay over the rim of the tub where her head rested, the ends just dusting the floor.

Bubbles surrounded her. Lots of them. Even though they hid her body, they merely enhanced that feeling of fire that grew within him. Fire that burned, and fire that brought...

Warmth. A warmth he didn't want to feel. She looked very tired, and defenseless. The porcelain beauty of her face had never been so evident. Then her eyes opened and she started violently. She had heard him.

For a moment—so brief a moment—he thought that he saw fear within her eyes. But then they were flashing, emerald and glittering, and very hostile.

He walked into the room, casting off his coat and his gun belt. She watched him all the while, her lashes fluttering as her gaze fell on his gun belt.

"I'm not going to shoot you," he told her. Then he paused for a moment in reflection. "Not yet, anyway."

She glared at him. He smiled and shrugged innocently.

"You're awfully good with them," she said.

"Yes, I am."

"And you're humble."

"It isn't a matter of being humble. I spent four years of my life using them almost daily. Yes, I'm good with them," he said wearily. He sat down on the bed, and took off his boots. She seemed to jump a mile when they thudded on the floor. Her eyes met his. They stayed captive there as he unbuttoned his shirt, button by button. Then he pulled the tails from his jeans and let the shirt fall casually to the floor. He stood. Once again, there was that look of panic about her. A pulse that beat like wildfire at the very beautiful base of her throat.

He walked closer to the tub. Then he knelt down beside it. Maybe that had been his mistake. The smell there was soft, a mingling of roses and clean femininity. Something twisted inside him. He itched to touch her, to wrench her from the tub, to have her then and there and look to the subtleties later. He ground his teeth again, determined that it wasn't going to be that way. Maybe she was one of Jack Leroux's sluts. Maybe, hell. Probably. But she was his wife.

He dangled his fingers in the water, just above her breasts. She hadn't moved. Just that pulse at her throat, and then the rampant rise and fall of her chest.

"Having second thoughts?" he inquired.

Her eyes met his. She shook her head. He smiled. She was plainly longing to hit him. Longing to really hit him.

"Think you've been in that bathtub long enough?"

She shook her head again. "If you'll just go away for a few minutes—"

He laughed out loud. "No, I won't just go away. We made a bargain. You're not trying to squirm out of it, are you?"

"No! I am not trying to squirm out of anything. Yes, I made a bargain! And I intend to keep every painful promise that I made!"

"Painful promise?" Shane said indignantly. "I beg to differ. I haven't ever had any complaints."

"The lamps are burning, I've no decent gown—"

"You certainly don't need a gown—"

"But the light! No decent folk would think of doing—what you're thinking of doing—with so much light—"

"I'm not so sure that we are decent folk, Mrs. MacAuliffe. And I just acquired a bride under very unusual circumstances. I intend to inspect every single inch of my new acquisition."

Her eyes went very wide, and suddenly he could take it no longer. Heedless of the denim breeches he still wore, he reached into

162

the tub, plucking her from it, bubbles and all. He lowered her onto the bed, sprawling halfway over her. A startled scream began to escape her lips and he covered them with the palm of his hand.

"You mustn't start shrieking with pleasure yet," he warned her sarcastically. "We've company. Daniel. He's probably sleeping by now. Alas, my love! And you thought that you'd be sleeping with him. Sorry, it's me!"

Fury flared in her eyes again, hot and green. Shane felt as if those flames ripped into his loins, and tore through the length of him. He had recognized her beauty so quickly. He had known that he was falling into some prison in the haunting emerald of her eyes.

He hadn't realized that he could want her this way. So damn desperately. That the flames inside him could burn and soar more brightly than the wicked tempest of a forest fire.

She bit his hand. He gave a muffled curse and pulled it back.

"I'm not about to shriek with pleasure," she assured him.

"Perhaps you will," he taunted. Her hands were pressing against his chest. "Then again, maybe you do want to renege."

"No! Get on with this wretched business!"

For a moment he paused, staring down into her face. It was Christmas. Let her be. Seek some peace.

No. It was Christmas, and they had formed a strange bargain. And it would probably be best if she knew from the very start that he had not taken a wife for her ornamental value, that she would fulfill every aspect of her bargain.

"I shall try to make it the very least wretched that I may," he told her softly.

There might have been a hint of tears in her eyes. The softest hint. Then she closed them.

And then he could truly wait no longer.

He kissed her eyelids. Lightly. The tip of her nose. Then he found her lips. Found the resistance within them. But he kissed her anyway. Her mouth was closed against him. Prim. He let his tongue tease and caress the softness of her lips until they began to part. He caressed the more tender, inner flesh. And when she began to give, he allowed passion and desire their free rein, freely, fully, forcefully knowing the secrets of her lips and teeth and tongue, and feeling the ever-expanding thunder of desire within his own loins.

Her fingers no longer pressed against him. He rose quickly, baring the whole of her body to his eyes as he stripped off his breeches. She was instantly on the defensive again, eyes growing very wide as she looked at him, her fingers groping for the covers.

"No!" he told her hoarsely, catching her hand and pausing for a minute.

There were no flaws on her anywhere. She was shaped like a goddess, with firm, full breasts, peaked with dusky rose nipples. She had a miniscule waist, softly rounded hips, and long shapely limbs. She was so stunning that he stared at her. Stared at her so long that her temper and defiance flared and her distress disappeared.

"Shall I stand, shall I walk around?" she demanded furiously.

Shane laughed. "Madame, I wouldn't mind one bit!"

"Oh!" she gasped, but he allowed her protest to go no further, sweeping down upon her, and covering her nakedness again with the bulk of his body. He caught her lips again, and kissed her until she surrendered to the kiss.

Then his lips left hers, and traced a slow steady pattern over the length of her body. His mouth paused at the soaring pulse at her throat. It played where the dusky rose nipples rose so hard and tempting before him. He listened to the catch of her breath, felt the twist of her body beneath him, and went on, burying his face against the sweet flat plane of her belly.

Her fingers tugged at his hair. She murmured some protests. He ignored them, twisting her body suddenly, stroking the length of her spine with his touch, and following that touch with the hot moisture of his tongue. He flipped her again and found her eyes on his. Her breasts rose and fell quickly. Perhaps she wasn't shrieking with pleasure, but she was trembling fiercely. So fiercely.

He smiled, and feathered his fingers over the length of her again, softly stroking over her breasts, her belly, and below. He pressed his lips against her flesh once again. Lower and lower. She cried out in protest, but he gave her no quarter, touching, stroking, caressing. When he rose high above her, her head was tossing against the pillow. He caught it, held it still, and met her eyes.

Dear Lord, but there was passion within them! If only he could draw out the warmth and the fire. She was trying so desperately to hold against him.

She was his wife.

He parted her thighs, his desire at a fierce and hungry peak.

Yet he held tempered that desire swiftly when he felt the barrier, heard the sharp intake of her breath. He met her eyes again and they were shimmering with moisture. "You weren't one of Leroux's whores."

"I told you who I was!" she cried. Her arms were on him now, hands that grasped his shoulders, bracing against the pain. He could stop, he could pull away. But the damage would be done.

And she was his wife. They were bound now. And she had assured him that she would do her "wretched" duty.

He held very still, then moved slowly. So slowly. And he began to feel the subtle change in her body, felt it give, felt it accept. Once again, the force of his desire tore through him. Surged and swept. The scent of her, the feel of her, even the emerald of her eyes, all swept into the force of his need.

She moved. He had touched something within her. Maybe he hadn't found the deep searing passion within her, but he had touched something. A soft sound escaped her lips. Her body moved beneath his.

The depth of his own hunger seized him. Shattering, volatile, it tore through him until it burst within him, and swept into her. The aftermath kept shudders raking through him as he eased his weight from her, coming to her side. She tried to pull away from him, choking, embarrassed.

"No," he told her softly.

"No, what! I've already fulfilled my bargain."

"That 'wretched' bargain!" Shane said. Dammit. He wanted to slap her. He knew that he had given her something. "Mrs. MacAuliffe, this has been one night. We've a lifetime ahead of us."

"But you—"

"I enjoyed this 'wretched' bit tremendously. Especially since I discovered..."

"That I wasn't one of Leroux's whores?" she demanded.

He stared at her; her ebony hair was a wild mane about her fine features. "Yes," he said.

She tried to pull away. He caught her arm, wishing that he hadn't begun the relationship with so much hostility. What relationship? he asked himself. He barely knew her.

He had mistrusted her from the beginning.

Hell, she was still an adventuress.

Maybe that wasn't so bad. Maybe they were all damaged shells that had once been people.

If nothing else, he figured, he had a tempting bed partner.

Fires could build and burn within him again so swiftly...

He held back, gritting his teeth. He had married her. He was going to make it work.

"Let's call a truce for Christmas," he said softly.

"What?"

"It's Christmas, Kaitlin. The season of good will, peace and all. Let's call a truce. We'll act like man and wife until tomorrow afternoon."

"Tomorrow afternoon?" Her beautiful green eyes narrowed suspiciously and he laughed.

"Yes, you'll appreciate this, I believe. I'm going to head back home without you."

The startled pleasure in her eyes was downright close to insulting.

"You have to have some clothing made, and New Orleans just might be the right place to have it done. I've got to get back. I've left Francesca, and a very big herd of cattle. You can follow as soon as you've acquired everything that you may need. You might want to look for household items, too. Buy some pots and pans that you might like. And draperies."

He wasn't sure what impression he had made, allowing her free rein on purchases. She studied him gravely as he spoke, then asked, "Who's Francesca?"

"My niece. She lives with me. She's almost ten."

"Oh," she said simply.

Anger, irrational perhaps, suddenly seized him. He rose over her, straddling her on the bed. "You can bear any hostility toward me that you want, Mrs. MacAuliffe, but don't you ever show it before her! And don't you ever raise a cruel finger to that child, do you understand?"

Emerald fire lit her eyes. "I shall be entirely grateful for her company over yours!" She stared at him in defiance, and then she seemed to realize his position, and their mutual nakedness. Her lashes lowered. "Honestly. I love children. Will you really leave in the morning?"

"Yes. It will probably be April before you see me again, by the time you'll be able to travel."

Her eyes opened wide to his. She nodded gravely. "That will be fine." She could be so damned prim at times. "I shall be very careful with your money," she said.

"You don't need to be so careful. You need to buy what you want, and what you need. I've managed to become a fairly wealthy man," he said. He thought that her eyes widened again. "The bargain is not such a one-sided one, Mrs. MacAuliffe. I think you'll like your new house. It's very gracious. Like I said, buy anything at all that you want."

Her eyes met his. "Thank you."

"Have we a Christmas truce?"

"Yes." It was barely a whisper.

"Then lie back, Mrs. MacAuliffe, for I see cold and lonely months ahead for myself—when I have just acquired a wife."

She swallowed hard. Then she wound her arms around him, and pressed her lips to his.

In his amazement, he stiffened and pulled back. "Is that for the clothing?" he asked her bitterly. "Or for the house?"

"Oh!" she cried out, and tried to twist away. "It was for neither! It was for Christmas."

He was sorry, so sorry. No matter what it had been for, she had made a tentative move in his direction.

And he did want her. His fascination with her had become something that beat within him, driving him. He wouldn't be able to get her out of his mind once he had left her. Not for a minute. He was sorry for his promise. He couldn't begin to foresee the months ahead without her.

"Kaitlin!"

She had rolled to her side beneath him. He caught her shoulder, pulling her back. "Kaitlin, I'm sorry. Come. Come love me for Christmas."

Those eyes of hers met his. Brilliant, beautiful.

She made no overtures toward him again, but neither did she fight him.

Well, she had said that she was determined to do her duty.

And still...

He made love to her slowly, completely. And his need for her reached peaks that startled him, they were so strong.

He touched something in return. Something. He knew that he didn't hurt her, that he gave to her. But she held back. No matter what emotions and feeling escaped her, there was something that she held back.

Maybe it didn't matter. Maybe it would come. Yet it left him with a sense of loss, of deeper hunger.

He had to have it.

That would be the future.

For that early, early Christmas morning, he slept with his new wife in his arms.

Christmas truce.

Chapter 3

Kaitlin didn't arrive at Three Mills until the end of May.

Shane and Daniel left in time to avoid the most wicked weather of the season. By the time that Kaitlin should have been on her way, the winter had become so harsh that Shane had sent a telegraph advising her to hold off her travel plans for a while.

Kaitlin had stared at the telegraph for a long time, wondering if he wasn't sorry about the whole thing already. He'd left her on Christmas day.

It hadn't been that terrible a Christmas. She'd awakened to find him gone from the room, and a box beside her bed. *Merry Christmas*, the tag read. And inside of it had been a beautiful dress of red velvet and silk, a Christmas dress. There had been a note embedded in the folds, too. *The fit may not be perfect, but it will get you through to do your own shopping.*

It had seemed rather difficult to rise and to walk that morning. Her body was sore, but still so warm!

And just thinking of the night, she could flush so easily. She had told herself that it would be wretched, but that she had resolve, she was strong, she could endure.

But in the end...

The night just hadn't seemed so wretched. Maybe there had been Christmas magic around them. Something warm, something very giving. It should have been so horrible.

It was remarkably pleasant. It made her think of her new husband in an entirely different light. There was something in his touch...

Whatever it was, one minute it had made her dread to see him again and long to do so the next. For one, their leave taking hadn't been in the least romantic. She had tried to thank him, not so much for the dress, but because he'd given her a Christmas present. It had seemed like forever since she had received one.

But by morning, in the light of the day, the gold eyes had seemed shrewd and assessing once again each time they fell her way. "I'd hardly have my wife in rags," he told her bluntly.

"Nevertheless, thank you," she'd said primly. "I—I don't have a gift for you."

His smile was wicked, taunting. "Last night was quite a present in itself."

She turned from him quickly, feeling as if bristles rose at her nape. He knew she'd never been one of Leroux's women. But he still seemed to condemn her for the fact that she was there to begin with.

She had begun to feel more than anger or fascination toward him. More than the startling electricity that had seemed to surround them last night. He was giving her what she wanted. A home. A family. A different world. And he was a unique man. He was...

Handsome. Wonderfully strong, powerful. He was built beautifully, tight and lean, with rippling muscles that were whipcord-hard and vibrant. That night, even when he had merely left the room, she had found herself remembering the feel of his arms, the heat of his flesh next to hers, the encompassing breadth of his shoulders. To her amazement, she didn't dread his touch at all anymore. She had slept absurdly sweetly with his sheltering arms around her.

But she couldn't let him know. He would think she was a whore and be all the more convinced that she should have stayed with Jack Leroux.

He could be kind enough. He could also be as hard as rock. She had to be careful, so careful, of what she gave. The war had taken too much from her. She just couldn't be hurt anymore. She wouldn't allow anyone to do so. She would be a good wife—she would just keep a careful distance. She certainly wouldn't fall in love with him.

And still, that Christmas day, in the hotel suite, was far more than she might have hoped for. Shane ordered up a Christmas goose, and she and he and Daniel sat down to it. And if Shane was quiet, his eyes hard on her the entire meal, Daniel was charming. She laughed and chatted with him throughout, trying to ignore the golden gaze upon her.

Then it was time for the men to leave. Shane had arranged for Kaitlin's board at the hotel, and she was supplied with steamship passage along the Mississippi, railway tickets once she reached the North, and stage fare from there.

She didn't think that her new husband was going to kiss her good-bye at all. But he did. Down in the street. He suddenly swept her into his arms, and she was startled by the strength of the fever that encompassed her with his touch. Startled, and frightened. She didn't want to care too much; it was dangerous to do so.

He set her down, and met her eyes. There was something almost gentle in his for a moment. "I'm sorry that this is your Christmas."

Her eyes widened. It had, in fact, been a wonderful Christmas. He just didn't know what her past Christmases had been. "It was fine."

"No tree, no decorations, no reading of Mr. Dickens 'A Christmas Carol' with the family warm by the fire."

"I... I'd like such a day. Surely."

"Next Christmas. Next Christmas, I swear. For Francesca. For you."

Then he was gone, and Kaitlin had been left to wonder after a while if any of it had really happened.

Then the weather had become so severe, and soon after that she'd received his telegraph warning her not to attempt to travel until some of the snow cleared. Then she began to wonder if he really wanted her to come at all, if he wasn't regretting his rash marriage with all of his heart and mind.

At the beginning of May, though, she'd received another telegraph. She wasn't sure how he had managed to pack so much anger into so few words. *You'd best arrive soon.* Then Kaitlin imagined that he was thinking her one of Leroux's women of the very worst kind, the type who would take payment and give nothing in return.

It made her angry, and it brought chills along her spine. She had to go. They hadn't made so simple a business deal. She was his wife.

And so she arrived in the spring. The mountains rose majestically, beautifully in the distance, the grass was endlessly green, and the small town was bustling. She had barely emerged from the stage before she saw all this, and more, for there was Shane, waiting on the steps of the Three Mills Travelers' Inn, a young girl before him.

At first, Shane drew her entire attention. There had been so many endless days and nights when she had both dreaded and anticipated their meeting again.

He was taller than she had remembered. Leaner, his skin more bronzed.

But she had remembered his eyes just right. Gold eyes that were touched with the most extraordinary fire.

She tore her gaze from his and looked at the little girl. Wide, hesitant eyes met hers. Big, beautiful brown eyes. Wary ones. The little girl had a lovely face, her features fine and delicate. Francesca was frightened of meeting her, Kaitlin thought. People hurt people so frequently, and Francesca knew it.

Kaitlin shivered, remembering her new husband's fierce warning about his niece. He didn't really care what else she did, as long as she was good to Francesca.

He needn't have warned her about such a thing, she thought indignantly. She'd never hurt the little girl. Never.

They hadn't stepped toward her. The stationmaster had handed her down from the coach. A sense of panic seized her. He'd been so cold, and then so angry. Was there really any kind of a welcome here for her?

He had promised her Christmas this year, she thought. Christmas, for her and Francesca.

She stepped forward, "Well! She's come! She's made it!" a voice called out. And Daniel Newton, leading a tiny and pretty and very pregnant woman on his arm, came bursting out of the hotel doorway. He didn't seem to realize that no one had really greeted anyone else and he left his wife's side to give Kaitlin a warm embrace, swinging her around. "See, she's here, Shane, Francesca. Oh, Kaitlin, this is my wife, Mary. She's been dying to meet you—and she's thrilled to have another woman near! We're quite a ways out from town, by you."

"Naturally," Mary said, extending her hand, smiling warmly. "Your husband gave us our property. It adjoins yours."

Kaitlin shook Mary's hand. "I'm truly delighted," she said. Then she turned to Francesca. "And I am truly delighted to meet you, too, Francesca."

The little girl blushed pink. She was pleased. "Thank you," she said softly.

"Well, come on, come on!" Daniel said. "Let's go inside and have something to eat. It's been an awfully long trip for Kaitlin. And we've got well over an hour's ride back home tonight, too!"

Daniel led the way with Mary, slipping his arm through Francesca's to urge her along.

Kaitlin felt as if a cold wind touched her. She met Shane's gaze again. She tried to smile. "You haven't greeted me yet, Shane." Her stomach was pitching. She felt as if her words sounded hollow. "Aren't you—aren't you glad that I've come?"

"Oh, indeed, I'm very glad that you've come. And don't worry. I'll greet you at home, Kaitlin."

Sizzles touched her spine. He took her elbow, and they followed behind the others.

They'd come into Three Mills with a big wagon, knowing that Kaitlin would be bringing goods from New Orleans. And she had a number of trunks with her, filled mostly with household goods. She had tried to go very sparingly on buying personal items. Shane eyed all the packages and trunks as they stowed them, but he didn't say a word to her then.

The trip out to his house was not so bad, or at least it wouldn't have been if Kaitlin hadn't been so nervous about going home with Shane. To distract herself, she thought about her other companions. Mary was a sweet, wonderful woman, one who really seemed to belong with Daniel, they were both so friendly and lighthearted. And Francesca...

Francesca watched her. Much like her uncle did.

The home that Shane brought her to might have been in the wilderness, but it was beautiful. It was a large, sprawling, two-story house that had been whitewashed and trimmed in a deep forest green to match the surrounding foliage. Her eyes were on it from the minute the wagon came to a halt. Her eyes remained on it when he lifted her down from the wagon.

"Did I keep my side of a bargain?" he asked softly.

"Yes," she replied.

"Then you keep yours," he told her.

Again, her stomach catapulted. She escaped his hold and turned to the little girl. "Francesca, would you show me the house, please?"

Blushing again, Francesca stepped forward. Tentatively, she took Kaitlin's hand. And then she led her in.

Inside, the house was beautiful too. There was a huge parlor, and an indoor kitchen and a wonderful large dining room. Up the stairs there were four bedrooms. "Here is mine," Francesca told her proudly, leading her into the first. And she should have been proud. There was a beautiful white knit comforter on the bed, which was covered with a fairy-tale canopy. Her furniture was painted white, and all in all Kaitlin couldn't imagine a more perfect room for a little girl.

"It's lovely," she said, smiling.

Francesca's lower lip quivered. "It is, isn't it? It's the first bedroom that I've ever had all to myself."

Kaitlin came down on her knees before her. "This house is really the first that I've ever had," she told her.

Francesca hesitated, then put her arms around Kaitlin and hugged her tight. Kaitlin held her, and gently smoothed her hair.

At length Francesca pulled away. "Come on, let me show you your room!"

"My room?"

"Well, yours and Shane's!"

Yes, hers and Shane's. She followed Francesca down the hallway, and found her room. Most of her bags were already there. Shane and Daniel and Shane's foreman, Chancey, had already been bringing things up.

Shane's room, she thought. It was a masculine room. The furniture was all deep mahogany, untouched by doilies or dust ruffles of any kind. The two armoires in it were large and heavy. The room wasn't that big. There were two more rooms down the hall... She met his eyes.

He must have been reading her mind. He smiled, and slowly shook his head.

She tore her gaze from his, her thoughts scattered. Daniel and Mary were still there. Chancey was a fine man with a warm handshake. She had already made friends with Francesca. There was a festive mood about the place. She had her own home. Her very own home. She was going to ignore Shane, and enjoy the celebration.

She wasn't quite able to ignore Shane then, for he invited her out to the barn. They weren't alone, for the others followed. He introduced her first to Jimmy and Jane, the harness horses, then Diablo, his own big black stallion, and then he brought her to a stall where she saw the prettiest horse she thought that she had ever seen, a mare with a deep dish nose and high flashing tail. "Genevieve," he told her. "I picked her up for you last week."

"She's—mine?" Kaitlin asked. She could barely imagine owning such a creature. Horses had become so precious in Georgia during the end of the war. She hadn't thought she'd even see anything like Genevieve again. "Mine?" The present seemed incredible. The mare nuzzled her, pushing against her chest. Kaitlin touched her warm, velvety nose and a rush of affection swept through her. "She—she's wonderful. Thank you."

Shane shrugged. "You need a good horse out here." He turned his back on her. She wondered what she had done wrong. Then she decided that she would enjoy the night, and enjoy her new life, no matter what. She was going to ignore Shane.

She did. Chancey had done his best with a meal of venison and summer vegetables, and Daniel—being Daniel—had supplied the champagne. They had a wonderful meal. And when it was done, they sat in the parlor, sipping coffee laced with just a touch of brandy.

Kaitlin sat on the love seat, and Francesca fell asleep with her head in her lap.

But then it was time for Daniel and Mary to leave, to go onward to their own home. And Shane lifted Francesca into his arms to take her up to bed. And finally there was nothing left for Kaitlin to do but go up to her own room and await her husband.

She'd bought a new flannel gown that buttoned all the way up to her throat and it was in that gown that she awaited him, in the darkness, in their bed. She thought about pretending to be asleep, but then she decided not to bother. And in a matter of minutes he was there with her. He opened and closed the door and leaned against it in the darkness.

"Time for that 'wretched' business again, eh, Mrs. MacAuliffe?"

"If you're going to make fun of me—"

"I'm not going to make fun of you. That is not my intention at all."

It wasn't. In seconds he was across the room. And the flannel gown was on the floor.

And suddenly, all the dread and anticipation of all the long months were with her. His kisses were hot and fevered. They did incredible and wonderful things to her. In the darkness, it seemed that the Christmas magic was there once again, the magic that had touched them when they'd wed. She could have returned his every touch, his every caress. She could have returned his passion. She fought so hard to hold back. She was so very afraid to give to him completely.

Yet later, it seemed that he was the one to withdraw. He didn't hold her but lay on his own side of the bed. She was suddenly certain that he could see in the darkness with those gold eyes of his.

But he said nothing to her. "Shane?" she asked softly.

He grunted. "Go to sleep. Sometimes it can be a hard life out here."

Perhaps it was a hard life. The next morning at five she was awakened with a firm hand upon her rump. Before she knew it, she was out of bed; and barely dressed and half-asleep, she was proving that she could cook by complying with his orders for a hearty breakfast. He was testing her, she thought irritably. She'd failed him somehow, and this was his way of having her make up for it. Well, she wasn't going to fail him. She could cook, and she did.

And she could keep house, and she did so. By the end of her first two weeks in Three Mills, she had changed everything about the place. Though the house was big and adequately furnished, it had lacked the little touches that only a woman could provide. Kaitlin gave the place those little touches. Now there were sunny yellow curtains at the kitchen window over the sink and water pump. There were beautiful draperies with valances in the parlor. Needlepoint pillows rested cozily upon the sofas in the living room.

And Francesca had become almost talkative.

The hour-long ride into town kept her from any regular schooling, but she was a very bright little girl. And Kaitlin had discovered that if she could dare to love anyone in this life anymore, it would be Francesca. She taught her far more than reading and writing and mathematics. When they finished with two hours of such basics every morning, Kaitlin went on with her, teaching her everything she could remember about etiquette, just the way that her mother had taught her. They would have tea, and laugh together as Kaitlin dramatically overdid the proper way to hold a cup. It was fun.

And busy. There was so much to do. It was a large house to keep clean. There were soap and candles to be made, linens to be washed, chickens to be fed, floors to be swept. And Kaitlin was determined to excel at it all.

For Shane noticed. Every move that she made, he noticed. He seldom commented, though, unless she asked him. "Do you like the parlor?" Or "Does the kitchen suit you?"

His grunts she assumed were by way of approval.

Except when he saw her with Francesca. Then he watched her very thoughtfully.

And then there were the nights...

The first two weeks were exactly the same. He came up to bed at ten, looked at her without expression, and took her into his arms.

And as the nights passed, she discovered herself more and more fascinated with her husband. Excitement stirred her blood as he came near her, wonder filled her at his touch. But she held back, so carefully, determined that she would not dare put too much trust into him, nor would she give him any opportunity to deride her.

Usually he stared at the ceiling when they were done, then eventually fell asleep.

But one night the end of May, he did not. He abruptly turned to her.

"In what way have I failed you?" he demanded. "You've come halfway across the country to a new life. You've my name, and my house. Why won't you uphold your part of the bargain?"

Kaitlin gasped, pulling away. How had she failed him? Had he found some fault with her? Did she simply do everything wrong?

"I've kept my part of the bargain!"

"No, no, you haven't!" he told her. His hands were on her shoulders. Though shadows crept between them, she could see him then. See the passion and the strength in his face. "Are you still in love with Daniel?"

"I was never in love with Daniel!"

"He was the man you wanted to marry."

"He didn't accuse me of awful things!"

"Well, I did find you in a whorehouse and gambling establishment."

"I told you—"

"Yes, you told me," he said wearily.

"I was a lady! Always!" she cried.

"Oh, yes, always. With your pinkie up as you sip your tea. It's wonderful. Just wonderful."

"If there's something wrong with me—"

"No, no, Kaitlin, there's nothing wrong with you. Even Chancey says he's never seen a more perfect or beautiful woman. You're a princess, Kaitlin. A damned princess. Ice princess!" he added softly.

She felt as if she had been slapped, and she turned away from him, fighting tears. "I don't know what you mean," she told him indignantly.

His fingers feathered down her back. "Don't you? Never mind. Go to sleep, Kaitlin."

She wasn't sure exactly how things changed after that. Perhaps she'd had a chance at happiness, and perhaps she had thrown it away.

Maybe it was just summer, and the Christmas magic was all gone.

Perhaps it was the situation with the Indians.

Whichever. But on the first of August, Shane was leaving. There had been confrontations with the Blackfoot Indians and since Shane had once signed his own individual treaty with Black Eagle, he promised the sheriff and the people of Three Mills that he would go speak with the chief once again.

Her heart seemed to be in her throat the day that he rode away. She was terrified that she would never see him again. She wanted to tell him that she...

That she what?

That she wanted him to come home, that she needed him. He had become her life. She cared for him.

That morning she discovered that she loved his eyes. Those gold eyes that could stare at her so shrewdly, always searching. She loved the planes of his face, the wry curl of his lips. She loved his shoulders, and the warm feel of his bronze flesh. She loved sleeping with him.

But there wasn't time. No time to say all of these things. War drums were sounding, and Francesca was at her side. And bright tears were in Francesca's eyes. Shane was staring at her, daring her to be anything other than perfect.

His perfect ice princess.

So she waved to him when he left, when he rode away, and she held tight to Francesca.

The days seemed longer. She didn't teach Francesca so long in the morning. The two of them started taking morning rides over to see Daniel and Mary. Kaitlin loved riding Genevieve. And she was

186

grateful for the company, and glad to be there for Mary, who was very nearly due. The days she could manage.

The nights she slept alone. And waited.

"I wouldn't worry about Shane," Daniel told her one day. "He's seen Black Eagle often enough in the past."

"I'm really not worried," Kaitlin lied.

She had barely said those words before Mary called out suddenly to them. The baby was coming.

Daniel, completely disconcerted, had to be reminded that he needed to ride into town for the doctor. Kaitlin, scared silly herself but determined that Mary not realize it, tried to remember all the proper things to do. They needed all kinds of clean linen and scissors for the cord, and the worst of it was that she needed to sit with Mary.

For the first two hours, Mary seemed to be fine. Then she cried and screamed out, and no matter what Kaitlin tried to say to her or do for her, nothing seemed to help. Mary was soaked with perspiration. She fell asleep several times, only to wake screaming once again.

Kaitlin walked to the window, watching for Daniel to return with the doctor. They didn't come. It began to dawn on her that things were going badly, very badly, and that there was no one there but herself.

She gritted her teeth, and waited some more. The ride into town was at least an hour. And an hour back out. The doctor would still come.

But two more hours passed. Then three. And Kaitlin realized in panic that the baby was going to come.

"I'm going to die," Mary said softly, looking up at the ceiling.

"You're not going to die! I simply won't let you. I'm not going to live out here without you," Kaitlin told her fiercely.

And I'm not going to live out here and have a baby, ever! she decided. It was too frightening, too dreadful, after all she'd been through already.

"Oh, Kaitlin, the baby is coming!"

The baby was coming. Kaitlin assured herself that she was capable, and she kept thinking of all the things that she must do. She had to deliver the baby.

And she did. The tiny head appeared in her hands first, and she urged Mary to push again. Then came one shoulder, and then the next.

And the baby seemed to pop right into her hands, and to her great relief, let out an ear-piercing cry, filling its lungs.

"Oh, Kaitlin! What is it?"

"What?" Kaitlin stared at the miracle in her hands, for even if it was a bloody mess, Mary's infant was a miracle.

"A boy!" Kaitlin said. "A boy!"

It was just minutes later that Daniel and the doctor did arrive. The doctor came in to see to Mary, and Kaitlin walked out into the hallway with Daniel.

"What happened? What took so long?" Kaitlin demanded. Perhaps she shouldn't be so rough on Daniel, she scolded herself. He looked as if he had just been through hell himself.

"When I went by the Thompson place, they told me that there was some worry about an Indian attack on white riders down the main road. I thought that I had best ride around the long way."

"Oh," Kaitlin said simply. She walked down the hall, her knees trembling. She did love Daniel—she loved him like she loved Mary. They were both good people.

But she was certain that Shane would never have left her in such a position. He would have ridden through every pack of Indians in the West to see that his child was safely delivered.

Except that she was never going to have a child. She was determined about it. Not after today.

Exhausted, she walked down the stairs and sank into one of their parlor chairs. She leaned her head back, just meaning to close her eyes, but she fell asleep. Sound asleep.

She was startled when a male voice awoke her. "Kaitlin. Kaitlin."

She opened her eyes, vastly disoriented. Then she realized that Shane was standing above her. He was back.

"Shane!" For a moment a wide smile lit up her face and she nearly leapt to her feet to greet him. He was back.

He seemed to be looking at her with a rather tolerant smile. "Yes. And I hear I've married rather a heroine. You delivered Mary's baby."

"I wasn't a heroine. I didn't mean to deliver the baby."

He kissed her forehead. "Maybe not. But he's beautiful. Big and beautiful. And wonderful. With any luck, maybe we'll soon have a son."

The smile faded from her lips. No. No, she didn't want to have a baby.

But he didn't see her expression at the moment. He was talking to Daniel, telling him about his meeting with Black Eagle, the chief of the Blackfoot tribe.

"I think that he'll call off his warriors. As long as we keep to our side of the bargain."

"I don't think that he can be trusted," Daniel was saying. "He's a heathen! Why, no man was more warlike before. Remember the Petersons? How they were killed?"

"Black Eagle's wife had been killed by that stupid trapper, Johnson, right before!" Shane said.

"You're defending him."

"I'm not defending him. I know him. He'll kill if he thinks it necessary. He promised that he'd even kill me if I disturbed him on his own ground again. But there is something about him..."

"What's that?" Daniel asked.

"He's always willing to listen."

Kaitlin was drifting off to sleep again, when she suddenly felt strong arms around her. Blinking, she met Shane's golden eyes.

"I'm taking my wife home, Daniel. Congratulations on your boy."

Kaitlin didn't ride home on her own horse. Shane held her on the saddle before him, with Genevieve trotting behind them on a lead.

* * *

By the time they reached their own home, she'd fallen asleep in his arms.

Shane looked at his wife a long while, then swallowed down his expectations for the night. He carried her up the stairs, and laid her down on their bed.

She was so beautiful. And strong, and courageous.

Maybe he'd been too hard on her. Maybe he owed her more. His bitterness over his first marriage had tainted his second. Yet when she had first seen him tonight, there had been something wonderful in her eyes. As if she had waited for him. As if she wanted him.

As if she loved him.

He smiled. Maybe he hadn't realized it, but perhaps she had been the best Christmas present he had ever received.

He didn't disturb her, but let her sleep. Her face was like porcelain, her skin ivory, her cheeks blushed a perfect rose.

He leaned down to kiss her forehead, not intending to wake her. She was very tired, and he was weary himself. And he was suddenly determined that he was going to woo her. Make her fall in love with him.

And maybe there he would find the warmth and the passion he sensed beneath the barriers she cast against him.

But as his lips touched her flesh, she opened her eyes. And she sat up quickly, as if she were suddenly frightened of him.

"What's the matter?" he asked.

"I'm—I'm tired. I'm so exhausted. Please..."

"Please what?" he demanded, aggravated.

She flushed and her lashes fell. "Please don't—er, force anything on me."

He gritted his teeth. "I didn't know that I did force things on you."

She rose from the bed. "I can go in the guest room and not bother you—"

"Get in here," he told her harshly. "I *will* force *this* upon you—you can sleep in your own bed. I never intended to touch you, Kaitlin. Not tonight. I *know* you're exhausted, what with the baby—"

"That's just it," she whispered. "I..."

"What?"

"I don't want a baby."

"What?" he said again, blankly.

"I don't want a baby. We—we have Francesca. I don't want to have a child out here in the wilderness where you can never reach a doctor—"

"Kaitlin, I would have reached a doctor."

"And children are so delicate. Look at what happened to Francesca. Look how she was passed around. Life can be so very cruel to children."

"Was it so cruel to you? My lady with her pinkie flying so elegantly in the air?"

"I grew up in a cabin with a drunkard for a father. Is that what you want to hear, Shane? The one good thing in my life was my brother, but the war took care of him. I was never Leroux's woman, but I was never a great belle, either. Are you happy? Whatever, it doesn't matter. I don't want a baby!"

A baby? Or his baby? Shane narrowed his eyes. "Well, we're in a sad state of affairs here, aren't we? I do want a baby."

She went very pale. He tried to remember his resolve to woo her. So what if unimaginable fires seemed to burn inside him when he was lying beside her? He wasn't going to force anything. Not for a while, anyway. She was tired. Upset. Maybe she just didn't see him as the charming, docile man she saw Daniel to be.

"Get in bed!" he roared. "I won't touch you. Not tonight."

Her green eyes luminous, she complied.

And lay beside him, her back to him.

His Christmas present...

Yes, but there was next Christmas. And it was coming soon, very soon.

For some reason, he felt a shiver race down the length of his spine.

Chapter 4

Thanksgiving came, and it was a wonderful day for Kaitlin. The house was warm and comfortable, there was a light snowfall, and Shane, ever-watchful in the background, seemed willing to let her have her way with everything.

Once filled, her table was nearly ostentatious. She'd cooked a huge turkey, a generous-sized ham, and a tender, spit-roasted side of beef. Their guests were Daniel and his wife and the baby, Kevin Richard Newton, and the Reverend Samuels and his wife, Jemimah—a wonderfully short and round woman with the most delightful smile Kaitlin had ever seen—who came out from town. All the day before, Kaitlin and Francesca baked and prepared, and the next morning, they started with all their meat dishes and fresh vegetables.

In the soft glow of the candles, the dining room was beautiful. Kaitlin was pleased to overhear the reverend telling Shane that he had indeed brought a beautiful and talented wife into the wilderness, and later she was doubly glad to hear Daniel telling Shane that he was one lucky fellow, Kaitlin was just amazing.

The pity was that she was entirely certain that Shane didn't find her amazing in the least, and lately it seemed more and more that he had grown very weary of her.

He hadn't been coming home until very late at night. Often past midnight. And she'd heard that there was a certain place in town, as establishment called Nelly Grier's, where ranchers were known to congregate.

Kaitlin wasn't quite sure why, because she *did* realize that she'd asked him to leave her alone and that that was exactly what he was doing, but she was furious with him.

Maybe it was because she didn't really want to be left alone anymore.

Or else she didn't want it to be so easy for him to leave her alone. She had wanted to make up, she just didn't really know how to do so. And once Mary had let it slip about Nelly Grier's place... well, then she'd been just too stubborn and angry to even think about trying to make things right with Shane.

Maybe he just didn't care at all anymore. That thought made her miserable, but it didn't really change anything. Night after night, they lay there, their backs to one another.

But then Thanksgiving came, and Kaitlin was determined to prove her worth, and it seemed that she was able to do so. The meal was delicious. Conversation flowed easily around the table—until the reverend mentioned Black Eagle and the Blackfeet who were really so very near Shane's property.

"You know the Indians attacked three riders just last week, Shane," Reverend Samuels said, pausing with a portion of turkey halfway to his plate.

Kaitlin glanced at Shane. He hadn't mentioned Black Eagle lately. In fact, he'd really said very little to her about his visit with the Indian. But then, they'd scarcely been talking since that night.

Shane shrugged. "So I heard. But I also heard that a fool trapper named Nesmith raided one of Black Eagle's camps and kidnapped one of his sons. If that's true, we might well have a major war on our hands very soon."

"Oh, dear God!" Mary Newton cried, hugging her baby close to her. "Are we in danger?"

Shane shook his head. "Not yet, at any rate. Except maybe..."

"Maybe what?" Kaitlin demanded.

"Maybe in the north woods, and the north fields. Black Eagle feels the roadway just beyond it was built on his land. He can be dangerous. Unless that little boy is found and returned to him quickly." He looked at Mary and smiled gently. "Don't be afraid. There hasn't been any real Indian trouble here in a long, long time."

Kaitlin's festive party had grown rather somber. She stood up. "Pumpkin and apple pies, coming right up. And we'll have coffee and brandy here at the table. Gentlemen, you are welcome to your cigars right here. We are not going to part ways on a holiday with the men going one way and the women another!"

She was very busy for some time then, collecting the dishes, putting out the pie plates and the coffee. But a little while later she had some time, and she insisted on taking little Kevin Richard Newton from his mother. She and Shane were going to be godparents and she was delighted. The little boy was an adorable little bundle of love, and all the fear and uncertainty she had felt when he was born was fading away.

While she held him, she was startled to find Shane staring down at her. She looked up, feeling guilty. "He's beautiful, isn't he?" she said.

"There's only one thing wrong with him."

"What's that?"

"He isn't ours."

Kaitlin's cheeks burned. "Well, Shane MacAuliffe, heaven knows you could have half a dozen children, from what I understand," she whispered, walking away from their guests, to the other side of the room.

"Really? And how do you understand this?" he asked, following her.

"Well, you've disappeared far more than half a dozen nights."

"I didn't realize that I was missed. And I didn't seem to have any reason to hurry home."

"As long as you seem so determined to visit Nelly's, you don't have any reason to hurry home. And as long as I have a choice—"

"You don't have a choice, my dear, lovely—*amazing* little ice princess! Just bear that in mind, and stay on my good side. And bear in mind this fact, too. This state of affairs is not going on forever!"

It didn't go on forever. It was stopped that very night, for some fever had swept into Kaitlin's system, and she was determined to cause him some heartache.

Perhaps it was because of her own.

But when all the guests were gone, when it was time for bed, she found that she was not really ready to lie down. Nor did she dress in anything prim or made of flannel, but chose an ethereal white gown of soft silk. And she stood before the window, watching the moon, brushing out her hair, certain that he would prove his point that the choice was not really hers at all.

He ignored her until her hair had been brushed at least two hundred times. Then he had told her irritably that he had a great deal of work the next day, even if she didn't.

Rejected, furious, she crawled into bed.

And then he let her simmer until she was just at the boiling point before he suddenly and forcefully pulled her into his arms.

She opened her mouth to yell at him, but he stopped her words with a kiss. Then, within minutes, the urge to stop him had disappeared.

Each time he touched her, the magic came more sweepingly upon her. And when it did seem to skyrocket through her at last, she buried her face in a pillow, determined that she would not cry out at the intense pleasure he'd given her.

She was not one of Jack Leroux's women, nor one of Nelly Grier's tarts.

No, she certainly was not, for in the morning, he apologized offhandedly for his tough treatment of her.

And in the evening, he came home very late.

Kaitlin wanted to rip him to shreds. She wondered why it hurt her so very badly, like knives tearing into her soul. Then she knew. It had happened slowly. It had happened for many good reasons.

She had fallen in love with her husband.

But love was a brutal emotion, one she didn't dare trust in. Once again, she decided that her best defense was to ignore him. It was incredibly difficult when he slept beside her, but she told herself that he wasn't getting anything from her again, anything at all.

Still, it was almost December. And she had a home this year, a beautiful home. He had given it to her. She could decorate as she chose, she could do anything she wanted.

And there was Francesca. Francesca who had learned so very little about the mysteries of Christ and Christmas and Santa Claus and caroling.

"It there a Santa?" Francesca asked her excitedly just a few days after Thanksgiving.

"Well, he is really Saint Nicholas, you see," Kaitlin said, winking. She and Francesca had done the laundry, and were now making the beds. "He was a bishop hundreds and hundreds of years ago and he was kind and generous and the patron saint of children and he loved to give out gifts. To the Dutch people who came to live in New York, he was 'Sinter Klaas.' So for us now, he is Santa Claus! And he comes every Christmas to bring gifts. A minister named Mr. Moore described him in a poem back in 1823—before I was even born!—and he is wonderful, Francesca, truly wonderful! He dresses in a red suit with white trim, and he is this huge roly-poly bear of a man, so kind, so very wonderful."

She heard a noise. It was early, but Shane was home. He was standing in the doorway, watching her.

Kaitlin finished the bed, and tried to walk on past him. He caught her arm. She gazed at him, waiting.

"Thank you."

"For what?"

"For giving her Christmas."

He touched her cheek. She was startled by the tenderness in his fingers. "You're just like her, you know. A child deprived of Christmas." And his voice was soft, so soft. "This year, we will have Christmas. We'll drink mulled wine before the fire. I'll chop down a fir tree and we'll decorate it with angels and stars. And we'll all put gifts beneath the tree. You will have Christmas, Kaitlin."

This kindness from him almost brought tears to her eyes. She pulled away. "I have no money of my own. I shall have no gift for you."

He laughed huskily. "Oh, but, my love, think of it, you do, you do."

And then the laughter was gone, and she was in his arms, held there so hard. "A son, Kaitlin, give me my son."

She pulled away from him. "You'll have to speak to God on that, sir, since I seem to have no choice in the matter."

"But you do. You run. You fight me."

"I don't seem to run fast enough," she informed him, her flashing eyes reminding him of the night so long ago when she had teased and taunted...

And he had won in the end.

He started to laugh, but then Francesca was suddenly there, looking worriedly at them both.

"What is it, Shane? Is something wrong?"

"Wrong?" Shane lifted her into his arms. "When I live with two of the most beautiful women in the Western world? Never! We were just discussing Christmas, Kaitlin and I. And Santa Claus is coming this year."

"He never came before," Francesca said.

"Well, he is coming this year. Right down the chimney."

"He'll singe his rump!" Kaitlin advised.

"Never. Santa Claus is invulnerable to fire."

Francesca laughed. "Will he come for us both, for Kaitlin and me?"

"Oh, yes. Santa will come for you. And for Kaitlin." He smiled at Kaitlin, his golden eyes afire. "Will he come for me, do you think?"

"I hardly know," Kaitlin said sweetly. "I hear it on good authority that you have not been a very good boy this year." And with that she swept by him.

At dinner that night Chancey came in with news and they heard that one of the ranches had been burned to the ground. The rancher and his wife had been spared, but Black Eagle's warriors had forced them to watch the destruction, and Black Eagle himself had said that they must warn the whites that there might be worse to come.

Shane came into the kitchen as Kaitlin was washing dishes. "It could prove to be dangerous here. I'm thinking of sending you and Francesca down south until this is over."

She dropped her dish and spun around. "No! I'm not going anywhere. We're going to have a family Christmas. We've—we've promised Francesca."

"Kaitlin, listen—"

"Please, Shane!"

He sighed, watching her. She wondered what lay behind the glitter of his eyes. Then he spoke softly. "Well, you've courage, my love. And a will of steel." He stared at her hard. "Yes, I'll grant you that."

Then he was gone.

It was the next day when Genevieve disappeared.

Kaitlin decided to ride into town. She didn't need the buggy because she wasn't going to make any major purchases, but she did want ribbon, red ribbon and green ribbon. She and Francesca were going to begin to decorate. Thanksgiving was over, they were into December. Perhaps it was a bit early, but Francesca was one child who had really had just too little Christmas in her life.

Maybe Shane was right. Perhaps Kaitlin was also a child who had really had too little Christmas in her life.

She was determined to make up for it.

But when she had brought Genevieve out of the stall to brush and saddle her, she had been distracted when Daniel had ridden by. He always had such a nice smile for her. She had stopped to talk. And when she had turned back, Chancey was just warning her that the wayward mare had broken loose and gone running off.

Right for the north field.

Kaitlin didn't really remember any of Shane's warnings. She was just desperate to find her affectionate little mare. Old Henry the plow horse was still in the bam and so she saddled him quickly and rode out. Chancey was shouting behind her, but she ignored him.

She rode straight for the north field. And she searched and searched, calling to her, but she didn't see a sign of the little mare.

Then she did see Shane, riding toward her on Diablo. He was furious. "What the hell are you doing out here, you fool!"

"I'm just—"

"You're just getting back to the house. Now!"

"I'm not your prisoner, Shane—"

"No, you're a damned idiot! Get back there, or *I'll* get you back there!"

She rode ahead of him, urging old Henry into as quick a pace as he could manage, and she and Shane fought all the way back. When they reached the barn she leapt down from old Henry and started for the house. She meant to reach it before he could yell anymore.

But his hand was on her arm.

"Dammit, Kaitlin, listen to me—"

"I didn't do anything—"

"Tell it to the Blackfeet when they find you the next time!"

She wrenched away from him. He didn't stop her. But as she started for the house, he was right behind her. And when she realized that he was following her into the kitchen, she headed for the stairway.

He followed her there, too. And when she would have slammed the bedroom door, he pushed it open and then slammed it shut behind him.

"I'm not worried about the Indians!" Kaitlin said sharply. "Chancey told me that they're a distance away."

"They're right on our border!"

"Living their lives. While we live ours—"

"Don't fool yourself, Kaitlin! The Blackfeet were the most warlike tribe in the area!"

"Yes, and they killed a lot of whites, and the whites killed them. But that's because the whites were infringing on their fur trade. And now we *buy* the furs from them and—"

"And that's supposed to make everything all better?"

"But the Indians don't come in this close—"

"The hell they don't! Ever since that fool trapper disappeared with Black Eagle's boy, the Blackfeet have been coming in closer and closer. All kinds of rumors are going around of Indian war—real, horrible, disastrous war. Damn you, Kaitlin, I know Black Eagle! I know him well. You stay the hell out of the north field and the north woods!"

"But Genevieve—"

"Genevieve is an Indian pony now. There aren't any finer horse thieves in the world than the Blackfeet. If you ever really cared for a living thing around you, she might not have disappeared!"

Kaitlin gasped, stunned. Tears teased her lashes. She'd tried so very hard...

"You're the only living thing around me that I don't particularly care much about, Shane MacAuliffe!"

Her words seemed to have been as sharp as a knife, for his eyes flashed and his jaw tightened. "I pulled you out of a New Orleans sewer. Maybe that's where you belong!"

She struck him. And suddenly she was being dragged across the room, and tossed on their bed.

"I've seen the fire in you," he told her. "I've seen you smile, and laugh. By God, it's there. It was there for Daniel Newton."

"Daniel's a gentleman—"

"And a half-assed fool. And he isn't for you. But damn you, Kaitlin, the fire is there. Within you."

"Maybe you haven't the spark to light any fire within me!" she snapped.

Shane's eyes narrowed. Then he spoke softly. Too softly. "Oh, but I do. Oh, but I do!"

She leapt up, suddenly afraid. She had never really been afraid of him before, but she had never, never seen him so angry.

He blocked the door with his body. She couldn't possibly reach it and throw it open.

"Well, let's see, we have agreed. You've courage, my love. And a will of steel. But that won't help you now. Not one bit. Whether I wooed you or won you, Kaitlin, I made you my wife. And you agreed to the terms. And I'll be damned if I'll let you try to cast me out one minute longer. You want a match, Mrs. McAuliffe? I'll light a boxful of them, Mrs. MacAuliffe, and so help me, we will find the fire within you!"

"Don't you dare talk to me so, Shane—" she had begun, lifting her chin and trying to walk on by. But she couldn't do so. His hand caught her arm tightly.

"You're right. Let's not talk."

She was stunned by the sudden ferocity of his kiss, swept away by the passion within it. Indeed, he had the match to light the fire within her, for within seconds, she felt the soaring heat throughout her body. She felt his touch on her flesh, and she seemed to feel it within her blood, too. And she wanted his kiss, wanted his touch, more than she had ever imagined wanting it before.

She heard the rent of fabric, and she thought with a certain amazement that he had actually torn her clothing. And it didn't matter. Not in the least.

But his eyes touched hers, in challenge, in defiance. She cried out, slamming her fists against his chest, but he didn't seem to care. They were falling together, and the softness of the bed was there to catch them. He whispered in her ear, soft. His kiss feathered against her throat.

And the heat began to rise.

His kiss was silk against her naked flesh. His whisper brushed her skin with tiny laps of flame. His hands caressed the length of her, so intimately. She was dimly aware that her fingers moved against his chest, stroked, caressed. She breathed softly against his lips, and they were locked within a frantic kiss once again.

Something was different. Her anger had dissipated, but an intensity remained. She was profoundly aware of his words, his whispers. The things that he said. Intimate things. Each touch became exquisitely keen. He was demanding so much, and yet gave to her so tenderly. Clothing seemed to melt away, and they were entwined as one, and everything that had been sweet before was ever more so now. Tonight, the stars seemed to explode in their room. She reached for the sky, and for a moment, her fingertips brushed it. And the stars burst out upon her with the most extravagant beauty she had ever imagined.

A cry tore at her throat. Just in time she swallowed it down, despairing that she might give so much to a man so determined to spend his nights away from her. She drifted down, down from the startling ecstasy, cloaked for long sweet moments in magic and mist.

Then she swallowed hard, careful not to speak.

Time passed slowly. She felt Shane's tension. Then he rose. And dressed.

"I'm sorry, Kaitlin. No, damn you, I'm not sorry. You're my wife. And I want you to be more than a cook. I'll not be stopping at Nelly Grier's when I've a black-haired beauty at home, even if she has emerald eyes flashing nothing but hatred my way. Black-haired, and black-hearted."

"No!" she cried. "No! It's not me, Shane MacAuliffe. You prove time and time again that you prefer the company at Nelly's to that at home—"

"Damn! I prefer a spark of warmth!"

Stark pain streaked through her. This afternoon, she had given to him...

She picked up her pillow and threw it at him with a vengeance. "I hate you, Shane! I hate you!"

The glittering passion in his golden eyes was deeper than she had ever seen it. She nearly cringed, certain that he meant to harm her.

But he did not. He turned, and left her. The door closed with a loud slam.

"No, no, that was a lie!" Kaitlin whispered. Too late. "I love you, Shane."

She jumped out of bed, splashed water on her face, and dressed quickly. It had already grown dark outside, but she didn't care. She raced out to the stables.

Chancey was there, working. He must have seen Shane come in and leave.

"Chancey, where's Shane?" she demanded.

"Why, I think he rode off to the north field. Said there was supposed to be some good hunting up that way." She barely heard him as he kept talking. "Course, what that fool man is hunting out in the dark, I don't know."

Kaitlin didn't answer him. She was busy saddling old Henry.

"Kaitlin, what do you think you're doing?" Chancey asked worriedly.

"I have to talk to him."

"Talk to him later."

"No, no, I have to talk to him now. It can't wait!"

Chancey kept calling after her. Kaitlin ignored him as she rode off. She pushed old Henry hard, racing a good twenty minutes into the night. There was a moon out to guide her.

Old Henry was quickly lathered, and despite the tempest in her heart, Kaitlin reined him in after a while. She would reach the north field soon enough. Perhaps she'd need to be careful. Shane might well shoot at her if he were there.

But he wasn't in the north field. Someone else was. She saw the horses before she recognized her danger.

Then she realized that the numerous horses moving in a semicircle were mounted by strange men. Indians.

Her heart began to pound. She stared at them, watching with an awful fascination. They were dressed warmly against the winter in their buckskins. She could dimly see that their faces were painted. She had seen sketches of Blackfoot war parties...

And she had just come upon one. A scream rose in her throat. She tried to wrench old Henry around. He snorted, fighting her lead. He hadn't been treated so rudely in years, Kaitlin was certain.

And he wasn't going to take it now. "Henry, damn you!" she cried, slamming her heels against his flanks. And he did begin to run.

At a slow lope. "Please, please!" she cried. She felt the cold wind against her face, but not strongly enough.

She looked to her side. The Indians were running her down. There was one to her left, and one to her right. Two of them had already raced their ponies ahead of her.

She was going to die. She was trapped. Within seconds, steel would pierce through her flesh.

But she didn't die. The Indian to her left brought his pony slamming against old Henry. He reached out, able to ride with only the tautness of his thighs keeping him upon his mount. He swept her up from her horse, and onto his own.

And began to race away.

* * *

Shane hadn't been anywhere near the north field. He'd ridden Diablo out to stare at the moon, his heart and soul still in a tempest.

I hate you, Shane...

She had said those words, said them clearly. But hadn't he given her every reason to do so?

Yet he hadn't believed it. She tried to hide things from him, but he knew her... better than she knew herself. And he believed with all his heart that he could please her. He knew exactly where he had taken her, and where they had been together when they made love.

She was wrong about Nelly Grier's. Hell, he couldn't even go there anymore.

Not since she had entered his life. Fulfilling every promise. His home was beautiful. Francesca was the happiest that Shane had ever seen her. They had everything...

If only they had one another.

He looked up at the sky and closed his eyes, a slow smile curving his lips. Maybe he should tell her. Just come out and tell her. Maybe it had happened slowly. Maybe it had happened at the very beginning. It didn't matter when. He didn't mean to ever hurt her, he didn't mean to ever force her into anything. He didn't even really care if they ever had a child, not if she didn't want one.

He just loved her, that was all. And he needed her.

Maybe if he just spoke to her, they could call a Christmas truce once again.

He turned Diablo and rode back toward home. At the stables he dismounted, but Chancey came hurrying out from the barn.

"Shane, Kaitlin's still out."

"Out? Where?"

"She come tearing out here right after you left. She said that she had to speak to you right away. She went on out to the north field. And she hasn't come back yet."

He felt as if his heart had jumped up into his throat. He leapt up on Diablo once again and spurred the horse into a gait like the speed of the north wind.

And yet he came to the field too late. There was no one there. He heard the sound of the wind in the trees, and nothing else.

Kaitlin was gone. He dismounted and walked the field. He knelt down.

There was one black eagle feather on the ground.

He cried out his agony, thundered it to the night. It didn't matter. There was no one to hear.

At length he gritted his teeth and rose, his hands clenched at his sides. He couldn't battle Black Eagle alone. Well, he could stage a one-man war against the Indian, but he wouldn't win. They'd kill him, and then they just might kill Kaitlin, too.

Jesu, he had to get Kaitlin back. He had to. She'd come like a Christmas gift, in truce, and she'd turned his life around, and now, he knew, he would have no life without her.

Shane exhaled slowly, then mounted Diablo once again.

There was a chance. There was a chance...

Black Eagle didn't celebrate Christmas, but maybe, just maybe, Shane could call a Christmas truce with the Indian, too.

He rode hard back for his house, praying that God would grant both him and Kaitlin the time that he needed.

Please, God, for Christmas...

* * *

Three... four... five...

Twenty-one... twenty-two... twenty-three...

Kaitlin stared at the last number etched into the skin of the teepee.

It was Christmas Eve.

"Dear God, please, for Christmas. Let him live. I'll never ask for anything again, I promise. Just let me see him again, let me tell him that I do have a gift for him this Christmas. Let me tell him that he's going to have his son. Oh, please, let us leave here together!"

Kaitlin whispered the words out loud. She continued to pray fervently.

Outside the teepee, the night wind howled.

Chapter 5

Kaitlin was startled by the sound of the buckskin flap rustling as Black Eagle entered the teepee. In the flickering shadows created by the small fire in the center, he appeared large and foreboding, menacing.

Her heart seemed to stop. He had killed Shane.

"Dear Lord!" she breathed. The world seemed to be spinning around her. A blackness reached out. She would have welcomed it. Anything other than accepting the fact that Shane might be dead. Her throat was dry, her eyes were filling with tears, blinding her.

"Come, Kaitlin," Black Eagle said.

No, she would never follow him anywhere. He could kill her right there, right where she waited.

"Kaitlin!" This time, a different voice. She brushed at her eyes, and stared toward the entrance. Shane was there. She leapt to her feet and went bounding the few steps toward him.

But Black Eagle stood in her way, dragging her back to his side. "I've not yet received my Christmas gift," Black Eagle told Shane.

Kaitlin stared at her husband, fear running along her spine. What was Shane up to? What was he trying to do?

Shane's eyes were on hers reassuringly as he spoke to Black Eagle. "That's right. You have not received your gift. Come, and I will bring you to your gift."

Shane left the teepee. Black Eagle set a hand upon Kaitlin's arm, dragging her along.

They came out into the snow-covered day. The sun was already falling. Pinks and oranges flared across the sky in dramatic streaks. The Blackfeet teepees, lined up against the horizon, appeared like a set of near-perfect, A-shaped hills in the soft pastel shadows that were beginning to form.

By the teepee, Black Eagle's people were lined up. Some were warriors, stripped of their paint now, yet standing just as proudly.

And the women were there. Beautiful Yellow Flower who had been the kindest to Kaitlin, heavy-set Cries Like the Wind who had mocked her with the most vengeance. Even the children flocked around, watching Black Eagle and Shane, the curious white man who had come among them before, and came among them now, despite the warnings that he might well be killed.

Diablo waited before the teepee. Black Eagle called out an order, and another horse was brought up. Kaitlin was surprised when Yellow Flower came forward, speaking softly to Black Eagle. She wondered if the chief's temper would flare at such an interruption, but Black Eagle paused, listening to the woman. Black Eagle grunted, then he actually seemed to smile. But he liked Yellow Flower, and Kaitlin was convinced that Yellow Flower was in love with Black Eagle. She didn't understand why the two were not man and wife, but standing there, shivering in the cold and waiting, she didn't really care. All that she could care about was Shane.

He had mounted Diablo, and he waited. Watching her.

So intently. His gold eyes blazed, and she longed so desperately to run to him. But his gaze warned her, too. He was still in the middle of negotiations.

"Kaitlin!" Yellow Flower said. Kaitlin spun around and gasped softly. Yellow Flower had gone for Genevieve. Her little mare stood before her, decked in an Indian rope bridle and an Indian saddle. Kaitlin stared at Shane, hesitating.

"Black Eagle has had her brought out for you."

Kaitlin caught hold of a handful of the mare's mane and swiftly leapt up on the horse. Black Eagle had mounted his paint, and the three of them were ready. One of the warriors said something to Black Eagle. Black Eagle laughed and answered in English.

"This man keeps his word, and his bargains. He will not injure me. Nor is he a fool. If he were to do so, you would kill him and his woman. Slowly. You are aware of this, MacAuliffe, right?"

"Very aware," Shane replied politely. "Shall we go?"

Black Eagle nodded and Shane urged Diablo forward. Kaitlin's mare followed at a brisk trot. Black Eagle kept pace behind them.

In a few moments, the A-line hill of teepees began to fade behind them as they left the winter village of the Blackfoot behind. They must have ridden for about twenty minutes before Shane reined in at last. Kaitlin couldn't begin to imagine where they were, and the shadows of night were beginning to fail around them. Then she heard a rustling and strained her eyes toward a group of trees. There had been some kind of a lean-to built there. And as she stared at it, a man suddenly appeared. Her eyes widened in surprise. It was Chancey.

"Shane?" he said cautiously.

"Yes, it's me," Shane said. "And Black Eagle is with us. He has brought my Christmas present, but I must now give him his before I am allowed to keep mine."

Even in the shadows, Kaitlin could see Chancey's broad smile. "Fine, Shane. That's mighty fine."

Shane dismounted and trudged through the snow toward the lean-to. He disappeared inside it.

Black Eagle waited in silence.

Then Shane reappeared carrying a little black-topped bundle wrapped in doeskin. For a moment, Kaitlin wasn't sure what it was.

Then she gasped as the bundle moved. Shane set it down. The bundle squealed and began to run.

It was a child. A baby really, Kaitlin thought, a little boy of no more than three or four.

Black Eagle answered the squeal with a hoarse, glad shout. He flung a leg over the neck of his pony and leapt gracefully to the ground, then ran to the boy, arms outstretched.

The boy was in his arms. Black Eagle rose and spun around in the shadows, cradling the boy against him.

Kaitlin looked at Shane. She could wait no longer. She ran to him, floundering a bit in the snow, nearly falling, but was then caught up in the strength of his arms.

"Kaitlin..."

She heard his whisper. Felt the warmth of it against her cheek. She wound her arms around him, not willing to be parted by the fraction of an inch.

Black Eagle did not come between them again. It was Shane himself who set her aside as the Indian walked up to him, still cradling his son.

"Your Christmas present is yours," Black Eagle said, "and mine... is mine. This is a good thing, this exchange of gifts."

"I think so, too," Shane said softly.

"It is an old custom? Part of your Christianity?"

Shane smiled. "Well, yes. You see, Christ was our god's gift to us. And on the night when he was born, wise men saw a star in the sky to follow, and they did so, bearing gifts for a newborn king. In honor of his birth, we bring gifts to one another."

Kaitlin felt a smile curve her lips as she watched Black Eagle. She had never imagined that such a man could be so tender, so gentle.

But all men, she realized, loved their children. Black Eagle was really no less—or no more—than any other man.

He looked at Kaitlin, then smiled at Shane. "You've given me a very fine gift."

"And you, sir, could have given me none finer," Shane replied.

Black Eagle stretched out a hand. Shane clasped it. Then the Indian turned with his little boy in his arms and mounted back up on his big paint. He glanced back.

"Kaitlin!"

"Yes, Black Eagle?"

"The mare is your Christmas gift."

She smiled. "Thank you. Thank you very much. I don't have anything for you. If—"

He interrupted her with his soft laughter. "Maybe you *have* given me a gift. I am going home now. I am going to tell Yellow Flower that she will be my Christmas gift. I have my son returned to me. His mother is dead a long time now. He will have another."

Black Eagle waved, and kicked his pony. Then he was swallowed into the shadows of Christmas Eve.

"Oh, Shane!" Kaitlin breathed.

Chancey cleared his throat. "I think we'd better be heading back now. Maybe we've got Black Eagle into the Christmas spirit, but I'd hate to count on the sudden conversion of his whole tribe."

"Right, Chancey, we'd better head back." But Shane was still holding Kaitlin, and Kaitlin was still looking up into his eyes. Neither of them could really care at the moment if they were surrounded by the entire Indian nation. "Chancey, you go on. You ride ahead and tell them all that everything is all right. That Kaitlin and I are coming home."

"I shouldn't be leaving you alone out here," Chancey muttered. "You're like a pair of babes in the woods right now, you are!"

He grumbled more as he drew his buckskin from around the side of the lean-to and mounted up. He was still grumbling when he cast his heels against the horse's side and started off through the snow.

They were alone. Alone in the white wilderness, with the last of the light fading fast, and stars beginning to appear above them, even as the light faded away.

"Oh, Shane..." Kaitlin whispered.

He kissed her at last. A kiss fueled with both passion and tenderness, a kiss that robbed the last of her breath away and set her heart to pounding fiercely.

She kissed him in return. With all barriers fallen, with all the warmth and desire and love he could have wished. They stood there, barely aware of the soft pelting of snow that began to fall upon them.

Then Kaitlin finally broke away, barely able to stand, so glad of his arms around her. "Oh, Shane, I do love you! I was trying to find you, trying to tell you—"

"And you found the Indians instead," he said softly. He cradled her fiercely against him. She was reminded of the way that Black Eagle had held his child, and she had never felt more loved, more protected, more cherished.

"Oh, Shane, it's true! You did find me in a New Orleans sewer. And I did come from an awful home, and it was torn to shreds by the war. And I wanted—material things. I never knew how little those things meant until I became so certain that I lost you. And I didn't mean to be so horrible, except that I was afraid. Shane, forgive me, please?"

"Kaitlin!" His arms swept around her again. So fiercely. "Kaitlin, I was horrible to you from the moment we met. But you see, I was fascinated with you then. I think that I was very afraid myself. You see, I risked love once. And I didn't dare believe in anything good."

"We were all wounded," Kaitlin whispered. "You, me—even Black Eagle. Maybe we've started to heal one another."

Shane smiled. A broad, tender, crooked smile. "Maybe," he agreed. "Did he—hurt you?"

She shook her head. "I think he meant to. But he saw your ring on my finger, and he refused to touch me because of his respect for you." She started to tremble. "Oh, Shane, even the Indians knew you better than I did!"

He laughed. "Not so, Kaitlin, but it doesn't matter. None of it matters anymore. I've got you back. And it's beginning to snow harder. Think we'd best head home."

She shook her head, her eyes dazzling as they met his. "No. I can't let you go."

"Then we'll ride Diablo together. I'll tie Genevieve to him so she can follow us home."

Once they were mounted, Kaitlin leaned her head against his chest, unable to believe that she was in his arms, and that they were on their way home. "How did you manage to come for me? Black Eagle had warned that he would kill even you if you disturbed him."

Shane's arms tightened around her. "I was nearly insane when I realized that you were gone, and what had happened. I would have ridden straight in for you, except that I knew that I couldn't save you alone, and that there wasn't enough manpower here to make any assault on Black Eagle and the entire tribe. Then I realized that I could make an assault on that fool trapper who had taken Black Eagle's boy, and so I rode on into his camp."

"Peacefully?"

"Guns blazing," Shane admitted, "but I had to convince him that I meant business. He gave up the boy to me, because I promised him a whole-scale war and an end to his future business trade if he didn't. Of course, I also promised him a bullet through the head. That seemed the most convincing argument."

Kaitlin laughed softly. "Oh, Shane... And I thought that I was going to spend Christmas in a teepee, unloved, unwanted!"

"Never, Kaitlin, never," he whispered huskily. "It was a year ago you came into my life. A year ago today, remember? And I told myself that you were a Christmas gift. I just didn't realize then that you were the greatest Christmas gift I was ever going to receive."

"Oh, Shane!" She turned in the saddle, flinging her arms around him, nearly unseating them both. She gave him a sloppy kiss, and he kissed her in return. Somehow managing to keep them balanced in the saddle. In time they parted. Diablo snorted as if he were certain his master and mistress had gone mad.

"All right, Diablo," Shane told him, "we're almost there."

And they were almost there. Francesca was on the front steps despite the cold, waiting. When she saw Kaitlin, she gave a glad cry and came racing down the steps and into the snow.

"You're home, Kaitlin, you're home! You're all that I asked for for Christmas, I prayed for you every night, and now you're here! Oh, Kaitlin!"

She hugged Francesca, hugged her and hugged her. And when she was done, she held on to her still. And Daniel and Mary were there, eager to hug and hold her.

Even the Reverend Samuels was there with Jemimah, all ready to greet her.

She had come home for Christmas. She had truly come home.

There was so much commotion for the longest time. Mary had seen to it that a hot bath filled with sweet rose scent awaited her first in the kitchen. Mary was convinced that she had to feel awfully dirty after her stay with the Indians. The Blackfeet had actually believed far more in bathing than a lot of white folk Kaitlin knew, but since Mary had gone through so much trouble to provide the delightful bath, Kaitlin decided to enlighten them later about the tribe. She smiled. Mary was a good friend. So was Daniel. They were wonderful people.

Just not quite so wonderful as Shane.

When she was bathed and dressed—wearing that beautiful gown Shane had bought for her the year before, the night they had wed— she came back to the parlor. Everyone wanted to speak with her, to be with her. To Kaitlin, it was fine. She sat there in the parlor, before the fire. Mary served her mulled wine, Francesca curled up next to her on the sofa with her head in her lap. There was a big fir tree in the parlor, too. Chancey had dragged it in. "Ain't decorated much, ma'am," he told Kaitlin, "but I was thinking that maybe you and

Shane and Francesca might want to get to that tomorrow. None of us ever gave up hope, you know. It was Christmas. And we just wanted you back for Christmas."

Kaitlin gave Chancey a big kiss, and that brought a blush to his cheeks. Then she realized that Shane had been very quiet all night. He was just standing there, leaning against the mantle, watching her.

Then, at last, it was time for everyone to go to bed for the night. They were all staying, the Newtons and their baby in one of the guest rooms, the reverend and Jemimah in another. It would be an early morning, with the lot of them traveling into town for Christmas services.

They'd have carols then, Kaitlin thought. She hugged Francesca close. There'd be carols in the church. And tonight, Santa just might come down the chimney.

Shane had said that he would give her Christmas. He had done just that.

And finally, she was alone with him. He hadn't let her walk up the steps. She assured him she hadn't been through any hardships, but he wouldn't let her walk up the steps anyway.

He carried her, his eyes locked with hers all the way. She wound her arms around his neck, smiling.

"Is Santa coming down the chimney for Francesca?" she asked softly.

"I think that Santa came tonight for Francesca, too," he said, smiling tenderly in return. "But yes. He's brought her a bright new dress and a beautiful doll. I'll have to see that he places it under the tree correctly very soon. He's coming for you, too."

"He came for me already," Kaitlin told him. "He came when I saw your face tonight."

"But there will be a present under the tree for you, too. I—" He paused. "I never gave up hope."

"Oh, Shane, I really won't have anything for you under the tree—" she began. Then she broke off. "Oh, but I do have something for you!"

They had reached their room. Shane still held her, closing the door behind them with his foot. Moonlight streamed into the room.

His eyes blazed down into hers. "I said that you were my Christmas gift. The finest gift that I have ever received. I truly need no other."

"But I have one, my love!" Kaitlin whispered. "I think we're going to have... no, I'm positive now. We're going to have a baby. Next year, I think that you'll have your son."

His arms tightened around her. "Kaitlin..."

For a moment he was utterly still.

Then he hugged her, set her down, and let out a cry, a joyous cry. It was something like a yell, something like a shout.

And Kaitlin was certain that it woke the entire house.

It did. There was suddenly a banging on their door.

Shane threw it open.

The Reverend Samuels stood there. "Shane, Kaitlin, is something wrong? Is someone injured—"

"No, no, we're fine!" Shane said quickly. "I was just receiving my Christmas gift."

The reverend gasped. Kaitlin giggled, realizing that the reverend had assumed that he was shouting about something indecent.

"Shane MacAuliffe, there's a child in this house—"

"And there's going to be another one! Good night now, all. No, not good night. It's past midnight. It's Christmas. Merry Christmas, everyone. Merry Christmas. Now go to bed!"

He closed the door with a firm snap. He smiled at Kaitlin. "Merry Christmas, my love!"

She smiled, and flew into his arms. "We do have the greatest gifts in the world," she whispered. "Gifts of love."

He held her tenderly, then kissed her lips. "Come, give me mine!" he whispered back.

And with the snow falling softly beyond the window, her home filled with the most wonderful Christmas spirit, Kaitlin curled her arms around him.

And gave him the gift of her love.

HOME FOR CHRISTMAS

A note from the Heather:

Since my father was Scottish, my mother is Irish and my husband and in-laws are Italian, Christmas dinner at our house is usually an unusual affair.

I love Christmas. With four children or more, the day is wild and woolly and wonderful. The house is all decorated, and we usually build a fire, even if it is eighty-odd degrees in South Florida that day. We tend to have a lot of family and friends every year, from thirty to fifty people, and my mother, sister, mother-in-law and everyone else cooks up something and brings it. We have turkey and gravy and potatoes and a big ham, and we also have lasagna and meatballs and Italian cheesecake.

One of my favorite Christmas recipes is a clam sauce I learned from my cousin-in-law, and it's a favorite recipe because it always tastes great and takes little time and effort. When unexpected company drops by, it can be whipped up in less than half an hour. It's also just about foolproof!

COUSIN JIMMY'S CHRISTMAS CLAM SAUCE

4 cans of chopped clams
2 ¼ lb. sticks butter or margarine
1 large garlic bulb (yes, that much!), chopped
1 tbsp olive oil
Fresh parsley, chopped

Sauté garlic in olive oil. Add clams and juice. (Use a little water to make sure all clams and juice are rinsed from the cans.) Add parsley. Heat mixture to almost boiling. Add butter or margarine and heat until the mixture bubbles lightly. Sauce can be served immediately or allowed to simmer on lower heat for about an hour.

Serve over linguine, tortellini or any other pasta of choice. It tastes even better when reheated.

I like to prepare the sauce using butter, but when I'm feeling health-conscious, I like it just as well made with margarine, or sometimes made with a stick of each.

Another Christmas tip:

For those who like stuffing cooked on the stovetop just as well as inside the turkey, cook the turkey without the stuffing. Instead, insert a stick of butter or margarine wrapped in a number of lettuce leaves. Cooking stuffing inside the bird dries out the turkey, while the lettuce keeps it moist, and the butter or margarine bastes the inside.

Prologue

Christmas Eve, 1864

A soft, light snow was falling as Captain Travis Aylwin stood by the parlor window. He could almost see the individual flakes drift and dance to the earth against the dove-gray sky. It was a beautiful picture, serene. No trumpets blared; no soldiers took up their battle cries; no horses screamed; and no blood marked the purity and whiteness of the winter's day.

It was Christmas Eve, and from this window, in the parlor that he had taken over as his office, there might well have been peace on earth. It was possible to forget that men had died on the very ground before the house, that lifeless limbs clad in gray had fallen over lifeless limbs clad in blue. The serenity of the darkening day was complete. A fire burned in the hearth, and the scent of pine was heavy in the air, for the house had been dressed for the season with holly and boughs from the forest, and bright red ribbons and silver bows. Hawkins had roasted chestnuts in the fireplace that morning, and their wintry scent still clung lightly to the room, like the mocking laughter of holidays long gone. He had not asked for this war! He hadn't been home for Christmas in four long years, and no scent of chestnuts or spray of mistletoe would heal the haunting pain that plagued him today.

She could heal the wound, he thought. She, who could spend the holiday in her own home, at her own hearthside. But she would not, he thought. And no words that he spoke would change her feelings, for it was almost Christmas, and no matter what had passed between them, no matter how gently he spoke, Isabelle took up the battle come Christmas, as if she fought for all the soldiers who rested in the field.

From somewhere he could hear singing. Corporal Haines was playing the piano, and Joe Simon, out of Baltimore, Maryland, was singing "O, Holy Night" in his wondrous tenor. There was a poignant quality to the song that rang so high and clear. Two people were singing, he realized. Isabelle Hinton had joined in, her voice rising like a nightingale's, the notes true and sweet.

She had forgiven the men, he thought. She had forgiven them for being Yankees; she had forgiven them the war. It was only him she could not forgive, not when it came to Christmas.

The sounds of the song faded away.

He closed his eyes suddenly, and it was the picture of the past he saw then, and not the present. Not the purity of the snow, the gentle gray of the day. He could not forget the past, he thought, and neither could she.

He tensed, the muscles of his arms and shoulders constricting, his breath coming too quickly. She was there. He knew she was there. Sergeant Hawkins had told him that Isabelle had requested an audience with him, and now he knew she was standing in the doorway. He could smell her jasmine soap; he could feel her presence. She would be standing in the doorway when he turned, waiting for him to bid her to enter. She would be proud and distant, as she had been the first day he met her. And just as it had that very first time, his heart would hammer within his chest as he watched her. She was an extraordinary woman. His hands clenched into fists at his sides. It was almost over. The war was almost over. He knew it; the lean, starving soldiers of the South knew it; she knew it—but she would never concede it.

He straightened his shoulders, careful to don a mask of command. He turned, and as he had known, she was there. And as he had suspected, she was dressed for travel. Her rich burgundy and lace gown was dated; her heavy black coat was worn, and beneath her patched petticoats, he knew, she would be wearing darned and mended hose, for she would take nothing from him except the "rent" for the house, and that she put away each month behind a brick in the fireplace. Once she had put it away for two brothers, but now one of them lay dead in the family plot that was hidden by snow, and so she put the money away for Lieutenant James L. Hinton, Confederate States Artillery, the Army of Northern Virginia, in hopes that he would one day come home. She took the money because the United States Army had taken over her house. Because she was determined not to lose her home, she had no choice but to let them use it. The Hinton plantation lay very close to Washington, D.C., and though the army had been forced to abandon the property upon occasion when Lee's forces had come close, they always returned.

Isabelle knew that. That he would always return.

Travis did not speak right away. He had no intention of making things easy for her, not that night, not when he felt such a despairing tempest in his soul. He crossed his arms over his chest and idly sat on the window seat, watching her politely, waiting. His heartbeat quickened, as it always did when she was near. It had been that way from the first time he saw her, and now that he had come to know her so well...

She was pale that night, and even more beautiful for her lack of color. She might have been some winter queen as she stood there, tall, slim, encompassed by her cloak, her fascinating gray-green eyes enormous against the oval perfection of her face. Her skin was like alabaster, and the darkness of her lashes swept beguilingly over the perfection of her flawless complexion. Her nose was aquiline, her lips the color of wine. Tendrils of golden hair curled from beneath the hood of her cape, barely hinting at the radiant profusion of long, silky hair beneath it. Watching her, he was tempted to stride across the room, to take her into his arms, to shake her until she cried for mercy, until she vowed that she would surrender.

But he would not, he knew. He had touched her in anger before, had shaken her to dispel the ice from her heart. He held the power, and sometimes he had used it, in despair, in desperation, and once in grim determination to save her life. But he would not touch her tonight. He loved her, and he would not force her to stay.

"Good evening, Isabelle," he told her. He had no intention of helping her. He would let her go, because he had to, but he would not help her abandon him to the barren emptiness of another Christmas without her.

"Captain," she acknowledged.

He didn't say a word. She lifted her chin, knowing they were both fully aware of why she had come, and that he would not make it easy for her.

With soft dignity she spoke again. "I would like an escort to the Holloway place, please."

"The weather is severe," he said noncommittally.

"That does not matter, sir. I will go with or without your escort."

"You know that you won't go two steps without my permission, Miss Hinton."

Her lip curled, and her rich lashes half covered her cheeks. "You would prevent me from leaving, Captain?"

Why didn't he do it? he wondered. He could turn his back on her, could deny her request. If she tried to leave him, if she tried to ride away into the snowbound wilderness, he need only ride after her, capture her, drag her back. It would be so easy.

But he had fallen in love with her, and he could never hold her by force. If she wanted to go, he would saddle the horse himself if need be.

"No, Miss Hinton," he said softly. "I will not prevent you from going, since that is your heart's desire."

He stood and walked to the desk, her brother's desk, his desk. It was a Yankee desk now, piled high with his paperwork, orders, letters, the Christmas wishes that had made it to him, the letters he had dictated to the parents and lovers and brothers and sweethearts of the men he had lost in their last skirmish, letters that had not yet been sent. He searched for his safe-conduct forms, drew out the chair, sat and began to fill in the blanks. Any Union patrol was to see to the safe passage of Miss Isabelle Hinton to Holloway Manor, just five miles southwest of their own location in northern Virginia. She would be accompanied by Sergeant Daniel Daily and Corporal Eugene Ripley, and she was not to be stopped, questioned or waylaid for any purpose.

He signed his name, then looked up. He thought he detected the glistening of tears behind the dazzle of her gray-green eyes. *Don't do this!* he longed to command her. Don't you see that in this very act you deny our love?

But she had never said that she loved him. Never, not while she was burning in the flames of desire, nor in the few stolen moments of tenderness that had come her way. And neither, God help him, had he ever whispered such words, for he could not. The war waged between them, and enemies did not love one another.

He stood, then approached her with the pass. Her gloved hands were neatly folded, but they began to tremble where they lay against her skirt.

"Isabelle..." He started to hand her the paper.

She reached for it, but her fingers didn't quite reach it, and it drifted to the ground. He meant to stoop to pick it up, but he didn't. His dark eyes locked with hers, and the room seemed to fill with a palpable tension. Suddenly he discovered that it was the woman he was reaching for, not the paper. He drew her into his arms and knew that she was not made of ice, that warmth flickered and burned within her. A soft cry escaped her lips, and her head fell back. Her eyes met his with a dazzling defiance, yet they betrayed things she would not say, that she would deny until the very grave if he allowed her.

"Isabelle!" he repeated, staring into her eyes, devouring her perfect features, his callused fingers coming to rest on the gentle slope of her cheek and chin. Once more he whispered her name, and he felt the frantic pounding of her heart just before he kissed her. He touched his lips to hers, and the fire seemed to roar behind him as he delved deeply into her mouth, stroking the inner recesses with his tongue and evoking memories within them both. His lips caressed and consumed hers, and flames lapped against his chest, his thighs, his loins, until he thought he could bear no more. Her breasts thrust explicitly against his cavalry shirt as he filled himself with the sweet taste of her, a taste that would so soon be denied him.

If she had thought to fight his touch, he had quickly swept that thought from her mind. In the power of his arms she did not—could not—deny him. The kiss evoked memories. Memories of blinding, desperate passion and need, memories of tenderness, of whispers, of golden, precious moments out of time, when love had dared and defied the reality of war.

The kiss was hungry, and it was sweet, and in those stolen seconds it meant everything to him that Christmas should. It simmered with passion, yet reminded him deep inside his heart of the times when they had laughed together. Of the times when he had held her against the world. It had begun in tempest, and yet it whispered of peace and the commitment of the soul. It promised years together, evenings before an open fire with children on their laps and the sweet sounds of Christmas carols dancing in their ears. It was everything that a Christmas kiss should be.

"No!" she cried softly, breaking away from him. Her small gloved hands lay against his chest, and the tears that had glazed her eyes now dampened her cheeks. "Travis, no! I must go! Don't you understand? I have to be with my own kind for Christmas, not in the bosom of the enemy!"

"By God, Isabelle! Don't you see? You *are* home. *This* is your home—"

"Not with you in it, Travis!" she interrupted, backing away from him. "Travis, please!" The desperate sound of her tears was in her voice. "Please, let me go!"

He felt as if his body was composed of steel, taut and hard and rigid, but he forced himself to breathe, and, watching her, he slowly forced himself to bend for the paper. He handed it to her, and their fingers brushed as she reached for it.

"Don't go, Isabelle," he said simply.

"I have to!"

He shook his head. "The war is almost over—"

"I cannot be a traitor."

"Loving me would not be turning your back on your own people. The war will end. The nation must begin to heal itself, to bind up its wounds—"

"The war is not over."

"Isabelle! Lee's men are wearing rags and tatters. They're desperate for food, for boots. Don't you see? Yes, they've fought and they've died, and they've run the Union to the ground, but there are more and more of us, and we have repeating rifles when half the boys in gray are dealing with single-shot muskets! I didn't make this war, and neither did you! Isabelle—"

"Travis, don't! I don't want to hear this!"

"Stay, Isabelle."

"I can't."

"You must."

"Why?" she demanded desperately.

"Because I love you."

She froze as he spoke the simple words, her cheeks going even paler. But she shook her head in fierce denial. "We're enemies, Travis."

"We're lovers, Isabelle, and no lies, no heroics, no denials can change that!"

"You're a Yankee!" she gasped. "And no gentleman to say such things aloud!"

238

A pained smile touched his features. "I tried, but a gentleman could not have had you, and I had to have you. Don't leave. It's Christmas. You should be home for Christmas."

"No!" She shook her head fiercely and spun around and hurried toward the door. She went through, then slammed it in her wake.

"Isabelle!"

Travis charged after her. He heard her lean again the door, and he paused, fingers clenching and unclenching.

There was nothing left to say.

"You should be home for Christmas," he repeated softly.

He heard her sob softly, then push herself away from the door. And then she was gone.

At length Travis wandered into the room and sat down before the fire. The flames leaped high, and he saw her face in the red-gold blaze. Come home! he thought. Come home, and be with me tonight.

He leaned back. It had been almost Christmas when they met, he thought.

From far away, he heard the piano again. The men's voices were raised in a rendition of "Silent Night." The fire continued to burn, and beyond the window the delicate flakes of snow continued to fall.

He could go after her, he thought. Maybe he should.

It had been almost Christmas, an evening like this one, when they had first met.

He closed his eyes, and he could see her again. See her as she had stood on the front steps, a woman all alone, ready to defy the entire Union Army.

Chapter 1

December, 1862

The snow had finished falling, but the house sat like an ice palace, like something out of a fairy tale. Rain had glazed over the white, newly fallen snow, and when the sun came out, the house and grounds seemed dazzling, as if they were covered with a hundred thousand diamond chips. The landscape seemed barren, a painting from a children's book. It was a place where the winter queen should live, perhaps—it certainly seemed to have no bearing on real life.

But real life was why they had come. Since the first shots had been fired at Fort Sumter, everyone had known that northern Virginia was going to be a hotbed—and that certain areas were going to have to be held by the Yanks if Washington, D.C., was to be protected.

Now, with the war raging onward, it was becoming more and more important to solidify the Union presence in Virginia. The Hinton house was just one of the places that had to be taken over. The little township was already filling with his men, and from studying his maps looking for strategic locations, Travis had known that the Hinton house would be the best place for his headquarters.

His occupancy would keep the Rebs away, while he would still have easy access to the town nearby if it became necessary to pull back. In addition, he would be in a good position to join up with the main army should he be called.

The day seemed very cold and still. Travis could hear only the jangle of harness and the snorts of the horses as his small company of twenty approached the house. The breath of men mingled with the breath of the horses as they plowed through the snow, creating bursts of mist upon the air. He reined in suddenly, not knowing why, just staring at the house.

It was such an elegant structure, like a grand lady in the crystallized snow. Great Grecian columns rose high upon the broad porch, tall and imposing. The house was white, and the white, diamond-like snowflakes caught on the roof and the windows. Even the outbuildings were covered in crystal. Through one window he could see a flicker of red and gold, and he realized that a fire was burning, warm and comforting against the snow and cold.

"Captain? It's mighty cold out here," Sergeant Will Sikes reminded him.

"Yeah. Yeah, it's mighty cold," he said. He nudged Judgment, his big black thoroughbred, forward. His men, cold and quiet, survivors of Sharpsburg and more that year, followed in silence. Everyone had thought the war would be over by May. A few weeks. The Yanks had expected an easy victory, while the Rebs had thought they could beat the pants off the Yanks—which they had done upon occasion, Travis had to admit—but they hadn't counted on the tenacity of Mr.

Lincoln. The President had no intention of letting the nation fall apart. He was going to fight this war no matter what. So the North had learned there was to be no easy victory, and the South had learned that the war could go on forever, and here it was, just a few days before Christmas, and they were all preparing to bed down in Virginia instead of returning home to their loved ones.

Of course, for some, Christmas was destined to be even gloomier. For some, the war had already taken its toll. Fathers, lovers, husbands and sons, many had returned home already, returned in packages of pine, wrapped in their shrouds, and for Christmas they would lie in their familial graveyards, home for the holiday.

He was becoming morose, he reminded himself, something he couldn't allow. He was in charge of this group of twenty young men and the hundred he had left behind in the town. He had no intention of letting morale fall by the wayside, nor was he of a mind to shoot any of his men for desertion.

"Seems a fair enough place, eh?" he called out, lifting himself out of his saddle to turn and view the troops. He was met with several nods, several half smiles, and he turned once again to face the house.

That was when he saw her.

She had come out to stand on the porch. She had probably heard the jingle of the horses' trappings, and she had known that men were coming. She must have hoped it was a Confederate company, yet it seemed she had suspected Yanks, for she had come out with a shotgun, and Travis was certain it was loaded.

For the life of him, at that moment, he couldn't care.

She was clad in blue velvet, a rich, sumptuous gown with puff sleeves and a daring bodice that left her shoulders bare and gave a provocative hint of the ivory breasts that surged against the fabric. She wore no coat or cloak against the cold, but stood upon the top step of the porch, that heavy gun swept up and aimed hard at him even as a delicate tumble of sun-gold curls fell in a rich swirl against the sights. She tossed her hair back, and he knew that she was young, and though he couldn't see the color of her eyes, he knew they would be fascinating. He knew that he had never seen a more beautiful woman, more striking, more delicate and fine. For several seconds he lost sight of duty and honor, even of the fact that he was fighting a war.

"She looks like she intends to use that thing," Will muttered, casting Travis a quick glance. "What do you think, Captain?"

Travis shrugged, grinning. She couldn't be about to shoot them. One lone woman against a party of twenty men. He lifted a hand and twisted in the saddle to speak. "Hold up, men. I'll do the talking and see if we can't keep this polite."

He urged his mount forward, leaving the others by the snow-misted paddocks and gate. She aimed the shotgun straight at him, and he pulled up his horse, lifting a hand to her in a civil gesture.

"Stop right where you are, Yank!" she commanded. The voice matched the woman. It was velvet and silk. It was strong, but with shimmery undertones that made her all the more feminine.

"Miss Hinton, I'm Captain Travis Aylwin of the—"

"You're a Yank, and I want you off my property."

He dismounted and headed for the steps that led to the porch. His heavy wool cape flapped behind him, caught by the breeze. He tugged his plumed hat over his forehead in acknowledgement that he had come upon a lady, but before he could take the first step he discovered himself spinning in astonishment. She had fired the rifle and just skimmed the feather on his hat.

"Son of a bitch!" he roared.

Behind him, twenty rifles were cocked.

"Hold it! Hold it!" he shouted to his men. He jerked off his singed hat and sent it flying down on a snowdrift, then glared at this southern angel, his dark eyes flashing with fury. "What the hell is the matter with you? If you had hit me—"

"If I had intended to hit you, Captain, you'd be dead," she promised softly, solemnly. "Now, get your men and move off my property."

He threw back his cape, set a booted foot on the first step, placed his hands on his hips and clenched his teeth. There was no easy way to take over a person's property, but this was war.

"So you didn't intend to hit me, huh?" he demanded.

"Don't you believe me, Captain?" An exquisite brow rose with the inquiry.

"Oh, yes, ma'am, I believe you. If I didn't, you'd be tied up and on the backside of a horse right now."

He watched her eyes narrow and a slow crimson flush rise to her cheeks. She started to aim the rifle again, and though he wanted to believe that she wasn't stupid or vicious enough to shoot a man—

244

even a Yank—he didn't want to take any chances. He leaped up the remaining steps, sweeping an arm around her waist to wrest the rifle from her grip. A soft gasp escaped her, but her grip was strong, and his efforts to dislodge the weapon sent them both reeling off balance. Suddenly they were tumbling down the steps and careening into a snowdrift. Travis instinctively attempted to keep his body lodged beneath hers. He didn't know why—-she wanted to shoot him. Maybe he just couldn't bear the idea of such a beautiful creature being hurt in any way.

When they landed, she was still seething and fighting. He wrenched her beneath him, securing her wrists, and spat out an oath. There was no nice way to do this, no nice way at all.

"Lady, in the name of the United States government—"

"The U.S. government be damned! This is the Confederacy! Don't threaten me with the U.S. government!"

"Lady," he said wearily, "this is war—"

"Get off my property!"

"In the name—"

"Get off me! I will not listen to a government that—"

He jerked her hands hard, dragging them high above her head, and leaned very close to her. "Don't listen to the government, then, listen to me. Listen to me because I'm twice your size, ten times your strength—and because I have twenty armed men behind me. Is that logical enough for you? Listen, now, and listen good. I'm taking this house. It's called confiscation, and it is something that happens during times of war. I'm sorry that your property happens to be so close to the border, but that's the way it is."

She blinked, and he noticed snowflakes clinging tightly to her eyelashes and dusting her cheeks. She was very white, and she was shivering beneath him. He didn't know whether it was the cold that made her shiver, or if she was trembling with rage. She moistened her lips to speak, and he found himself staring in fascination at her mouth, her pink tongue as it moved over her lips. They were wonderful lips, well defined, full, sensual, beautiful. He wanted to touch them. He wanted to feel the sizzling warmth he knew he would find within the recesses of her mouth.

He blinked, straightening against the cold of the day.

She spoke then, the breath rushing from her in a gust. "You're not going to burn the house?"

He almost smiled. She might hate having a pack of Yankees on her property, but she did want her property to survive.

He shook his head. "I'm taking the house for my headquarters. These fellows will bunk here—I have another hundred men in town. We'll do our best to compensate you for what we use."

She was still staring at him, unblinking now. Her velvet gown was wet with snow, her golden hair lying like curious rays of golden sun against it, and her gray-green eyes were startlingly bright and deep against the pallor of her cheeks. He felt her tremble again and saw that the snow was touching her bare shoulders and her breasts where they rose above her bodice. Little flakes fell deep into the shadowed valley between them. Lucky snowflakes, Travis thought, then he realized that she was freezing and silent in her misery. He thought with a sudden, unreasoning fury that she was what the South was made of, that she would suffer any agony in silence, that her pride was worth everything to her. This war would go on until eternity because of all the damn Southerners just like her. They had something that all the Yankee weaponry and numbers could not best, that sense of pride, of honor.

"Get up!" he snapped suddenly.

"I can hardly do that, sir, when you're lying on top of me!" she returned, but he had already thrust himself upward and reached down to help her. She didn't want to take his hand, but he allowed her no nonsense, taking hers. He drew her to her feet and swept his cloak from his shoulders, then threw it over hers. "I don't need Yankee warmth!" she protested.

"Whether you need it or not, you'll take it!" he growled and prodded her toward the steps. "Who else is inside?"

"General Lee and the entire army of Northern Virginia," she said sweetly.

"Sergeant! Draw a detail of five and shoot anyone inside that house who lives and breathes!"

"No!" she cried out in protest. She spun around, caught within his arms, but meeting his eyes again. "I'll tell you who's inside!" she snapped. "Peter, the butler, Mary Louise, my maid, Jeanette, Etta and Johnny Hopkins, all of them house servants. In the barn you'll find Jeremiah, the blacksmith, and five others, field hands. That's it. Just the servants—"

"Just the slaves?"

She lifted her chin, smiling with such a supreme sense of superiority that he wanted to slap her. "My parents are dead; and my brothers are fighting. The *servants* are all free men and women, Captain. My brothers saw to that before they left for the fighting. All free so that they could leave if trouble came—and not be shot by the likes of you!"

Her blacks were far more likely to be shot by renegade Confederates, but he wasn't going to argue the point with her. He turned around, trusting her suddenly, because she had no more reason to lie. "Sergeant, bring the men in. It's getting damn cold out here. Oh, excuse me, Miss Hinton." He bowed to her then bent to pick up his hat from the snowdrift. He started up the steps, then paused, for she was staring at him with pure hatred. "Lead the way, Miss Hinton."

"Why, Captain? I'm not inviting you in."

He walked down and caught her arm, a growling sound caught in his throat. He had assumed that the Southern belle he had to wrest the house from might have the vapors, or faint at the sight of a Yankee detail. He hadn't expected her to come after him with a shotgun, nor had he expected this defiance.

"Fine. I can escort you elsewhere."

"What?" she said.

"I can see that you are sent elsewhere, if that is your wish. I can pack you south, Miss Hinton. Where would you like to go? Richmond, New Orleans, Savannah, Charleston?"

"You intend to throw me out of my own house?"

A tug-of-war was going on within her beautiful eyes. She didn't want to be near him—but neither did she want to desert her home. He smiled. "Lady, the choice is yours."

"Captain, you're not going to be here long enough to do anything to me."

"I won't be?"

She smiled serenely. "Stonewall Jackson rides these parts, sir. And Robert E. Lee. They'll come back, and they'll skewer you right through."

He smiled in return. "You hold on to that thought, Miss Hinton. But for now... well, you can talk to Peter about something for dinner, or I can send my mess corporal down to raid your cellars. My men are good hunters. They can keep you and yours eating well. Just don't interfere."

"Interfere—"

"God in heaven, woman, it's cold out here!" He grasped her arm hard and jerked her along, opening the door to the house and thrusting her in before him.

The servants she had spoken of stood along the elegant carved stairway that led from the marble-floored foyer to the second floor above. Doors lined a long, elegant hallway to the right and another to the left, but Travis was certain that she hadn't lied, that the servants were the sole occupants of the house. They were all staring at him now with eyes wide. That must be Peter, a tall, handsome man dressed in impeccable livery, and that would be Mary Louise at his side. The others were peeking out from behind them.

"Hello." He doffed his hat to them, smiling, aware that Sergeant Sikes was coming up behind him with half the men. Peter nodded gravely, then looked at Miss Hinton.

"Speak to them," Travis suggested.

She moistened her lips. "Peter, this is, er, Captain Travis Aylwin." He thought she was about to spit on the floor, but the manners she had learned long ago on her mammy's lap kept her from doing so. "Oh, hell! The damn Yanks have come to take over the house."

"They're not a-gonna burn us—" Peter began.

"No!" she said quickly, then shot Travis a furious stare. "At least, the captain has promised they're not."

"I don't remember promising anything," he said pleasantly. "But, Peter, it is not my intent to do so. Not unless your mistress is a spy. She isn't, is she?"

Peter's eyes went even wider. "No, sir. Why, you can see how it is here, winter and all. You can hardly go house to house in these parts, much less find an army to spy for!"

Travis laughed. He had to agree. They were just about snowbound for the moment, except that he was going to have to get word through to intelligence about his location and the situation here. "There are twenty of us here, Peter."

"And we're colder than a witch's teat and hungry as a pack of bears!" Sergeant Sikes said.

"Sergeant!" Travis barked.

But Sikes already appeared horrified at his own words. He was staring at their unwilling hostess as if he were too mortified for words. Travis found himself grinning. "I'm certain Miss Hinton has heard such words before, even used a few herself, perhaps, but an apology is in order."

She cast him a scathing glare, but her lips curled into a curious smile. "If I haven't used such language, Captain, I'm quite sure that I shall before I have seen the last of you."

"Supper, Miss Hinton?" Peter asked.

She lifted a hand. "Feed the rabble, since we must, Peter." She pulled away from Travis's side, letting his military cape fall to the floor. "Do excuse me, Captain, but I choose not to watch your ruffians eat me out of house and home."

She started up the stairway. He watched her warily as she went, but he did not stop her. She might very well be going up to find a bowie knife or a pistol, but for the moment, he would just let her go. It was time to settle in.

"Where is Miss Hinton's room, Peter?" he asked.

"Second floor, second door to the left, sir," Peter said uneasily.

Travis merely nodded and smiled. "Thank you, Peter. Sikes, you find a room in the house, and find one for me, too. As for the men—"

"The barn has a full bunkhouse," Peter advised him. "Fireplace, wood-burning stove, all the amenities, sir. Sleeps thirty easily."

"But that leaves Sergeant Sikes and me alone in the house, doesn't it, Peter? You wouldn't be planning something, would you?"

Peter shook his head.

"But your mistress might be."

Peter lowered his head, but not before Travis saw acknowledgement in his eyes. She was dangerous, Miss Fairy-tale-princess Hinton. But he could handle the danger. "Fine, Peter, thank you. The men will take the bunkhouse. Sikes and I will find rooms here, and if you value your Miss Hinton's life, you'll take care to see that she behaves."

Peter nodded, but Travis had the feeling that he wasn't at all sure he was up to the task.

"I'll sure try, Captain. I'll sure try," Peter told him.

Travis started to walk along the hallway to find a room he could use as an office. He paused, turning back. "Why?" he asked Peter.

Peter grinned, his white teeth flashing as he smiled. "I don't want to see her shot up by you Yanks, Captain, and that's a fact."

Travis nodded, grinned and started down the hallway. He waved a hand. "See to the men, Sikes. And to yourself. Peter, when's dinner?"

"I can fix you up in an hour, Captain."

"An hour. Everyone in the house. It isn't quite Christmas Eve, but we'll pretend that it is. Everyone at the dining table except for a guard of two."

"Only two, sir?" Sikes asked.

"Only two. The enemy lurks within the house tonight," he warned, then wandered down the hallway.

* * *

Isabelle Hinton didn't appear for dinner. The men ate, warming their hands by the fire and gazing at the fine plates and silver and the crystal goblets as if they hadn't seen such luxury in years. It had been forever since they had sat down to this kind of meal. It seemed as if they had spent the entire year in battle. The worst of it had been at Sharpsburg, by Antietam Creek. Travis had never seen so many men die, never seen the bodies piled so high, never smelled so much blood. Great fields of corn had been mowed to the ground by gunfire. Yankees and Rebels had died alike, and that battle alone had taught them all that war was an evil thing.

While the men were in the parlor playing the piano and singing Christmas carols, Travis retired to the den he had found to use as his office. He sipped from a snifter of brandy and rested his booted feet on the desk, staring at the flames that burned in the hearth. He closed his eyes, and for a moment he felt the sun again as he had that day at Sharpsburg. He remembered how eerie it had felt to lead a cavalry charge, then watch as the men were mown down around him. He had taken grapeshot in the shoulder himself and wondered if it wouldn't be easier just to die than to wait for infection to set in. But he hadn't lost the arm, and he hadn't died—he'd lived to fight again.

The men were singing a rousing rendition of "Deck the Halls." The warmth of the fire enveloped Travis, and the pain of battle drifted slowly from his memory. He wondered what he would be doing if he was home. Well, he wouldn't be at his own house. Since his wife had succumbed to the smallpox, he had avoided his own house for the holidays, but never his family. He would have headed into town to his mother's house. There would be a huge turkey roasting, and the scent of honey-coated ham would fill the house. His sister Liz would be there with the kids, and Allen would be asking him all about West Point, while Eulalie would want a horsey ride on his knee. Jack, his brother-in-law, would talk about the law with his father, and all the voices would blend together, the chatter, the laughter, the love. They would go to church on Christmas Eve, and they would all remember, even in the depths of the deepest despair, that it was Christmas because a little child had been born to rid the world of death and suffering. And somehow, no matter how dark an hour they seemed to face, he would believe again in mankind. And even now, even here, far from home, he knew that Christmas would always convince him that there could be love again. He just wished that he were home.

The men were no longer singing; the house had grown quiet. Travis set his brandy snifter on the desk, rose and stretched. He had a pile of maps on the desk, but he would get to them tomorrow. Right now, he wanted to get to bed.

He found Peter in the hallway, returning the last of the crystal glasses to a carved wooden rack on the wall. "Upstairs, Captain. We done give you the master suite, third door to the right."

"Thank you, Peter. Sikes?"

"He's gone up, sir. Third floor, first door to your left."

"It's a big house, Peter."

"Lordy, yes. Needed to be, before the war. There was parties galore then, cousins coming from all over the countryside to sleep for the whole weekend. Why, around now, at Christmas..."

Peter's voice trailed away. Travis clapped an arm on the man's shoulder. "Christmas is kind of hard all around right now, Peter. Good night."

Travis climbed the stairs and found the door to his room. The master suite. It was a huge room, with a four-poster bed against the far wall, two big armoires, a secretary facing a window and a cherry-wood table with a handsomely upholstered French chair beside it by the fire.

He draped his sword and scabbard over a chair and unhooked the frogs of his jacket, then cast that, too, over the chair. His shirt followed. Then he sat to tug off his boots and socks before peeling away his breeches. He would have slept in his long underwear, but there was a big pitcher of water and a bowl on a small washstand by one of the armoires, so he stripped down to the flesh and found that the water was still a little bit warm. There was a bar of soap there, too, supplied by Peter, he was certain, and not his hostess. It didn't matter. He scrubbed himself the best he could, then dried himself, shivering, before the fire, before slipping into the bed. It wasn't quite home, but it was a good soft mattress and an even softer pillow, and it was, in fact, so comfortable that he wasn't sure he would be able to sleep.

He closed his eyes, and he was just starting to doze when he heard the sound. He opened his eyes, then closed them again swiftly, before allowing them to part slightly. Firelight danced on the walls, and for a moment he didn't know what he had heard. The door to the hallway had not opened.

But he wasn't alone. He knew it.

He waited. Then he sensed the soft rose fragrance of her perfume, and he knew that she had invaded his bedroom, though for what purpose he didn't know. He could see her through the curtain of his lashes. All that lush blond hair of hers was free, flowing like a golden cascade over her shoulders and down her back. She was dressed in something soft and floor length and flannel, but the firelight ignored the chasteness of her apparel, playing through the material and outlining the alluring beauty of her form. Her breasts were high and firm, her waist slim and tempting, her hips and buttocks flaring provocatively beneath it. She carried something, he saw. A knife. And she was right beside the bed.

He snaked out an arm, capturing her wrist, pulling her down hard on top of him. She gasped in surprise, but she didn't scream. Her gray-green eyes met his with a fear she tried desperately to camouflage, but with no remorse. He tightened his grip on her wrist, and the knife clattered to the floor.

"What good would it have done to kill me?" he asked.

She tried to shift away from him. He gave her no quarter; indeed, some malicious demon within him enjoyed her flushed features and the uncomfortable way she squirmed against him. He hadn't dragged her into his bedroom; she had come of her own accord.

"I wasn't going to kill you!" she protested.

He skimmed both hands down the length of her arms, then laced his fingers through hers and drew her to his side, leaning tautly over her. She swallowed and strained against him, but still she did not scream, and she tried very hard not to look his way. "I see," he said gravely. "You came to offer a guest a shave, is that it?"

Her eyes fell to his bare chest. He could feel the rise of her breasts, the outline of her hips, the staggering heat coming from her skin. He knew that she was aware of the desire rising in him. She couldn't help but feel the strength of him hard against her.

"I—I just..." Her voice trailed off.

"You came here to murder me!" he snapped angrily.

"No, I..."

"Yes, damn it!"

Suddenly her eyes met his. They flashed with fury, with awareness, then fear. Then something more. "All right!" she whispered. "I—I thought that I would kill you before you violated my home! But then..."

"Then what?" he demanded.

She moistened her lips. Her lashes fell, and she was so beautiful he could barely restrain himself. He wanted to live up to the reputation Yankee soldiers were given in the South; he wanted to wrap his arms around her, to have her, to make love to her at all costs. He would have traded every hope he had of heaven just to fill

257

his hands with the weight of her breasts; he would have sold his very soul to the devil to feel himself within her.

"I realized that you were a man, flesh and blood.... I..." Her words trailed away, and her eyes met his. She had never seen the deaths at Sharpsburg; she hadn't watched them fall at Manassas. But tonight she had played with death, and she had discovered that it was not glorious, not honorable.

She had recognized him as a human being.

"I still wish you were dead!" she snapped, surging against him suddenly as if she was horrified that she had forgotten their fight. "You're still a damn Yank and—" She broke off, breathing raggedly. He smiled, because they were both all too aware that he was human, and very much a man.

"Please, Captain, if you would be so good as to let me up now...?"

He started to chuckle softly. She could still be such an elegant, dignified belle, so regal despite their position.

"Sorry," he said.

"Sorry!" she gasped, realizing that he had no intention of letting her go. "But—but..."

"I can't take the chance that you might decide you're capable of killing me after all," he said, rolling over and dragging her with him. He had to forget modesty to bring her along with him so he could find a scarf. She tried to fight him, to look anywhere but at him, but he was ruthless as he pulled her along in his footsteps until he found

258

a scarf, then brought her back to the bed, where he tied her wrists together, then laid her down with her back against him.

She swore and she kicked and she protested, and she wriggled and fought until his laughter warned her that her movements were pulling her gown precariously high on her hips.

Then she merely swore. Like a mule driver. Sergeant Sikes could have learned a thing or two.

"Go to sleep!" he warned her at last. "Aren't you afraid I'll remember that I'm a raiding, pillaging, murderous—raping—Yankee?"

He heard her exhale raggedly. She didn't know how close she had come to forcing him to discover that a desperate monster lived in every man.

But in time she slept, and so did he, and when he awoke, his arm was around her, his hand resting just below the fullness of her breast. His naked leg lay entwined with hers, while the golden silk of her hair teased his nose and chin. It felt so good to hold her. To want her, to long for her. Even to ache. Just seeing her, just touching her, evoked dreams. Dreams of a distant time, dreams of a peaceful future. In those first seconds of dawn, she seemed to be the most wondrous present he had ever received.

She twisted in his arms, instinctively seeking warmth. She cuddled against his chest, her fingers moving lightly across his skin, her lips brushing his flesh. He pulled her against him. As the morning light fell into the room, her lips were slightly parted, slightly damp, as red as wine.

Carefully he untied her wrists, freeing her hands.

Then he kissed her. He touched his lips to hers, and he kissed her. A soft sound rumbled within her throat, but she didn't awaken right away. Her lips parted farther, and his tongue swiftly danced between them, and he tasted, fully and hungrily, everything that her mouth had to offer. Heat rose within him, swift and combustible, swamping him, hurting him, making him ache and yearn for more. His fingers curled over her breast, and he found it as full and fascinating as he had imagined. He touched her nipples beneath the flannel that still guarded them and he felt her stir beneath him as he drew his lips from hers.

Her eyes opened slowly, and he realized that she had been lost in her own dreams. Their gazes met, then a horrified whisper left her lips. She suddenly seemed to realize what the situation was, and she twisted violently away from him.

And he let her go. She leaped away from the bed, her fingers trembling as they touched her lips, her arms wrapped tightly around herself. She stared at him in fury. "You... you Yank! How could you, how dare you, how—"

"You tried to murder me, madam, remember?"

"But you tried to—" She broke off. He hadn't really used any force against her. "You know what you did! You are no gentleman!"

"I never make any pretense of being a gentleman when I'm in the midst of trying to stay alive!" he told her angrily.

"A Virginian, sir, would have been a gentleman to the very end. A Virginian—"

She broke off as her gaze fell over him, over his nakedness, and she turned to run.

He caught her arm and pulled her hard against him. His eyes burned into hers. "I *am* a Virginian, Miss Hinton. And trust me, ma'am, nothing has hurt so bad as this war. I have cousins in blue, and cousins in gray, and do you know something, Miss Hinton? Every single one of them is a gentleman, a good, decent man. And sometimes I wake up so scared that I can't stand it because I just might find myself shooting one of my very decent cousins someday. My gentlemanly cousins. Most of the time I wake to my nightmares. This morning I woke to see you. It was like a glimpse of paradise."

The blood had drained from her face, and when her eyes met his they were filled with a tempest of emotion, but she did not try to pull away. For the longest time they just stood there, then he lightly touched her cheek. "Thank you. It was just like a Christmas present."

She didn't move even at that. Her hand rose, and she touched his cheek in turn. She felt the texture of his skin, rough from lack of shaving.

Then suddenly it was gone, that curious moment when they were not enemies. Her hand fell away, and she seemed to remember that she was flush against a naked Yankee. With a soft cry she whirled and headed across the room, and he discovered that there was a door in the wall, very craftily concealed by the paneling.

She disappeared through it without a word.

* * *

261

Later that day she found him in her den, which he had taken over as his office. She wore a bonnet and cloak, and her hands were warmed by an elegant fur muff.

"You said that I could go where I chose, Captain."

His heart hammered and leaped as he looked up from his work. It would be best if she left. He would cease to dream and wonder; he would be able to concentrate more fully on the war.

He didn't want her to go. He would never know when she intended to pull a knife again, but he was willing to deal with the danger just to enjoy the battle.

"Yes," he told her.

"I wish to go to a neighbor's."

"Oh? You're not going to stay to protect your property?" he said, trying to provoke her. His eyes never left hers. Her lashes fell, and she reddened very prettily. She was remembering that morning, he thought, and he was glad of the flush that touched her cheeks, just as he was glad of the totally improper moments they had shared.

Her eyes met his again. "Don't worry, Captain. I'll be back. I just don't care to spend Christmas with the enemy."

He looked down quickly. She was going to come back. He opened his drawer, found a form and began writing on it. He looked up. "I don't know your given name."

"Isabelle," she told him.

He stared at her. "Isabelle," he murmured, a curious, wistful note in his voice. In annoyance, he scribbled hard. "Isabelle. Isabelle Hinton. Well, Miss Hinton, where is this neighbor?"

"Not a mile on the opposite side of town."

He nodded. "Sergeant Sikes and one other soldier will serve as an escort for you. How long do you plan to stay?"

She hesitated. "Until two days after Christmas."

"Sergeant Sikes will return for you."

"I hardly see why that will be necessary."

"I see it as very necessary. Good day, Miss Hinton."

She turned and left him.

* * *

Christmas dawned gray and cold. Restless, Travis went out into the snow with a shotgun. He brought down a huge buck and was glad, because it would mean meat for many nights to come.

At the house, Peter and the servants were almost friendly. There was a long and solemn prayer before they started eating the Christmas feast, and there was general good humor as the meal was downed. Travis tried to join in, but when he realized that his mood was solemn, he escaped the company of his soldiers and returned to the den. He did not know when Christmas had become so bleak. Yes, he did. It had become gray and empty when Isabelle Hinton left.

* * *

He didn't hear her return. He had spent the day poring over charts of the valleys and mountains, pinpointing the regions where Stonewall Jackson had been playing havoc with the Union Army. A messenger had arrived from Washington with orders and all kinds of information gleaned from spies, but Travis tended to doubt many of the things he heard.

By nightfall he was weary from men coming and going, as well as from the news of the war. Peter had brought him a bowl of venison stew and a cup of coffee, and that had been his nourishment for the day. Exhausted, he climbed the steps to his room, stripped off his cavalry frock coat and scrubbed his face. Then it seemed that he heard furtive movements in the next room.

His heart quickened, but then his eyes narrowed with wariness. He hadn't forgotten how she had come upon him that first night, even if she had stopped short of slitting his throat. Silently he moved across the room, wondering what she was up to. He found the catch of the secret door and slowly pressed it. The door opened, and he entered her domain.

A smile touched his features, and he leaned casually against the door, watching her, enjoying the view. Miss Isabelle Hinton was awash in bubbles, submerged to her elegant chin, one long and shapely leg raised above the wooden hip bath as she soaped it with abandon. Steam rose from the tub, whispering around her golden curls, leaving them clinging to her flesh. From his vantage point, he could just make out the rise of her breasts, just see the slender column of her throat and the artistic lines of her profile.

Then she turned, sensing him there.

Her leg splashed into the water, and she started to sit up straighter, but then she sank back, aware what she was displaying by rising. She lifted her chin, realizing that she was caught, and from his casual stance against the door, she knew he wasn't about to turn politely and leave.

"Welcome home," he told her.

She flushed furiously. "What are you doing in my room, Captain?"

"Seeking a bit of southern hospitality?"

She threw the soap at him. He laughed, ducking.

"No gentleman would enter a lady's bedroom!" she snapped angrily.

"Ah, but no lady would venture into a man's bedroom, Isabelle, and it seems that you did just that to me. Admittedly, you came to do me in, but you barged in upon my, er, privacy nonetheless."

Ignoring him, she demanded, "Get out, or you shall be gravely sorry."

"Shall I?"

So challenged, he strode across the room toward the tub. Her eyes widened, and she wrapped her arms around her chest, sinking as low as she could into her wealth of bubbles. He smiled, crouching beside the tub. She stared at him in silence for a moment, then called him every despicable name he had ever heard. He laughed, and she doused him with a handful of water, but he didn't mind a bit, since her movement displayed quite a bit of her.

"I'll strangle you!" she promised. But he caught her wrists when her fingers would have closed around his throat, and then, even as she struggled, he kissed both her palms. Then he stood, releasing her and stepping back.

"Damn, I forgot to be a gentleman again," he apologized. "But I was just wondering whether you had a knife hidden under that water or not. Do you?"

She inhaled sharply. "No!"

"I could check, you know," he warned.

Her look of outrage made him laugh. He gave her his very best bow, then returned to the door that separated their rooms.

"I'm changing rooms!" she called to him.

He paused in the doorway, looking at her. "No, you're not. You chose it this way the night you planned my early demise. So now it will stay."

"I'll move if I choose."

"If you move, I'll drag you back. Depend on it. If you stay, I promise that we're even. I won't pass through the doorway unless I'm invited. A threat, and a promise, and I will carry out both, Miss Hinton."

Thick honeyed lashes fell over her eyes. She was so lovely that he ached from head to toe watching her. "You will never be invited in, Captain," she said.

"Alas, you have a standing invitation to enter my room, Miss Hinton. Of course, I do ask that you leave your weapons behind."

Her eyes flew to his. He offered her a curiously tender smile, and she did not look away, but watched him. She was as still and perfect as an alabaster bust. Her throat was long and glistened from the water. Her golden curls clung tightly to her flesh, and if she were to move, he knew she would be fluid, graceful, a liquid swirl of passion and energy.

I'm falling in love, he thought. "I missed you on Christmas, Isabelle," he told her. She did not answer, and he slipped through the door, closing it behind him.

Chapter 2

Isabelle Hinton had never wanted to like the Yankee commander who had come to take over her home. She spent hours reminding herself that the boys in blue were causing the war, that the South had just wanted to walk away in peace. She reminded herself of all the atrocities taking place; again and again she remembered that her brothers were out there, facing Yankee bullets daily, but nothing that she could tell herself seemed to help very much. He'd never claimed to be a gentleman, and indeed, his behavior had been absolutely outrageous at times. But still, as the days went by, he proved himself to be a true cavalier underneath it all.

She tried to ignore all of them at first. But one evening, when she knew that he was dining alone, her curiosity brought her to the table. Though she tried to bait him, he was calm and quiet during the meal, the flash in his dark eyes the only indication that she touched his temper at all. He was a good-looking man—she had admitted that from the start. His eyes were so dark a mahogany as to be almost coal black; his hair, too, was dark, neatly clipped at the collar line. He was the perfect picture of an officer when he set out to ride, his cape falling over his shoulders, his plumed hat pulled low over his forehead, shading those dancing eyes. Beneath the beard, his features were clean and sharp, his cheekbones high, his chin firm, his lips full and quick to curl with a sensuality that often left her breathless, despise the condition though she might. Even his tone of voice fascinated her; his words were clear and well enunciated, but there was something husky about them, too, just the trace of a slow Virginia drawl. And, of course, she was very much aware of the rest of him; even if she didn't see much daily, the picture lived on vividly in her memory.

She hadn't had a great deal of experience with men's bodies, but she did have two older brothers, and after a few battles she had gone to the makeshift hospitals to help with the wounded. She had gone from ladies' circles, where she and others had rolled bandages, to being thrust right into a surgeon's field tent, and she had learned firsthand a great deal of the horror of war. She had cleaned and soothed and bandaged many a male chest, but none of them had compared to the very handsome chest that belonged to Captain Travis Aylwin. His shoulders were broad and taut with muscle and sinew, and the same handsome ripple of power was evident in his torso and arms. His waist was trim, and dusky dark hair created a handsome pattern across his chest, then narrowed to a thin line before flaring again to... well, she wouldn't think about that. She had been raised quite properly, she reminded herself over and over again, but that didn't keep her from remembering him, all of him, time and time again. She couldn't cease her wondering about him, nor could she keep him from intruding upon her dreams.

She always awakened before anything could happen, though her cheeks would be dark with a bright red blush, and there was a burning behind her eyes as she longed to crawl beneath the floor in humiliation.

She tried hard to stay away from him. He respected the distance, as he had promised when he had left her room after Christmas, but she always knew he was there at night, just beyond her door. His men were perfectly courteous and polite, and they were good hunters; there was always plenty to eat. So much so, she knew, that when she mentioned that some of her neighbors were facing hard times, the Union officers were quick to leave a side of venison before a door, or a half dozen rabbits, or whatever bird had ventured too close to the hunters. It was Travis's leadership that led to their generosity and care, she knew. Travis did not relish war.

She began seeing him and his troops not as faceless enemies but as men, just like the friends who had come to her parties, just like the young Southerners who had come to her home to laugh and dream, to fall in love and plan a future. She had to tell herself that they were the enemy, and that she did not want her enemy to be flesh and blood.

It was late January when she came down to dinner with him again. He had been reading some papers, but once he masked his astonishment at her appearance, he quickly set them aside, rose and held out her chair. She sat, quickly picking up the glass of wine that had just been poured for him and swallowing deeply. He sat down again, a touch of amusement in his eyes. He must have been a true lady-killer back home, she thought. He was full of warmth and laughter, a quiet strength and a subtle but overwhelming masculinity. His eyes held so much, and his lips were so quick to curve into a smile. But he could be ruthless, too, she knew. She had learned that the first night, when he had held her beside him until dawn.

"To what do I owe this honor?" he asked her softly. He barely needed to lift his hand. Peter was there with a second setting almost immediately. More wine was poured for him. Peter glanced her way worriedly. She winked, trying to assure her servant that she was, as always, in charge.

"The honor, sir? Well, actually, I was hoping that the snow would be melting, that you might be marching out to do battle again soon."

He sat back, watching her. "Perhaps we will be. Will that really give you such great pleasure?"

She rose, not believing that he could make her feel ashamed for wanting the enemy to fall in battle. She walked around the room, pausing before the picture of her family taken by Mr. Brady just before the war. Her brothers stood on either side of her, and her parents sat before them. But already the boys were dressed in their uniforms, and every day she prayed that they would return. If they sat in some northern house, would a girl there wish them into the field of battle, to bleed, to die?

"I just want you out of my house," she told him, turning back.

He had risen and was staring at the picture, too. He walked around to it. "Handsome family," he told her. "Your parents?"

"They died in 1859, a few days apart. They caught smallpox. My brothers and I were safe, I think, because we had very mild cases as children. Neither Mother nor Father caught it then, but one of the neighboring babies came down with it and then..." She left off, shrugging.

"I'm very sorry."

"It's a horrible death," she murmured.

"I know," he said, turning from her. He stood behind his chair. "Shall we have dinner?"

She sat. Peter served them smoke-cured ham from the cellars, apricot preserves and tiny pickled carrots and beets.

"Where is home, Captain?" she asked him.

"Alexandria."

Alexandria. The beautiful old city had been held since the beginning of the war because of its proximity to Washington, D.C., but many of its citizens were Unionists. It was a curious war. Already the counties in the west had broken away and a new state had been born, West Virginia.

"You're going to get your home back, you know, Miss Hinton," he told her.

"Am I?"

"Of course."

She set her fork down. "How do I know you won't decide to burn the house down when you leave?"

He set his fork down, too. "Do you really believe I intend to do that?" he asked her.

She watched him for several long moments. He buttered one of Peter's special biscuits, then offered it to her.

"General Lee lost Arlington House," she said. "And, I admit, I'm quite surprised that you Yanks haven't burned it to the ground."

He set the biscuit down and sipped his wine. "It's a beautiful house," he said softly. "And it overlooks the Capitol. General Lee knew the moment he chose to fight for the South that he would have to leave his home. His wife knew, his family knew, and still he made his decision. Some people were bitter. Some of the men who had fought with him or learned from him before the war wanted to burn the place down. It is Mrs. Lee I pity—she grew up there. And as George Washington's step-granddaughter, she has always had a great sense of history. She's a magnificent lady." He paused, as if he had said too much. Then he shrugged, setting down his wineglass. "They're not going to burn the house down. They've been burying Union soldiers there since the beginning of the war. The land will become a national cemetery."

"And Lee will forever lose his home."

"The South could still win the war," he told her.

Startled, she stared at him. She hadn't realized that she had displayed such a defeated attitude. "The South *will* win the war!" she assured him, but then she frowned. "You sound as if you're quite taken with the Lees."

He pushed back his chair. "The general is my godfather, Miss Hinton. We all lose in this war. He made his choices, and so did I. A man must do what he feels is right. And yet I tell you, Miss Hinton, that this fratricide must and will end, and when it does, if we are blessed to live, then he will be my friend and mentor again, and I will be his most willing servant."

She jumped up, wrapping her fingers around the back of her chair, staring at him in fury. It was almost blasphemy to speak so of General Robert E. Lee; he was adored by his troops, by the South as a whole.

He was a magnificent general and a soft-spoken gentleman.

"How dare you!" she spat out, trembling.

He took a step toward her, grabbing her wrist, holding her tight when she would have fled his presence. "Would you make monsters of us all?"

"I've read about the things that have happened. I know what Yankees do."

"Yes, yes, and *we've* all read *Uncle Tom's Cabin,* but I've yet to see you whip or chain or harness your slaves. By God, yes, there is injustice, and some horror is always true, but must we create more of it ourselves?"

"I'm not creating anything." She jerked free of him and spun around, hurrying from the room, but he called her back.

"Isabelle!"

She turned. He stood tall and striking in his dress frock coat and high cavalry boots, his saber hanging from the scabbard strapped around his waist. His eyes touched her, heated and dark.

"I am not a monster," he told her.

"Does it matter what I think?" she demanded.

A rueful smile touched his lips. "Well, yes, to me it does. You see, I... care."

She gasped in dismay, "Well, don't, Yankee, don't! Don't you dare care about me!"

She fled and raced up the stairs.

* * *

That night and every night after that she lay awake and listened to his movements, but he never touched her door, and he never mentioned anything about his feelings again. He was always unerringly polite to her, and though she felt that she should keep her distance from him, she couldn't. She came down to a meal occasionally, usually when Sergeant Sikes or one of the other men was joining him.

Sometimes he disappeared for days at a time, and she suspected that he had ridden away to supply information about troop movements, or to receive it.

At the beginning of April, Isabelle awoke to find that the house was filled with activity. The way the men were bustling around, coming and going from the office, she knew that something was going on.

She came down the stairs and presented herself in the den. Travis's dark head was bent over a map in serious study. He sensed her presence and looked up quickly.

"What's happening?" she asked without preamble.

He straightened and studied her as thoroughly as he had the map, a curious shadow hiding any emotion in his eyes. "We're pulling out. There's a company of Rebels headed this way."

"You're going into battle?" she asked him.

"That's what war is all about," he returned, and there was just the slightest trace of bitterness in his voice. He sat on the edge of his desk, still watching her. "You should be pleased. Maybe we'll all die."

"I don't want you to die," she said. "I just want you to go away."

He smiled and lifted a hand in the air, then let it fall back to his thigh. "Well, we're doing just that. Tell me, Isabelle, will you miss me at all?"

"No."

He stood and walked toward her. She stepped back until she was against the door. It closed, and she leaned against it, but he kept coming anyway, until he stood right before her. He didn't touch her, just laid his palm against the door by her head. "You're lying just a little, aren't you?" he whispered.

She shook her head, but suddenly she found that she could not speak, that her knees were liquid, that her palms were braced against the door so she could stand. He smelled of soap, of leather and rich pipe tobacco. His eyes were ebony coals, haunting her; his mouth was full and mobile.

"I could die a happy man if you would just whisper that you cared a little bit," he told her, the warmth of his breath creating a warm tempest against her skin while the tenor of his voice evoked a curious fire deep within her.

She kept her eyes steady and smiled sweetly. "I'm sure you say those words to every woman whose home you confiscate."

He smiled slowly. "Yours is the only home I have ever confiscated." He leaned closer. "And you've known for some time how I feel about you."

She wanted to shake her head again, but she discovered that she couldn't. His lips brushed hers, and then his mouth consumed hers as the roar within her soul came rushing up to drown out the rest of the world. She fell into his arms and felt the overwhelming masculine force of his lips parting and caressing her own; she felt the heady invasion of his tongue, so deep it seemed that he could possess all of her with the kiss alone. His hands, desperate, rough, massaged her skull, and his fingers threaded hungrily through her hair, holding her close. But she couldn't have left him. She had never known anything like that kiss, never known the world to spin in such delirious motion, never known the hunger to touch a man in return, to feel his hair, crisp and clean, beneath her fingers, to feel his body, his heat and his heartbeat throbbing ferociously against her breasts. The sweet, heady taste of his mouth left her thirsting for more and more, until sanity returned to her, some voice of reason screaming within her that he was the Yankee soldier who had taken over her home, a Yank who was leaving at last.

She pulled away from him, her fingers shaking as she brought them to her lips.

He watched her, his eyes dark and enigmatic, and sighed softly. His rueful smile touched his lips again. "Will you care if I come back, Isabelle?"

"You're a Yank. I hope you never come back," she told him. She wiped her mouth as if she could wipe away the memory of his kiss, then turned and hurriedly left the room.

But later, in her room, she lay on her bed and knew that she had fallen in love. Right or wrong, she was in love with him. In love with his eyes and his mouth and his voice... and with all the things he said. And he was riding away. Perhaps to die.

She rose when she heard the sergeant call out the orders, and she raced down the stairs two at a time. She forced herself to slow down and walk demurely out to the porch. There he was at the head of his troops, his magnificent plumed hat in place, sitting easily on his mount.

He saw her and rode closer, his horse prancing as he came near. He touched his hat in salute and waited.

"Well, I do hope that you don't ride away to get killed," she told him.

He smiled. "Not exactly a declaration of undying devotion, but I suppose it will have to do." He leaned closer to her. "I will not get killed, Isabelle. And I will be back."

She didn't answer him right away. She didn't remind him that she could hardly want him to come back, for if he did, it would mean that the Union was holding tight to large tracts of Virginia.

"As I said, I hope that you survive. And that is all."

His smile deepened as he dug his heels into his horse's flanks and rode hard for the front of his line.

Isabelle watched the troops until they were long gone.

* * *

News came to her in abundance as spring turned to summer. There was a horrible battle fought at Chancellorsville. The Union had over sixteen thousand troops killed, wounded or captured; the South lost over twelve thousand, and though the South was accepted to be the victor, she had received a crippling blow. Stonewall Jackson was mistakenly shot by one of his own men, and he died on May tenth from his wounds.

Isabelle prayed for more news. She volunteered for hospital duty again. She worked endless hours, fearful that every Confederate soldier might be one of her brothers, anxious that any Union soldier who fell into their hands might be Travis.

She was working in the hospital in July when news came through that a horrible battle had been fought in a little town in Pennsylvania called Gettysburg. The losses in human life were staggering. And General Lee and his Army of Northern Virginia were in retreat. Men whispered that it was the turning point of the war. The South was being brought to her knees.

Isabelle hurried home, anxious to hear about her brothers, anxious to hear about Travis. In town she waited endlessly for the lists of the dead, wounded and captured to come through, and when she was able to procure a sheet she eagerly sought out her brothers' names. When she did not find them, she thanked God in a silent prayer, wincing as she heard the horrible tears of those who had lost sons, fathers, lovers and brothers.

She swallowed tightly, wondering about Travis, and prayed that he had made it. Shaking, she drove her carriage home. And that night she admitted in her prayers that she loved Travis Aylwin, and that even if he was a Yankee, she wanted God to watch over him always.

* * *

In September she was busy picking the last of the summer vegetables from her small garden when she heard Peter calling to her anxiously. She came running around the house, wiping her hands on her apron. Peter was on the porch, anxiously pointing eastward. Isabelle shaded her eyes from the afternoon sun. Riders were coming. She could see them. Her heart began to beat faster. There were about twenty or thirty men on horseback. In Union blue.

Her heart thudded. Travis was alive!

But what if it was not Travis? What if it was some other Yankee who lacked Travis Aylwin's sense of right and wrong, even in the midst of war?

She turned toward the porch and raced up the steps, shoving Peter out of her way. At the end of the hallway she tore open the gun case and reached for her rifle. With trembling fingers she attempted to load it. A hand fell on her shoulder, and she screamed, spinning around.

"You're going to shoot me again? Damn, I didn't survive Chancellorsville and Gettysburg just to be shot by you, Isabelle!"

He was thin, very thin and gaunt, and yet his dark eyes were alive with fire. She started to move, and the gun rose with her movement. His eyes widened, and he grabbed it from her, sending it flying across the floor. Then he swept her into his arms and kissed her hard, and she couldn't begin to fight him, not until he eased her from his hold. He clutched her tightly to him, his fingers clenched around her upper arms. "Tell me that you missed me, Isabelle. Tell me that you're glad I'm alive!"

She swallowed hard. She was a Southerner. A Virginian. Her heart was alive, and it seemed that her breath had deserted her, but she could not surrender while the South fought on. She pulled away from him. "I'm glad you're alive, Yank, but I wish heartily that you were not here!"

She ran upstairs, where she paced her room while the Yankees settled in. When darkness fell, she listened to his footsteps in the room beside hers. She heard them come close to her door; she heard them retreat. Again and again.

It wasn't two weeks later that the Yankee rider came racing to the house. He slammed his way into the house, then hurried into the den with Travis. Isabelle came hurrying down the stairs, wondering what was happening. Men were rushing into her house, knocking glass from the windows, then taking up positions with their rifles at the ready. Travis came out of the den in time to see her at the foot of the stairway. "Isabelle, you've got to get down to the cellar."

"Why? What's happening?"

"Rebels. Clancy's brigade."

281

"Clancy's brigade?" she said, her face paling.

"Yes, Clancy's brigade," he repeated. "They're on their way here. They heard that Yanks were holding this house and the town, and they want a battle."

She was going to fall, she thought. She was too weak to stand.

"Isabelle, what is it?"

"Steven is with Clancy's brigade. My brother Steven."

She saw in his eyes that he felt her pain, but she saw, too, that at that moment he was in command of his men, that this was war, and that he had to fight to win. "You've got to get down to the cellar."

"No!"

Travis turned to the butler, who had just come on the scene. "Peter! Peter, I don't know who is going to win or lose here today, but I'll be damned if I'll let Isabelle become a casualty of this war! Get her downstairs."

Peter put his arm around her and rushed her toward the cellar stairs. Dazed, she let him force her down them.

When she heard the first cannon roar, she screamed and clapped her hands over her ears. Then the house shuddered, and she heard a burst of fire and shells, and the screams of horses and men. She never knew what goaded her, but she couldn't bear it, knowing that Steven was out there, bombarding his own house. She escaped Peter and hurried out, ducking as bullets whizzed through the open windows. She didn't know what she hoped to accomplish—of course she wanted the Confederates to win. But there was Private Darby with his freckles, crooked teeth and easy smile, and there was blood pouring out of his shoulder, and he looked as if he was in shock. Isabelle crawled swiftly to the window by his side, ripping at her petticoat, finding cloth to bind up his wound, to staunch the flow of his blood.

"Thank you, Miss Hinton, thank you," he told her over and over again. She stretched him out on the floor; then she heard Travis shouting her name in fury.

"Isabelle!" It was a roar. He came rushing over to her, spinning her away from the window, pressing her against the door. "You could be killed, you little fool!"

She didn't hear his words. She was looking out the window, and she wanted to scream. Steven, in his battered gold and gray, was coming nearer and nearer the house, sneaking toward the rear. He looked so close that she could almost reach out and touch him. Then he stiffened, and red blossomed all over the gray of his cavalry shirt, and he fell onto the grass.

"Steven!" She screamed her brother's name and jerked free of Travis to race toward one of the windows. She felt nothing as she slipped over the windowsill with its shattered glass. She knew no fear as she raced across the battle line to her brother's silent form. "Steven, oh, Steven!" she cried desperately.

"Get down!"

Travis was behind her, throwing himself on top of her, bringing her down to the ground. Bullets flew by them, lodging in the house, in the ground so very near them. "Fool! You'll get shot!"

"That's my brother, I will not go back into the house without him!"

"You have to!"

"He could die!"

"Get in the house! If you go, I'll bring him back. I swear it. By all that's holy, Isabelle, I have a chance! You have none!"

He rolled her away with a shove. Then, before she could protest, he was up himself, racing across the lawn to reach Steven. A Confederate soldier stood up, his sword raised for hand-to-hand combat. Travis was unprepared, and he fell with the man onto the verdant grass. Isabelle bit the back of her hand, repressing a sob. Then she saw Travis again, saw him reach Steven, saw him lift her brother and stagger toward the house.

When he neared it, several of his own men hurried out to meet him. Steven was carried in and set on the floor of the parlor. Isabelle fell beside him, ripping open his shirt, finding that the bullet had pierced his chest, frighteningly near his heart. She staunched the flow of blood, discovered that the bullet had passed cleanly through him and wrapped the wound, with her tears falling down her cheeks all the while. She realized suddenly that the sound of the battle had receded, that no more guns blazed, no more shouts or Rebel yells rose upon the air. She turned toward the doorway. Travis stood there, leaning in the door frame, watching her.

She moistened her lips. The Yanks had held their ground, but he had brought Steven to her. She owed him something. "Thank you," she told him stiffly.

He smiled his crooked smile, doffing his hat. "It was nothing, ma'am, nothing at all."

But then he suddenly staggered and keeled down hard on the floor, and she heard herself screaming as she saw the blood pouring forth from his chest.

* * *

Travis was going to live. The Yankee surgeon promised her that, although he had lost a good deal of blood, he was going to live. He was tough that way. Steven's injury was by far the worse of the two.

The Yank worked hard over her brother. And he seemed to be an enlightened man, using clean sponges for each man, washing his bloodied hands with regularity. She could not have asked for better care for her brother. The Yanks had morphine, and they kept him out of pain. They gave him their best.

But that night Steven died anyway. She held him in her arms as he breathed his last, and then she held him until dawn, sobbing. No one could draw her away from him.

She was only dimly aware, when morning dawned at last, that Travis was with her. In breeches and bare feet, his chest wrapped in bandages, and none too steady on his feet, he came to her. He curled his fingers over hers, and she slowly released her grip on the brother she had loved. He whispered to her, he soothed her, and she fell against his shoulder and allowed her tears to soak his bandage. Then she realized who was holding her, and she tried to pull away, slamming her fists against him. She didn't see him wince at the pain, and, indeed, it meant nothing to him. Though he had seen men die time and again in war, he'd had little opportunity to see what it did to the loved ones left behind.

And he loved Isabelle Hinton himself.

"Let go of me, Yankee!" she ordered him, but he didn't release her. And finally her sobs quieted. In time he lifted her into his arms, and carried her upstairs, where he laid her on her bed.

It was hours later when she awoke. And he was still with her. Bandaged and in his breeches, he stared out the window at the September fields where the war had come home. Where the blood of her brother still stained the grass.

"Travis?" she whispered, and tears welled in her eyes, because she wanted to believe that it had all been a dream, a nightmare. He came to her bedside, silent and grave. He stared into her eyes and found her hand, squeezing her fingers. "I'm sorry, so very sorry, Isabelle. I know you would have rather it had been me, but I swear that we tried—"

"Oh, God, Travis, don't say that, please! I—" She broke off, shaking her head. Her tears were very close to falling again; she felt that she had been destroyed in those moments when Steven had breathed his last. "Thank you," she said primly. "I know how hard you tried to save him. And you—you shouldn't be up. You're wounded yourself." Indeed, he seemed drawn and weary and haggard, and he had aged years in the months since he had been gone.

"I'm all right," he told her.

She nodded slowly. "So am I," she whispered.

286

"I'm always here if you need me."

"I *can't* need you!" she whispered.

He inhaled deeply, but he released her hand, turned and left her.

That afternoon they buried Steven. They stood by his grave, and the chaplain said that he had been a brave soldier, fighting for what he believed. Then Travis ordered that the musicians play "Dixie." Isabelle wasn't going to cry again, but she did. Then she ran away from the gravesite and retired to her room. She spoke to no one for days. Peter brought her food on a tray, but she ate very little of it.

Steven had been dead for almost two weeks when a sharp tap on her door and then a thundering brought her from her lethargy. She swung the door open, furious that her privacy was being abused, but when she would have protested she fell silent instead. It was Dr. Allen Whaley, the surgeon who had tried so hard to save Steven. He looked grave and worried.

"The captain is dying, Miss Hinton. I thought you should know."

"What?" she gasped incredulously. "But he was fine! I saw him. He was fine, he was—"

"He shouldn't have been up. He lost more blood, and he courted infection. Now he's burning up with fever."

Isabelle raced to the door connecting her room to Travis's. She thrust it open and raced to his bedside.

He was burning up. The bandage around his chest had been curtailed to cover just the wound, and the flesh all around it was slick and hot. Sergeant Sikes had been sitting by him, ineffectually dabbing at his flesh with a wet cloth.

"Up, Sergeant!" Isabelle ordered quickly. She took over the task of soothing Travis's forehead and face with cool water. She touched his wrist and felt for his pulse. She flinched from the fire of his skin and glanced toward Doctor Whaley, who nodded his approval of anything she might try. She bathed Travis from his waist to his throat with the cool water. She began to talk to him, and she talked until she was hoarse.

Later Doctor Whaley came and they rebandaged the wound. The doctor lanced it, and they drained the infection, then wrapped it again. And still his fever burned on.

"Tonight will tell," Doctor Whaley told her. "If you would pray for a Yank, Miss Hinton, pray for this one tonight."

She tried to pray, and she kept moving. She soaked him again and again, trying to cool him. She wiped his forehead and his cheeks; she saw where the war had engraved lines around his eyes, and she thought of how dearly she loved his fascinating, handsome face. If he died, he would have died for her, she realized. She had wanted Steven. He had gone for Steven for her.

"Don't die, don't die, damn you! I—I need you!" she whispered fervently to him.

It couldn't have been her whisper. It really couldn't have been. But he inhaled suddenly, a great ragged breath, and then he went so still that she thought he had died. She laid her ear against his chest and heard his even breathing. She touched his flesh, and it was perceptibly cooler. She started to laugh as she sank into the chair by his bedside. "Oh, my God, he is better!" She breathed the words aloud.

And then Doctor Whaley was by her side, lifting her up. "Yes, he's better, Miss Hinton. And now you'd best get some rest before you fall apart on us!"

He led her away, and when she slept that night, she slept soundly, a smile curing her lips for the first time since Steven had died. There *was* a God in heaven; Travis had lived.

* * *

He stayed in bed for a week before he summoned sufficient strength to stand. Isabelle kept her distance from him, not trusting herself with him anymore.

She heard him, though, the day he first rose. He shouted now and then when one of his men seemed to think he needed more help getting around than he did. His soldiers walked around that day with pleased grins, ignoring his tone. They were just glad to have him up.

Isabelle wanted to see him, but she couldn't bring herself to do so. She avoided the dining room; she avoided his office. She was afraid of getting too close to him.

November faded away. December came, and Isabelle made her plans to leave for Christmas. She was packing when she realized that someone was watching her from the open doorway.

That someone was Travis.

He was completely healed now. He was still gaunt, but his features were so striking that his thinness only accentuated the clean lines of his face. His eyes followed her every step, and wherever they fell, she was touched with warmth, with fire. He was striking in blue wool breeches, his high boots and regulation cavalry shirt, his officer's insignia upon his shoulder. "What are you doing?" he asked her.

"Packing."

"Why?"

"I'm leaving for Christmas."

"Why?"

"Because it is not a holiday to be spent with the enemy."

"I am not your enemy, Isabelle."

She shrugged and kept packing.

He slammed the door shut and strode across the room, catching her by the shoulders, wrenching her from her task. His eyes bored into her like ebony daggers.

"Let me go!" she cried.

"Why, Isabelle?"

"Because, because—"

"No!" he cried, and he tossed her leather portmanteau to the floor, bearing her down upon the bed. His fingers curled around hers, holding her hands high over her head.

"Travis, damn you!"

"I need you, Isabelle. I need you!"

She wanted to fight him. She wanted to deny everything that had happened, everything she felt, but then she thought that perhaps it had always been coming to this, from the very first, when they had fallen together to the snow. She opened her mouth to swear, to protest, but his whisper was already entering her mouth.

"I need you, Isabelle, my God, I need you!"

Then his lips were on hers, his kiss fervent, building a fire within her. He whispered against her mouth, and his lips burned a fiery trail across her cheeks, to her throat, against her earlobe, then back to her mouth again. His tongue teased her lips, then delved between them.

She wrapped her arms around him, her fingers burrowing into his hair, and she came alive, rejoicing in the feel of his hair, in the ripple of the muscles in his shoulders and back. She wasn't sure when it happened, but it seemed that his shirt melted away, and she was torn between laughter and tears when her hands moved across his bare flesh, luxuriating in the warmth of him, in the feel of life. She touched the scars where war had torn his flesh, and she placed her lips against them as tenderly as possible. But after that few things were tender, as the tempest flared between them with a sudden swirling desperation. Her bodice had somehow come undone, and his face lay buried against the valley between her breasts. And then he was taking one into his mouth, his lips and teeth warm upon one pebbled, rosy peak, and the sensation was shattering, sending tremors of fire and yearning through her. She gasped, clinging to him, then she gasped again as she felt his hands upon her naked hips, then between her thighs. She moaned, closing her eyes, shuddering and breathing deeply against his neck as his touch became bold and intimate, stroking, delving, evoking need and searing heat and molten pleasure...

His breeches were shed; her gown was a pile of tangled froth around them; his features were both hard and tender as he rose above her. He gently pulled and tugged away the tangle of her clothing until she lay naked and shivering beneath him. And yet she trusted him, the enemy; he saw it in her eyes. He laid his head against her breasts, then he shuddered with a frightening force. "My God, I've needed you, Isabelle. I may be your enemy, but no enemy will ever love you so tenderly. No friend could swear with greater fervor to be so gentle."

She cried out, finding his lips, drowning in his kiss. As they kissed, his hands traveled the length of her. He touched and stroked her endlessly, boldly, intimately.

And gently, tenderly.

Finally passion rose swiftly, wantonly, within her. Desire had bloomed so completely and surely in her that she knew nothing of distress or pain, and everything of the driving, blinding beauty of being taken by a man who gave her love. She knew the fury of his passion and the wealth of his rapture as he brought her to a peak of ecstasy so sweet that it was heaven on earth before he shuddered violently and fell beside her, the two of them covered in the fine sheen of their own sweat.

They were silent for the longest time. Then he reached out and touched a curl against the dampness of her cheek. "I'm sorry, Isabelle, I had no right...."

She caught his hand. "No! Shh. Please don't say such things, not now!"

He rolled over, stroked her cheek and stared unabashedly at the rise and fall of her breasts. "I love you, you know."

"No! Don't say that, either!"

She tugged away from him, trembling as she reached for her clothing.

"Isabelle," he said, rising, trying to stop her.

She didn't know why she was so upset. She wanted him—she had wanted him desperately! And she loved him, too.

But there was a war on.

"Travis, leave me alone. Please."

"Isabelle, I didn't—"

"No, Travis, you didn't force me. You didn't do anything wrong. You were—you were the perfect gentleman! But please, leave me alone now. I have to be alone."

He turned angrily and jerked on his shirt and breeches, then his boots. "I'll expect you at dinner tonight," he told her.

She watched him leave, then she washed and dressed and finished her packing. She walked down the stairs and into his office.

"I want to leave for Christmas, Captain," she told him.

He stood up, staring at her across the desk. "Don't leave, Isabelle."

"It's war, Captain."

"Not between us."

"I can't stay! Don't you understand? I can't spend Christmas with the enemy!"

"Even if you sleep with him?"

She slapped him. He didn't make a move, and she bit her lip, wishing she hadn't struck him. She didn't know what she was doing to either of them anyway. It was just that the sound of Christmas carols made her cry now. She wanted so badly to be home for Christmas, but she didn't know where home was anymore.

"I'll write you a pass immediately," he said curtly. "Sergeant Sikes will see to you."

"Thank you."

He scratched out the pass and handed it to her, then looked at the work piled on his desk.

Isabelle turned and headed for the door, then hesitated. She wanted to cry out to him; she wanted to run back.

But she couldn't. Something deep inside her told her that it just wasn't right. She might be in love with the enemy, but it was still wrong to spend Christmas with him.

Chapter 3

Isabelle spent Christmas and New Year's Day with Katie Holloway. Katie's place was an old farmstead, and Katie was as solid and rugged as the terrain that surrounded her. She had watched the British siege of Fort McHenry during the War of 1812, and she had lived long enough to say and do and think what she wanted.

"It's dying down now, mind you, Isabelle. This war, it's almost over."

"That's not true! Our generals run circles around theirs. Time and time again we've won the day with far less troops and—"

Rocking in her chair, Katie clicked her knitting needles and exhaled slowly. "When our men die, there's none left to replace them. Aye, we fight fine battles! None will ever forget the likes of Stonewall Jackson. But he and many of his kind are gone now, cut down like flowers in the spring, and we cannot go on without them. Not even Lee can fight this war alone. It's over. All over except for the dying."

Isabelle didn't feel like arguing with Katie; she just felt like crying. She didn't know how life would change when it was all over; she only knew that she had seen enough of it, and she was ready for it to end. She had buried one brother; she wanted the other to live.

She wanted Travis to live.

"I think I'm going to go home tomorrow," she told Katie. It was late January, the snow was piled high, and she wasn't supposed to go home alone. Sergeant Sikes or one of the men came by every couple of days to see if she was ready to leave. No one was due for a few days—she had been determined to say that she wasn't going back. Not until the snows melted. Not until the men went to war again.

But now, suddenly, she didn't want them to go to war. She didn't want *Travis* to go to war.

She hopped up and kissed Katie's weathered cheek, then she hurried into the bedroom to do her packing.

It was the end of January, and not even high noon brought much warmth. Despite Katie's protests that she shouldn't travel alone, Isabelle was going to ride home.

"You should wait for an escort! Captain Aylwin is not going to be pleased."

"Well, Katie, they haven't won the war yet. I can still do as I please," she assured her friend.

She mounted her bay mare and drew her cloak warmly around her. She determined not to go through town—there were too many Yankee soldiers she didn't know there. So she headed east, past small farms and decaying mansions. Everything was winter bleak, and her mare snorted against the cold, filling the air with the mist of her breath. Trees were bare, and the landscape was barren. It was always like this during winter, she told herself. But it wasn't. It was this barren because of the war.

She had ridden for an hour when she came upon the deserted Winslow farm. Thirsty and worried about her mare, she decided to stop to see if the trough had frozen over. She dismounted into the high drifts and led the mare toward the trough. She sighed with relief, because the water had only a thin layer of ice over it. She broke through with the heel of her boot, then patted the mare as she dipped her head to drink. Then she heard a noise behind her and turned around.

A soldier had come out to the porch. He was dressed in ragged gray and butternut, his beard was overgrown, and his eyes were hard and hostile and bleary. At first her heart had soared—one of her own. But as the man leered at her the sensation of elation turned to one of dread. She knew instantly that he was a deserter, and he was here hiding from the Confederates and the Yanks.

She pulled the reins around swiftly, ready to mount, but to no avail. The man threw himself against her, dragging her down into the snow. She pounded her fists against him desperately, and her screams tore the air, but neither had any effect on him. His breath was horrible and rancid, he was filthier than she had ever imagined a man could be, and the scent of him terrified her beyond measure. She knew what he intended, and she thought wildly that she really might rather die than let him touch her. But she was unarmed; she'd had no reason to travel with a weapon—Travis had always seen to her safety.

And now she was alone.

"Hey, ma'am, I'm just looking for some good old southern hospitality!" he taunted.

She freed a hand and smashed at his face. A hard noise assured her that she had hurt him. She took the advantage and kneed him in the groin with all her strength. He screamed with the pain, but took hold of her hair and wrenched her to her feet, then dragged her toward the house. She started screaming again, but it didn't matter; he dragged her up the stairs and through the doorway. A fire was burning in the open hearth, and he tossed her down before it. She tried to scramble up, but he pounced on her. She twisted her face, frantic with fear, when he tried to kiss her.

Then, suddenly, the man was wrenched away from her and tossed hard across the room. Travis was there. Travis, in his winter cape, his dark eyes burning with an ebony fury. As Isabelle scrambled away, she saw the Rebel deserter draw his pistol. "Travis!" she shrieked in warning. She heard an explosion of fire, but Travis did not fall. A crimson stain spread across her attacker's shirt, and she realized that Travis, too, had pulled a pistol. He wasted little time on pity for the Reb but strode quickly to Isabelle, jerking her to her feet.

"What were you doing out alone?" he demanded.

"I was coming home."

His hands were on her. He was shaking; he was shaking her. "Fool!" he exploded, and he wrenched his hands away from her, turning his back on her. She wanted to thank him; she wanted to tell him that she was grateful he had come. She even wanted to cry out that she loved him, but she couldn't. He was the enemy.

"Thank God I decided to come for you myself this morning! Damn it, Isabelle, don't you know what could have happened? He could have raped you and slit your throat and left you in the snow, and we wouldn't even have known it!"

She moistened her lips. She couldn't tell him that she had been anxious to come home because she had been anxious to see him. He caught her arm and pulled her along with him—until they got outside. Then he lifted her up on her mare before mounting his own horse, and they started off in silence. The silence held until they reached the house, where he dismounted and came over to her before she could get down herself. He lifted her down, his hands fevered and strong. Her hair tumbled in reckless curls around her face, golden beneath the sun. "What?" he asked suddenly, angry. "Are you upset that I killed the Reb? He was one of your own, right? A good old Southern boy!"

"Of course not!"

"Friend or enemy, is that it, Isabelle? And am I forever damned as the enemy?" His eyes were alive with fire, and his fingers were biting into her upper arms.

"What do you want from me?" she cried.

His grip relaxed slightly, and a slow, bitter smile just curved the corners of his lips. "Christmas," he told her quietly. "I want Christmas."

And suddenly Christmas was everything—everything he wanted and everything she could not give. She pulled herself from his arms and ran into the house.

* * *

Travis damned himself a thousand times for the way he had handled things. But finding her in the arms of that deserter had scared him to the bone, and he trembled to think that he would not have been there if he hadn't determined that morning to go to Mrs. Holloway's himself and bring her back.

And he had done that only because his orders had come. They were pulling out again. He was to lead his men to ride with Sheridan. Grant was in charge on the Eastern front now, determined to cage the wily Lee, whatever the cost. Grant knew that the other Union generals had been overmatched by Lee's abilities—and overawed by his reputation.

He had only a few days remaining to him here. Right or wrong, he was in love with her, and after the endless months of torture, he had found that she was not all ice and reserve, but that she could be fire and passion as well. He wanted a taste of that fire upon his lips when he rode away again.

But it was lost now, he thought.

He sat in the dining room alone, waiting for Peter to serve him. But then he grew impatient with himself, with her. He slid from the table and strode up the stairs to his room, and, once there, he burst through the connecting doorway.

He paused sharply, for he had found her this way once before. She was cocooned in a froth of bubbles, one slender leg protruding from the water as she furiously soaped it. Her eyes met his as he entered the room, and a crimson flush rose to her cheeks. But she didn't deny his presence, and she even smiled softly. "I was coming to dinner," she said quietly. She bit her lower lip. "It's just that I felt so... dirty after today."

Golden-blond ringlets were piled on top of her head, some escaping to dangle softly against her cheeks and the long column of her neck. He had no answer for her other than a hoarse cry and the long strides that brought him to her. He didn't reach for her lips, but paused at the base of the bath, smiling ruefully as he dropped to his knees, then caught the small foot that thrust from the bubbles, and kissed the arch, teasing the sweet, clean flesh with the touch of his tongue. His eyes met hers, which were shimmering with mist and beauty, and he heard the sharp intake of her breath. Her lashes half fell, sensual, inviting. Her lips parted, and still her gaze remained upon him. He stroked his fingers along her calf, soaking his shirt as he leaned into the water, but he didn't care. Brazenly he swept his hand along her thigh. Then he lifted her, dripping and soap-sleek, from the tub. He held her in front of the fire, kissing her, before he walked with her to the bed, cast aside his sodden shirt and breeches and leaned down over her.

No woman had ever smelled so sweet; no skin had ever felt so much like pure silk. She was the most beautiful thing he had ever imagined, with her high firm breasts, slender waist, undulating hips. He kissed her everywhere, ignoring her cries, drinking in the sight and taste and sound of her, needing more and more of her.

That night she dared to love him in return, stroking her nails down his chest, dazzling him with her fingertips. Dinner was forgotten. The night lingered forever. He didn't leave her, didn't even think to rise until the sun came in full upon them and he heard a knocking at his own door.

He kissed her sweetly parted lips and rose. Scrambling into his breeches and boots, he hurried to his own room and opened his door.

There was a messenger there from Sheridan, Sikes told him. He was needed downstairs right away.

He found a clean shirt and hurried down the stairs, where he closeted himself with the cavalry scout and received the latest news.

He had only until the fourteenth of February to meet up with other troops north of Richmond.

* * *

Isabelle came down later. She wore her reserve again, as another woman might wear a cloak. "You're leaving?" she asked coldly, sitting down across from him.

"Soon."

Her fingers curled around her chair, her lashes lowered. He rose and came to stand before her, then knelt down, taking her hands. "Marry me, Isabelle."

"Marry you!" Her eyes widened incredulously. Gray-green, brilliant against the soft beauty of her face, they were filled with disbelief.

"I love you. I would die for you. You know that."

She swallowed painfully, then shook her head. "It's not over yet. I can't marry you."

"Isabelle, you love me, too," he told her.

She shook her head again. "No. No, I don't." She paused for a second, and he sensed the tears behind her voice. "I *cannot* love a Yankee. Don't you understand?"

She leaped up and was gone. She didn't come down to dinner, and he wouldn't go to her. He ate alone, then drank a brandy, before he finally dashed the glass into the fire and took the stairs two at a time. He burst in upon her and found her clad in a soft white nightgown of silk and lace, a sheer gown, one that clung to the exquisite perfection of her form. She was pacing before the fire, but when she saw him, she paused. He strode over to her, wrenching her into his arms, shaking her slightly so that her hair fell in a cascade down her back, and her eyes rose challengingly to his. "If you can't marry me," he said bitterly, "and you can't love me, then come to bed with me and believe that I, at least, love you!"

At first he thought she would lash out at him in fury. He bent over, tossing her over his shoulder, and the two of them fell together onto the bed. Her eyes were flashing, but she only brushed his cheek gently with her palm.

"I cannot love you, Yank!" she whispered. But her lips teased his, her breath sweet with mint, and her body was a fire beneath him. Her mouth moved against his. "But I *can* need you, and I need you very much tonight!"

* * *

It remained like that between them for the days that remained. By day she kept her distance, the cool and dignified Miss Hinton, but by night she was his, creating dreams of paradise.

But neither paradise nor dreams could still the war, and in due course he rode out for his appointment with battle. She stood on the porch and watched him as he mounted his horse. And then, as he had before, he rode as close as he could to where she was standing on the porch.

"I love you," he reminded her gravely.

"Don't get yourself killed, Travis," she told him. He nodded and started away.

She called him back. "Travis!"

He turned. She hesitated, then whispered, "I'll pray for you."

He smiled and nodded again, then rode away. The war awaited him.

* * *

They said that the South had been losing the war since Gettysburg, but you couldn't tell it by the way they were fighting, Travis thought later.

At the end of February, when Travis was joining up with Sheridan's forces, General Kilpatrick staged an ill-conceived raid on Richmond. Papers found on the body of Colonel Dahlgreen indicated an intention to burn the city and assassinate President Jefferson Davis and his cabinet. Meade, questioned by Lee under a flag of truce, denied such intentions vigorously, and Lee accepted that the papers were forgeries. Travis was glad to hear that both sides could question something so heinous, and that even in the midst of warfare, some things could be discussed.

In May, Travis and his troops were engaged in the Battle of the Wilderness, which would stand out in his memory forever. Rebels and Yanks alike were caught, confused and horrified, in the depths of the forest. Soon the trees were ablaze, and more men died from the smoke and fire than from bullets.

From there the survivors moved to the Battle of Spotsylvania. Next Travis followed Sheridan into the Battle of Yellow Tavern, where the cavalry, ten thousand strong, met up with Stuart's southern troops on the outskirts of Richmond. Stuart brought over four thousand men, and the fighting was pitched and desperate, but Travis managed to survive. The great Confederate cavalryman Jeb Stuart was mortally wounded, however. He died in Richmond days later.

Late in June, Isabelle became aware of a man approaching the house on foot. She was upstairs in her room, and she watched from the window. She bit her lower lip, perplexed. He wore a gray uniform, but she couldn't trust Confederate soldiers anymore, not after what had occurred on her journey home from Katie's.

Travis had given her one of the new repeating rifles, and she hurried downstairs to the gun cabinet to get it. She loaded the gun and hurried to the window, but her worry fell away when she saw the man coming closer. With a glad cry she set the gun down and raced outside, flinging herself into the mart's arms. It was her brother, James.

"Oh, my God, you're home!" She kissed him, and he hugged her and swung her around, and she laughed, and then she cried. And then they were in the house, and Peter was there, and the other servants, too, all eager to welcome him home. He only had a few days' leave; he was a lieutenant in the artillery, and he had been lucky to receive even that much time.

Isabelle was determined to make his time at home perfect. She ordered him a steaming bath, dug out his clothes, supervised dinner, and when he was dressed and downstairs again, she was ready to sit with him for a meal of venison stew. He smiled at her, a very grave young man with her own curious colored eyes, slightly darker hair and, now, freshly shaven cheeks. He started to eat hungrily, as if he hadn't seen such a meal in years. Then he suddenly threw down his fork and stared at her, his eyes filled with naked fury.

"This is Yank stew!"

Isabelle bolted back in her chair, sitting very straight. She stared at her hands.

James stood, walking around the room behind her. "I just realized what this means. The house is standing, and there's food in it. What did you pay for those concessions, Isabelle?"

She gasped and leaped to her feet. "I didn't pay anything for concessions!" Guilt tore at her, but she had never paid for anything. She was protected, yes, but she had never paid for that protection. She had simply fallen in love. "They use the house as their headquarters—that's why it's still standing. And there's food in the larder because they bring it in, for their own use, and ours, too."

"And you stay here!" he accused, his hands on his hips.

"I stay here, you fool, for you and Steven! I stay so that they won't burn the house down around us. I've even taken the Yankee dollars Sergeant Sikes gives me as rent, and I've stowed them away to keep this place alive so that you and... and Steven would have a home to come back to!"

He strode from the dining room, down the hall and into the den. With a fury he pushed Travis's papers from their father's desk. Something fluttered to his feet, and he bent to pick it up. It was a record of her safe conduct form to the Holloway home for Christmas. He stared from the form to Isabelle. "What is this?"

"Safe conduct. I—I always leave for Christmas."

Suddenly he started to laugh, but she didn't like the sound of it. "Oh, this is rich! You play the whore all year, but then you leave for Christmas! Oh, Isabelle!"

She itched to slap his face, but he was too gaunt from all he'd been through, and besides, she felt the horrible truth of his words. She turned, a sob tearing from her, and raced up the stairs. She burst into her room, where she lay on her bed and sobbed. It was odd, she thought. It was Christmas she was suddenly crying for, and not the war, the death, the pain. It was the peace of the holiday that had been lost, the peace and the gentle dreams, and the belief that man could rise above his sins.

Her door opened. James came in and sat beside her on the bed, then scooped her into his arms. "I'm sorry, Isabelle. I'm so sorry. The war has warped me. I know you, Isabelle. You're the sister who bathed all my cuts and bruises when I thought I was too big for my friends to see me cry. The one who stood by our parents. The one, Peter tells me, who ran out in the midst of a barrage of bullets to reach Steven. Isabelle, I love you. If some Yank has kept you safe, then I'm glad. Can you forgive me?"

She hugged him tight, because no words were necessary between them. Then they went down to their cold dinner, and when they had eaten, Isabelle took him out to Steven's grave, and she told him how odd it had been to hear Yankee musicians playing "Dixie."

He slipped his arm around her, then gave a silent salute to Steven before they walked to the house together.

Over the next few days he drew her out. He listened to the accounts of his brother's death, and he listened when she haltingly told him about the deserter who had attacked her. He also listened to her talk about Travis. He gave her no advice, only warned her, "Isabelle, you're in love with him."

She shook her head, watching the fire. "Even now he could be dead. He's fighting somewhere south of here." She swallowed. It was the front that James would soon return to.

James leaned toward her. "You *are* in love with him. And it sounds like he loves you."

"He is still the enemy."

"Will he marry you?"

"James, I cannot marry the enemy!"

"The war can't go on forever, even if it seems so. But it has taught me that life and love are sweet, and too easily stolen from us before we can touch them."

James left the next day. She forced herself to smile as she buttoned his coat and set his hat on his head. "You'll be home soon for good!" she told him.

He smiled. "Yes, I promise. I promise I'll come home for good." He kissed her cheek, and she walked him as far as the porch. He had to go a few miles on foot, since he was in Yankee territory. Somewhere to the south he would be picked up by a transport wagon. Horses were rare now, and he refused to take her mare. "They'll just kill her down there, Isabelle. Let her survive this thing. I may need her when I come back!"

She hugged him one last time, fiercely, and then he started out. She watched him from the porch, and he suddenly turned around. "Isabelle, don't marry him, if you feel you can't. But give him Christmas. He deserves Christmas."

Then he walked away, and she prayed that the war would soon be over. She assured God that she really didn't care in the least if the Yankees won, just so long as someone ended the damn thing.

* * *

The battles were fought fast and furiously on the eastern front as summer progressed. Women were desperately needed to nurse the wounded, and Isabelle found transport south to the outskirts of Cedar Creek, where an old church was being used as a field hospital. A horrible battle had been fought on October nineteenth. The South had nearly taken the day, but in the end the Union had prevailed.

Rebels and Yankees both were being brought in, and Isabelle was grateful to see that no injured man was being left on the field.

Still, each time she saw a blue coat with a cavalry-red stripe on it, her heart sank. Travis had ridden away to join Sheridan, and Sheridan's men had won this battle. Had Travis, too, ridden victoriously away?

At last she discovered that he had not, for she turned to a sheeted form one afternoon to discover it was Travis.

His face was as white as death, and he was barely breathing. She ripped open his uniform to discover that a saber had savagely slashed his side.

Isabelle turned to search out one of the surgeons. She wanted Dr. Hardy, a man with a keen belief in hygiene. If the wound didn't kill Travis, infection might.

"His pulse is good, his breathing is steady and, so far, no fever," Dr. Hardy told her a little while later. "Keep his wound clean, and he should make it."

She did as he'd said. She was careful to tend to all the men, but she reserved time daily to wash and rebandage Travis's wound.

On the third day he opened his eyes. He stared at her incredulously; then his eyes fell shut again. The effort to hold them open was too much. "Water," he croaked.

She dampened his parched lips, warning him not to drink too quickly. He managed to open his eyes again, and she tried not to smile. Despite his long hair, he was still so handsome. His dark eyes filled with dismay when he realized that he was in a Confederate hospital.

"You might as well let me die," he told her.

"Don't talk like that."

"Andersonville *is* death," he reminded her sharply, and a cold dread filled her heart, because rumor said it was true, that Union soldiers died like flies in the Confederate prison camp.

"You're far too ill to be sent to Andersonville now," she told him, then moved away.

The next morning she was dismayed to find that Travis had stirred an interest among the Southern women helping out as nurses. She was unable to find him alone. If he was going to get that much care, she decided, she was going to keep her distance.

He healed more quickly than anyone had expected. Two weeks after his arrival, she was making the bed beside his when his fingers suddenly clamped around her wrist, and he pulled her to face him.

"What are you doing here?" he demanded sharply of her.

Her brows arched. "Helping!" she snapped.

He shook his head. "You should be home. Oh... I see. You want to find your brother."

"My brother is well, thank you very much. He was home on leave during the summer." She pulled away. "Perhaps I was looking for you, Captain," she told him quietly. Then she left him. It was becoming altogether too disturbing to cope with him.

She didn't have to cope with him much longer. Three days later, when she came in, he was gone. Trembling with raw panic, she asked Dr. Hardy what had happened to him.

"The Yank? Oh, he's gone."

"Andersonville?" she whispered in horror.

Hardy shook his head, watching her closely. "He escaped. Not that we have many men to watch the prisoners around here. He just slipped away in the night."

Three days later Dr. Hardy called her, and when she turned, he took her by her arm and led her outside. She held her breath, terrified that he was going to tell her that Travis had been shot during his attempt to escape.

But Hardy hadn't called her about Travis. He cleared his throat and squeezed her hand as they walked along the barren meadow. "Isabelle, Lieutenant James Hinton is on our list as a prisoner of war. He was taken at Petersburg."

"No!" She screamed the word, then sank to the ground, denying Hardy's news with everything in her. She wanted to scream, to keep screaming, to make the words go away.

Hardy knelt beside her. "Isabelle, listen—"

She didn't listen. She grabbed his arm. "Was he injured? Are they taking him west? Do you—"

"He wasn't injured, he was just forced by overwhelming odds to surrender. And he's being taken to Washington. Isabelle, he's alive! And well. He'll probably even be able to write to you. Isabelle, many men died at Petersburg! Be grateful that he's alive. He might be better off in that Yankee prison. He might have Christmas dinner."

She tried to smile, tried to believe Hardy.

Two weeks later, December was upon them and the place was just about cleared out. The injured men had been sent home to recuperate, or back to the battlefield, or they had died.

312

Hardy called Isabelle into his makeshift office and handed her a sealed document. She looked at him. "You're going home, Isabelle. Confederate soldiers will escort you to the Union line. That letter should give you safe conduct. You need to go home. The war is digging in for winter. I'm moving on to Petersburg."

He stood and kissed both her cheeks. "Merry Christmas, Isabelle."

She kissed him in return. "Merry Christmas."

He smiled and slipped something from his pocket, then handed it to her. "I was afraid you wouldn't think it was a very merry Christmas. I just received that letter two hours ago. It's for you. From your brother, James. He'd heard that the Yanks were in and out of the house, so he wrote through me."

She stared at him, then ripped open the letter, tears stinging her eyes. He was alive; he was eating; he was lucky, considering what could have happened to him.

He ended his letter with a command: "Merry Christmas, Sister! Have faith in the Father, and who knows, perhaps next Christmas will bring us all together again."

She kissed Dr. Hardy again, then she ran out, pressing the letter to her heart.

* * *

As Dr. Hardy had promised, she was escorted to the Yankee line by two cavalry soldiers; then her papers were handed over, and she was given an escort through the lines to her doorstep. She had worried the whole way about Travis. He must have been weak after his ordeal; he hadn't been strong enough to return to battle. She hoped fervently that he would be there when she reached home.

He was.

Travis was waiting for her on the porch. The Yankee sergeant with her papers saluted him sharply and respectfully, and said that he had brought Miss Hinton home at the Union's command, and that he needed permission to return to his own unit. Travis quickly granted him permission, saluting in return. He stood tall and straight as he watched Isabelle dismount, then ordered one of his men to take her horse. When she walked up the steps, she saw that his eyes were alight with a pleasure that belied his solemn features.

She walked past him and entered the parlor, shedding her worn travel cloak and hat and tossing them on a chair. Seconds later Travis was behind her, pulling her against him, pressing his lips to her throat, whispering things that were entirely incoherent.

She turned, ready to protest, ready to reproach him, but no words would come. She didn't give a damn who was in the house, who saw what, or what they might think. Not at that moment. She wrapped her arms around his neck, and he swept her into his arms, then carried her into the huge master suite that he'd claimed as his own. A fire was burning in the hearth, hot and blazing. Darkness was falling, but the fire filled the room with a spellbinding glow. Travis laid her down on the bed, his fingers shaking as he removed her clothing. Then he shed his own and straddled her, and the loving began.

The fire cast its glow over them as the night passed. In that curious light he was sleek and coppery, and she couldn't keep her lips from his skin or her fingers from dancing over his rippling muscles. More scars were etched now across his flesh, and she touched them gently, kissed them with tenderness. She had wanted him so badly, and now he was hers. Right or wrong, she loved the enemy.

When morning came, Isabelle made no pretense of denial. She kissed him eagerly by the light of day, met his eyes openly, honestly, and smiled at his hoarse cry as she was swept into the ardent rhythm of his love-making.

She dined with him that evening. He told her about the battles, about Wilderness, about Cold Harbor, Chancellorsville. There was so much sadness in him. She kept a tight rein on her own emotions as she told him that James had been taken prisoner at Petersburg, but that she had heard he was in Washington, not Camp Douglas, in Chicago, which the Rebs feared so greatly.

Two nights later the men started playing Christmas carols. They came in and used the piano, and they played their sad harmonicas. She felt for them, for their longing to go home.

She didn't run away when they sang, and when Sergeant Sikes prodded her, she even rose to sing herself. To the tune of "Greensleeves" she sang about the Christ child's birth, and when she was done, the room was silent and still, and the eyes of every man in the place were on her. At last Sikes cleared his throat, and Private Trent laughed and said that he had made a wreath, and he went out and brought it in. She told them that they could find the household decorations in the attic, and they raced up to bring them down. Soon the place looked and smelled and glowed of Christmas.

Travis, who had watched her from beside the fire, turned and left the room. She heard his footsteps on the stairs.

Rising, she determined to follow him.

He was in the room they shared, staring down at the half-packed portmanteau she had set in one corner. She stared at him in silence as his eyes challenged hers.

"You're leaving again?"

"Yes."

He walked across the room to her, pinning her against the door, his palms flat against the wood on either side of her head. He searched her eyes for a moment, then walked away to stand in front of the fire, his hands clasped behind his back.

"There's something for you on the table," he told her.

"What is it?"

"Go see for yourself."

She hesitated, then walked across the room to the round oak table by the window. There was an official-looking document there wrapped in vellum and red ribbon.

"Travis...?"

"Open it," he commanded.

She did so, her fingers shaking. There was a lot of official language that she read over quickly and in confusion, and then she saw her brother's name. Lieutenant James L. Hinton. She kept reading, trying to make sense of the legal terms and the fancy handwriting. Then she realized that James was to be exchanged for another prisoner, that he was going to be sent home.

She cried out and stared at Travis. She didn't know *how* he had arranged it, only that he had. She started to run toward him, then she stopped, her heart hammering.

"Oh, Travis! You did this!"

He nodded solemnly. "Merry Christmas. You never let me give you a gift. This year I thought you might."

"Oh, Travis!" she repeated; then she raced into his arms. He kissed her, and it was long and deep, and as hot and glowing as the fire. Breathless, she pressed her lips against his throat. "Travis, it's the most wonderful gift in the world, but I have nothing for you. I would give you anything—"

"Then marry me."

She was silent. She saw the fever in his dark eyes, the shattering intensity.

"I—I can't," she said.

Disappointment banked the ebony fires. His jaw hardened, and she could hear the grating of his teeth. "And tomorrow afternoon you will come down to the office as if we were perfect strangers, and you will ask my blessing to leave."

"Travis..."

"Damn you! Damn you a thousand times over, Isabelle!" He turned away from her.

"Travis!" she called again, and he turned to her.

He stared at her for several agonizing seconds, and then his long strides brought him to her, and he wrenched her hard into his arms. His kiss was laced with force and fury, and his hands were less than tender as he touched her. She didn't care. She met his fury.

"Isabelle!" Her name tore from him raggedly as his fingers threaded into her hair. In the end, the loving was sweet, agonizingly sweet, and accompanied by whispers that he loved her.

Lying with her back to him, she repeated the words in silence. *I love you.* But the war was still on; he was still the enemy. She couldn't stay, and she couldn't tell him how she felt.

Not even for Christmas.

* * *

Travis lay by her side and watched the moonlight as it fell on the sleek perfection of her body. Her back was long and beautiful, and the ivory moon glow caressed it exquisitely. Her hair was free and tangled around him, and he thought with a staggering burst of pain about how much he loved her, how much he needed her. And perhaps God was good, because he *was* alive and able to hold her, and she was here with him. And, damn it, he knew that she loved him!

But he knew, too, that tomorrow would come, and that she would indeed enter the study and demand safe passage.

Suddenly he smiled ironically. He could remember being young, could remember his parents asking him to choose the one thing he wanted most for Christmas. He would think carefully about it, and they always gave him the gift he chose.

318

If only someone would ask him now. He wouldn't need to think. There was only one thing he would ask for.

Isabelle.

He mouthed her name, then rose, dressed and stepped into the hall. The smell of roasting chestnuts was in the air, along with the scent of the pine boughs the men had brought in.

Tomorrow would be Christmas Eve. She would come down for her safe-passage form, and he would give it to her.

* * *

He had been right. At noon Sergeant Hawkins came to tell him that Isabelle had requested an audience with him.

And now he was alone.

Chapter 4

Christmas Eve, 1864

With her safe-passage permit in her hands, Isabelle closed the door to Travis's office behind her and leaned against it. Didn't he understand that it hurt to leave him, but that it was all that she had left? She was among the nearly beaten, the bested. She was a part of the South. Once she had thrilled to the sound of a Rebel yell; once she had believed with her whole heart that Virginia had had a right to secede; once she had followed that distant drum.

It was true, perhaps, that the end was near, but the South had yet to surrender, so how could she do so?

She hurried along the hallway. Sergeant Sikes was there, waiting for her with his light blue eyes clouded, his face sad and weary. "So, you're leaving, Miss Hinton. I had hoped that you might stay this year."

She adjusted her gloves, and smiled. "It's Christmas, Sergeant. We should be with our own kind, don't you think?"

"It ain't up to me to think, ma'am. I'm just the sergeant." He turned, opening the door for her. "Seems to me, though, that

Christmas means we ought to be with the ones we love. Yes, ma'am, that's what it seems to me."

"Sergeant," Isabelle said sweetly, stepping onto the porch, "didn't you just tell me that you weren't supposed to do any thinking?"

"Um." He whistled, and their horses were brought up by one of the privates. She mounted without his assistance, and he sighed and mounted his horse. They started out, Sergeant Sikes riding behind her. Even so, he was determined to talk. "We celebrate a day when a little baby was born. Oxen and lambs flocked around him!"

"Right, Sergeant," she called back.

"There were angels floating around in heaven. Wise men made a journey following a star. Why, ma'am, God looked down from heaven, and he actually smiled. Miss Hinton, even God and the army know that Christmas is a time for peace!"

She turned around, smiling, "You love him a lot, don't you, Sergeant?"

"Captain Travis? You bet I do, ma'am. He's a great officer. I've known him for years. I've watched him put his personal safety behind that of his men every time. I've seen him rally a flagging defense with the power of his own energy, and I've seen him demand that the killing stop when the war turned to butchery. Damn right—'scuse me, ma'am—I do love him. And you do, too, don't you?"

She opened her mouth, not at all sure what she was going to say. In the end she didn't say anything at all. She only stared across the snow-covered fields and saw that another party was out that day, three Union soldiers heading south, trailing a hospital cart behind them. They were headed for the farmstead where she had been attacked the year before.

"Sergeant! There's a man on that cart."

"That's the way it looks, Miss Hinton."

"Come, then, let's see if we can be of help!"

She urged her horse on, then realized that she had forgotten the men were Yankees. Maybe it was Christmas magic that made her so concerned for the unknown soldier in the cart. She didn't know.

Her mare plowed through the dense white snow until she was nearly on top of the first soldier. "Sir! What's happened? I've been a nurse, perhaps I can be of some assistance."

The young officer paused, reining in, looking back as one of the other soldiers lifted a body from the cart and headed for the house. "I don't think so, ma'am. The old fellow isn't going to make it. We found him on the trail, barefoot and fever-ridden, and we've been trying to help him along, but, well, it doesn't look very promising."

Isabelle stared at him, then dismounted, tossing the reins over the porch railing. She caught up her skirts and hurried along the steps and inside.

One of the soldiers was working diligently to start a fire. The other was beside the old man, who he had laid on the sofa, and was holding a flask to his lips.

Isabelle stepped closer, and the Yankee soldier moved politely away. She gasped when she saw that the man on the couch was not a Yankee at all, but a Reb dressed in gray, with gold artillery trim. He was sixty, she thought, if he was a day, yet he had gone out to fight, and he had tried to walk home through the blistering cold with nothing but rags on his feet.

She knelt beside him, pulling the blanket more tightly around him. "I've done what I can," the Yank beside him said. He inclined his head politely. "Frederick Walker, ma'am, surgeon to the Ninth Wisconsin Infantry. I promise you, I have done all that is humanly possible."

She nodded quickly to him, but she didn't leave the old man's side. She took his hand.

"He wanted to get home. Home for Christmas. We were trying to see that he made it, but... well, sometimes home is a very long way away."

"Is he comfortable?" Isabelle asked.

"As comfortable as I can make him."

Suddenly the old man's eyes opened. They were a faded blue, rimmed with red, but when he looked at Isabelle, there was a sparkle in them. "God alive! I've gone to heaven, and the angels are blond and beautiful!"

Isabelle smiled. "No, sir, this isn't heaven. I saw the Yanks bring you in and came to see if I could do anything. I'm Isabelle Hinton, sir." She flashed a look at the doctor, wondering if she should be encouraging the old man to talk. The doctor's eyes told her that it was a kindness.

The old man wheezed, and his chest rattled, but he kept smiling. "What are you doing out on Christmas Eve, on a day like today? You should be warm and safe at home, young lady."

"And you shouldn't have been walking in your bare feet!"

"They weren't bare. They were in the best shoes the Confederacy has to offer these days!" he said indignantly. He sighed softly, then caught her eyes. "Oh, girl, don't look so sad! I knew my game was up. I was just trying to see if I could make it home. These nice young fellows tried to give me a lift." He motioned to her, indicating that she should draw near. "Yanks!" he told her, as if she hadn't noticed. Then he smiled broadly. "The doc here knows my boy Jeremy. Jeremy is a doc with a West Virginia division. They've worked together on the field. In Spotsylvania and Antietam Creek. Even at Gettysburg. Isn't that right, Doc?"

"Your son is in the Union?"

"One of them. Both my boys with Lee are still alive, and my daughters, they're back home. But you know, Miss Hinton, every year, whoever could get leave came home for Christmas. Not that we could get many leaves but... no matter what, we all wrote. My boys all wrote to me no matter what, no matter what color uniform they were wearing. And having those letters, why, it meant everything. It meant that I was home for Christmas." He broke off, coughing in a long spasm. Isabelle worriedly patted his chest. The young Yankee doctor offered him another drink. It soothed the coughing. Then he lay back, exhausted, but he looked at her worriedly. "Don't you fret so, girl. I'm going to a finer place. I'm going where the angels really sing.

Can you imagine what a Christmas celebration is like in heaven? Where the war don't make no difference? Quit worrying about me. Go home. Go home for Christmas."

She shook her head, swallowing. "I—I don't want to leave you."

His eyes closed, but he smiled, his lips parched and dry. "Then stay with me. But when I'm gone, promise me that you'll go home."

"I don't know where home is," she whispered beneath her breath.

But he heard her. His eyes opened, soft and cloudy, but she knew that he was seeing her.

"Home is where there is love, child. Surely you know that. It don't matter if it's a shack or a palace or a blanket beside a fire, home is where love is."

His eyes closed again. Isabelle squeezed his hand, and he squeezed back. Then his lungs rattled again, and the pressure of his hand against hers faded.

Tears flooded her eyes and spilled over his blanket.

Someone was touching her shoulder. Sergeant Sikes. "You come on now, Miss Hinton. Let me get you to Katie Holloway's place."

She let him lead her to the door because she could hardly see. She couldn't bear the injustice of it, that the old man had to die so close to home.

She shook free of the Sergeant's touch and turned back. The old man seemed entirely at peace. The lines had eased from his face. He even seemed to be smiling.

She walked into the snow. Someone came to assist her into the saddle, and Sergeant Sikes remounted, too.

They could go on. She could go to Katie's for the holiday.

Or she could go home.

She cried out suddenly, pulling the reins with such force that the startled animal reared and pawed the air, spewing snowflakes everywhere.

"Miss Hinton—" the sergeant began.

"Oh, Sergeant Sikes! He hasn't died in vain, has he? He's in there smiling away, even in death. Because he's home. And I'm going home, too. It's Christmas, Sergeant!"

Let the Yanks think that she was crazy. It was true that the war wasn't over yet. But for her it was. At least for Christmas.

She felt that she was flying over the snow. It was a day that promised peace to all mankind.

The snow was kicked up beneath the mare's hooves, and the wind whipped by them as she raced across the barren countryside. Sikes was far behind her, but he needn't have worried. She knew the way.

At last she saw the house. Through the window she could even see the fire that burned in the hearth in the office.

She leaped from her mare and raced, covered in snow, up the steps. She tore open the door, leaving it ajar, and flew on winged feet to the den. She didn't knock, just threw open that door, too. And then she stopped at last, completely breathless, unable to speak.

Travis was behind the desk. He stared at her in astonishment, then leaped to his feet, coming quickly around to her. She sagged into his arms.

"Isabelle! Are you hurt? What's happened? Isabelle—"

"I'm not hurt!"

"Then—"

"Nothing has happened."

"Then—"

"I'm just home, that's all. I've come home for the holidays. Oh, Travis, I love you so much!"

He carried her to the hearth and sat before the fire, holding her on his lap, his eyes searching hers. He whispered her name and buried his face against her throat, then repeated her name again.

"I do love you, Travis. So very much."

He shook his head, confused. "I think I've loved *you* forever. But you left...."

"I had to stop. Some Yanks were taking an old Rebel home, but he didn't make it. He died, Travis."

"Oh, Isabelle, I'm sorry."

"No, Travis, no. He was satisfied with his life. He'd known all kinds of love and... and he'd never cared about the color of it. It's so hard to explain. He just made me see... Travis, love is fragile. So hard to come by, so hard to earn. As fragile as a Christmas snowflake. Oh, Travis!"

She wound her arms around him, and kissed him slowly and deeply. Then her eyes found his again. "I—I'd like to give you something. What you did, getting James freed, was wonderful."

"Isabelle, you're my Christmas present. You're what I have wanted forever."

She flushed. "Well, I was hoping you would say that. Because I don't have anything to wrap for you. I've been so stubborn, so horrible."

"Isabelle—"

"Travis, do you really love me?"

"More than anything in the world, Isabelle."

"Then may I be your Christmas gift?"

"What do you mean?" He started to smile, but his eyes were suspicious.

"I mean, well, it would be a present for me, too, really. You—" She paused, took a deep breath and plunged onward. "You said you wanted to marry me. Our minister has gone south with the troops, but your Yankee chaplain is with you, and the church is just down the lane. Travis, I'm trying to say that I'll marry you. For Christmas. If you want to, that is."

He was silent for the longest time. Then he let out a shriek that rivaled the heartiest Rebel yell she had ever heard. He was on his feet, whirling around with her in his arms. He paused at last to kiss her; then he laughed and kissed her again.

When his eyes finally met hers again, they were brilliant with the fires of love, and his hands trembled where they touched her.

"Isabelle, there has never, never been a greater Christmas gift. Never. God knows, there is no gift so sweet or so fine as the gift of love."

She smiled, winding her arms more tightly around him. "And the gift of peace, Travis. You've given me both."

* * *

It wasn't hard to arrange. The men tripped over themselves to decorate the church, and though little else could be done on such short notice, they did manage to bring old Katie Holloway in for the ceremony.

Isabelle stood at the back of the church, while Katie insisted she take her mother's pearl ring. "Something borrowed, love. You must wear the ring."

Isabelle smiled. Her dress was light blue silk, her undergarments were very old, and her love... her love was new. She was all set to become a bride.

"I wonder what's taking them so long!" she said, looking toward the back of the church. Travis was outside in the snow, along with half his men. He turned around suddenly, saw her and ran into the church. To her amazement, he dragged her out into the snow. "Isabelle! Do you believe in Christmas?"

"What are you talking about?" she demanded. "Travis, you're behaving like a madman."

He started to laugh, then he shoved her around in front of him. "Isabelle, all we were lacking was the proper person to give you away. Now, well, we have that, too:"

For long moments she stared at the man in the gray uniform standing in front of her. Then she screamed with happiness and tore away from her prospective groom to catapult into the newcomer's arms. Travis, tolerant of her display of affection for another man, watched the dazzling happiness with which she greeted her brother.

"Isabelle!" James hugged her, then looked around at the blue uniforms surrounding them.

"Well, Yanks, is it a truce, then, for a wedding?"

Hats were ripped off and went flying into the air. A cheer went up.

Moments later they were all inside the church. James led her down the aisle and handed her over to Travis. The chaplain began the service, and she and Travis stated their vows. And when they were solemnly promised to one another, the chaplain stated, "On this date, Christmas of 1864, with the power invested in me by God and the state of Virginia, I declare Travis and Isabelle husband and wife. Captain, kiss your bride."

He kissed her and kissed her. And kissed her.

Sikes had found rice to throw at them, and James was quick to join in. Laughing, the newlyweds ran from the shower of rice to the supply buggy that had brought them, then headed to the house.

Peter had made the most sumptuous Christmas and wedding dinner imaginable, given the state of their larder, and though his feelings would change with the coming of the new year, James seemed willing enough to ignore the fact that the men in his house

330

were Yankees, and the Yanks were more than willing to accept him as one of their own.

It was Christmas.

* * *

Later, when most of the soldiers had gone to their sleeping quarters, when Sikes and James were half asleep in front of the parlor fire, Isabelle realized that her new husband was nowhere around.

She found him out on the chilly porch, looking up at the sky. She hooked her arm through his, and he smiled at her.

"What are you doing out here?" she whispered.

"Following a star," he told her softly. He brushed her hair from her face. "I thought I was far away from home for Christmas, but now I know I'm not. I am home. Wherever you are, love, that's where I live. Forever, within your heart."

She said nothing, and he lifted her into his arms, preparing to carry her from the cold porch into the warmth of the house, and then to their room.

But he paused just before he stepped through the floor, and he stared at the North Star, whispering a silent prayer.

Thank you, God! Thank you so much. For Isabelle... for Christmas.

ABOUT THE AUTHOR

New York Times and USA Today bestselling author of more than 125 novels, HEATHER GRAHAM has been featured in the Double Day Book Club and the Literary Guild. She has won numerous awards as both a romance writer and an author of thrillers, including: The Romance Writers of America Lifetime Achievement Award and the Thriller Writers Silver Bullet Award.

Heather hosts the Writers for New Orleans Conference each year in the city that she loves NOLA.

Find more information and links on Heather Graham and 13Thirty Books, and be sure to sign up for the 13Thrity Newsletter at 13Thirtybooks.com

Made in the USA
Monee, IL
02 December 2019

17815844R00187